Adventures With Blu

Adventures With Blu

Tedd Adamovich

NPI

Northwest Publishing, Inc.
Salt Lake City, Utah

NPI
Adventures With Blu

All rights reserved.
Copyright © 1995 Tedd Adamovich

Reproduction in any manner, in whole or in part,
in English or in other languages, or otherwise
without written permission of the publisher is prohibited.

For information address: Northwest Publishing, Inc.
6906 South 300 West, Salt Lake City, Utah 84047
JAC 1.19.95

PRINTING HISTORY
First Printing 1996

ISBN: 1-56901-736-0

NPI books are published by Northwest Publishing, Incorporated,
6906 South 300 West, Salt Lake City, Utah 84047.
The name "NPI" and the "NPI" logo are trademarks belonging to
Northwest Publishing, Incorporated.

PRINTED IN THE UNITED STATES OF AMERICA.
10 9 8 7 6 5 4 3 2 1

1. Eagle River Ordeal

    High pitched yelps are tearing at my heart as I slide down snow and ice covering the rocky bank of Eagle River. To prevent the powder in the flashpan from getting wet I hold my rifle high. I'll be needing it, and soon.
    The cold, black river lies before me, eerily discernible under the moon and star lit Arctic sky. My friend is out here somewhere being torn apart by wolves and I can't make out a body I can bury some lead into.
    My head is strained backward and my eyes shut tight as a loud, "*Aaaaaaaaaaaa!*" bursts from my mouth. It carries with it the pain, fear, and anger that beg for release within me. It also expresses unmistakable challenge. My stockinged feet hit

hard on the rocks of the river bed. I'm near panic. I scan up and down the bank for sight of my dog and the wolf pack that is killing him.

"Blu! Where, boy?!"

Nearing the bottom of the slide I had drawn back the hammer of my flintlock. It's ready to put a double ball in the first murderous critter that draws my attention, but my eyes cannot present me with a target. They anger me. I force them to delve deeper into the night.

"*Ooouuuu!*" another pitiful cry splits the icy air and I answer with another of my own. But how can it be? It's coming from the river. I search the blackness of the swift water out beyond the edge of the bank ice. Lord, the night has become cold.

Awakened by Blu's howls, I had had no time to do anything but grab hold of my rifle. Not even taking time to unzip the sleeping bag, I had pushed and slid my way out, slipping and falling two or three times in the process. At the time it seemed like the thing to do. Now I stand facing the frigid world in socks and long underwear. There is no wind but the cold is easily finding its way through my woolen long johns. So cold it burns.

No more than a minute has elapsed since I first heard his urgent cry. I still have hope, but I have to locate the combat quickly. He's fighting bravely and powerfully, I'm sure, but if the wolves hamstring him...God, don't let the wolves hamstring him!

There's something! Even blacker than the inky current. Not more than fifteen yards from me at the edge of the ice and another fifteen downstream. No wolves, only Blu! He's scratching frantically at the ice trying to drag himself out of the water. Now the issue is clear. But what can I do about it?

"I'm comin', boy! Hang on!"

Thumb and trigger finger instinctively return the hammer to a safe position while my eyes follow the ice upstream. There, at that broken rim. That's where Blu must have fallen in.

We'd made camp shortly after dark. The sun goes down early this far north. He and I had then strolled down to the river. The ice, though thick, was unstable. The river's rise and fall and its swift current made it so. The only way to safely venture onto it was by distributing my weight. I had told Blu to sit on the bank while I belly crawled out over the ice to the water's edge. There I had filled my coffee pot.

Near the edge, the ice was even more precarious so I had extended the pot my full arm's length to fill it. After I had returned to solid ground Blu had gamboled his way out for a drink. He was lighter than I, and naturally distributed, so he'd had no problem. Then we returned to camp.

After dinner I had turned in early intending to rise early. Evidently, Blu had returned to the river while I slept. This time, however, the fickle ice had given way under him.

Had the near-full moon not risen into a clear sky, I never would have seen his black form against the black open waters. Our association would have come to an end then and there in the dark and lonesome and frighteningly cold Alaskan wilderness.

Blu is slowly being carried downstream, his front paws digging at the ice. It's too thick for him to break with only the weight of his front legs. If I walk out on it though, it will give way under mine. If I crawl, he'll be far downstream by the time I get to the edge.

The rate he is going downstream is increasing as he weakens. All I can do is try to keep up. I stumble along the large rocks trying to keep pace with his descent. He's still fighting, but it's only a matter of time before this cold saps him of all his strength. Soon he will slowly release his last grip on life and be swept away.

"*Ouuuuu!*"

"Hang in there Bluper! I'm comin'!"

I haven't gone very far. Maybe thirty yards. My toes, heels and ankles have been smashing against the rocks repeatedly. What's that ahead? Damn! Sheer rock walls silhouetted by the moonlight. They come down to the water's edge on both sides of the river. They're only a few minutes away. If I can't get to Blu before he enters that canyon, he's lost.

"*Ahhh! Ouuu!*" I struggle to get up after falling. Boy, that knee hurts!

"*Ouuu!*" If I keep falling like this I'll never gain! After half standing, I push off some large boulders while stooped over using my knuckles for crutches.

By golly I'm finally getting ahead of him. I think I've got a chance to get to the edge of the ice before he goes by. Not enough time to crawl, though. I'll have to hazard walking on it.

Wait! What's that ahead? There, where the river makes that bend to the left. By golly, the current slamming into the bank is keeping the ice from forming over the water. I only see ice where it's splashing up onto the rocks and dirt. The opening is right in Blu's path. He ought to come within three or four feet of shore.

But how will he get up that perpendicular bank? The river's washed it out three, maybe four feet higher than the water. With most of his strength gone, he can't climb that. The canyon walls are the next obstacle, an obstacle impossible to surmount. I've got to get to that hole!

"Ouch! Damn you rocks!"

Intent on nothing but getting to this hole, I have lost sight of Blu. There can't be more than a few moments before he goes by. If he hasn't already. How deep is this hole?!

"Oh, hell!" I drop my rifle and jump in.

God, aren't my feet ever going to..."*Oooahh!*" At least the bottom is a flat rock. The waters are beating into my chest and splattering up into my eyes. Blindly I take two steps out into the river with arms outstretched and hands wide open. They ache to embrace anything that floats by.

Something just bumped the back of my left forearm. My arms close on it like a Venus fly-trap and pull it to my breast.

It's furry but unresponsive. Was that a whine? Thank God! There's life. Not much, but some is flowing. Tears stream down my cheeks as I scream even louder than before, but this time for joy.

"Gotcha now, boy. It's okay fella. We'll make it."

Fighting the current I turn toward shore. My feet and legs are so numb that I no longer feel the rock that supports them. Our trial is only beginning. We are both alive. Now we have to reach camp before the unrelenting cold removes our instinctive desire to stay that way.

Reaching the bank I strain to hoist Blu to safety. The cold has nearly claimed all of my strength. "Come on, boy, pull! That's it, pull harder, boy! Just a little more!"

Between my feeble attempt at lifting then pushing, and Blu's even feebler effort pulling, we manage. He crawls just far enough to assure that he won't slide back down and lies still without even shaking off water. Now it's time to get my numb body out of the hole.

Sinking my arms deep into the swirling black of the river, I clasp my frozen hands behind a knee and lift my legs one at a time. My feet feel nothing. The only way I can tell if they have a foothold into the side of the bank is when they stop moving downward. Pushing with lifeless feet and knees and pulling with numb fingers and elbows I manage to win the lip of the bank.

I think I'll just lie here next to Blu for awhile. Somewhere

I've got to find more strength. All I'm doing, however, is growing colder. Free of the relatively warm waters of the river, the subzero temperature of the night is draining my wet body quickly. I'm beginning to doze.

Unceremoniously my head bounces off the nightstand and I awaken. I'm breathing heavily, my heart is slamming violently against my breast bone and cold sweat drenches me. But I am alive! Safe in my bedroom in Colorado Springs. Again I've relived the nightmare of Blu's and my Eagle River ordeal.

No chance of getting back to sleep now. I'll reminisce awhile.

I remember the day I discovered that Alaska had become a state. It had been during recess at Phil Sheridan Grammar School. My buddies and I were on hands and knees in the gravel at the north end of the playground, immersed in a game of marbles. One of the fellas brought up the subject of Alaska's newly acquired statehood.

No one else paid much attention to his remark. A wealth of marbles was at stake. But for the rest of that day and all that night and for many countless days and nights thereafter, I thought of nothing but the far north and how someday I would like to go there. I lost a lot of marbles in that game.

That was many years ago and far away in a south-side neighborhood of Chicago. As I lay on that frozen bank, Lord, how I remember wishing that I were there instead of that unforgiving country.

The comfort of unconsciousness was nearly upon me and hard to discard in favor of the misery of the real world. If I had surrendered though, I knew that the moment of rest my mortal body deceptively begged for would have in reality become an eternity. I wasn't ready for that yet.

We had to get to camp and start a fire. My body had been

shaking out of control. Fatal symptoms were beginning. Hypothermia had stopped knocking and was opening the door. Once inside, my ability to reason would have been gone. Unwittingly I would have succumb to the sublime call of a permanent sleep.

I pulled myself to my knees and began rubbing Blu's still body. "Let's go, Bluper. After all this trouble what say we don't croak three hundred yards from camp."

Eventually he began to purr almost like a kitten. Blood began to flow in my own arms and hands as well. Then I sat back and began rubbing some life into my legs and feet, preparing for our odyssey.

Pain was shooting through my whole frame as I finally pulled myself to a standing position. Uncomfortable, yes, but grateful because the pain meant that blood was beginning to flow into places with which it had become unfamiliar. Thank God there was no wind and that I had been wearing wool, albeit scant.

I had to kick at Blu with my feet and swat at him with my hands to rouse him from sleep. "I said come on, Blu! Let's go!"

Then I shouted and kicked harder to get him to move. We must have looked like two beings out of a horror movie walking stiffly and with great effort toward our fire pit. My long underwear, socks and hair were covered with ice. Blu likewise was frozen. I was thankful that my feet were only half thawed. They had taken a beating chasing after Blu. Along with the beating they were taking on the way back, I knew that hibernating beneath their frozen exterior slept the monster known as misery.

Less than a hundred yards from camp I was shaking so violently that I didn't think I'd be able to take another step. Somehow, though, my legs knew what to do and kept moving one after the other. The right wouldn't budge till the left was firmly planted and then the left wouldn't until the right was.

It seemed each was carrying a washtub of cement.

Never had I been as tired as when we reached camp. Blu sank to the ground and was instantly unconscious. The urge for me to crawl into my sleeping bag, wet longies and all, was difficult to fight, but a fire was the only thing that could save us.

With my two hands frozen into the shape of hooks I scraped the wood I had gathered for our breakfast fire into the fire pit. I reached for my small Svea stove that I always carry in my pack for emergencies. Holding it in both hands and the wrench for opening the fuel tank cap in my teeth, I unscrewed it. I was shaking so fiercely that when the cap popped open quite a bit of the fuel splashed over my hands and face. I poured most of the contents onto the wood in the pit. The cold wrench tore skin from my upper lip as I removed it.

Striking a match with stiff hands was like trying to play piano with my knees. I held the match with both hands placing my fingertips all the way to its head so that there would be little chance of breaking the match stick. Reaching across to a rock that bordered the far side of the fire pit I set the match head on it and dragged the match toward me. After the third or fourth try the little blue bulb burst into flame and I simply dropped it into the fuel-soaked wood as I sat back. The exploding flame was good.

"Think we'll live now, Blu boy." Blu heard but didn't respond.

I threw on large logs until the flames were dancing as high as my chest. The warmth reached Blu. He crawled a few feet closer.

The coffee pot had at least a cup of frozen coffee in it. It had been meant for breakfast but it seemed like an ideal time for a cup. I pushed it closer to the fire. Then I removed my socks, long underwear, undershorts, and T-shirt. I hung the wet clothes on nearby branches to dry, unzipped my sleeping bag all the way, and pulled it up over my head and shoulders. I stood there stomping my feet on my hooded sweatshirt while the sting of returning blood continued biting at every inch of me. Oh, how my feet began to hurt.

After facing death and defeating one of his better efforts, I felt renewed, revitalized. That country was unforgiving, but certainly not unconquerable. Nowhere else had I ever felt so alive. What was that I had wished earlier about being back in Chicago? That thought left me.

From Blu's breathing I could tell he was resting more comfortably. He was no longer sprawled out every which way, looking so vulnerable. He was curled up close to the fire, lying on the ground cloth that had been under my sleeping bag. Every now and again I saw his chest heave as he took in a deep breath. He'd let it out with a long sigh of relief and a slight shiver.

The stinging had left my body but I still felt cold and quivered some. I temporarily let fall the sleeping bag while I donned my wool shirt, sweater and pants, and pulled my wool cap down over my ears. Then I rewrapped in the sleeping bag.

Within minutes, with the fire still burning high, I felt nice and toasty. So much so that I was confident in dozing off for a while without the concern of not awakening. But first, some hot coffee. The warm liquid hitting home made me even more drowsy. Sitting on a log by the fire I dropped my head slightly forward and was gone.

After a short catnap I awoke and checked on Blu. Though signs of life in him were far more pronounced than they had been down by the river, he still did not seem in the best of health. I doubted that spending the rest of the night immobile like he was would be good for him. He could rest for as long as it took my clothes to dry. Then I'd pack up and we would make our way back to Big Jack's and the shelter of his Garden of Eden Lodge.

Big Jack's place had been our starting off point on many an adventure. Situated at the very end of Eagle River Road it was the beginning of the Alaskan outback. By the time you were out of sight of the lodge upriver, you were in country as wild as could be found anywhere on earth. Grizzly, moose and wolf ruled the land.

Big Jack and his wife Irma had homesteaded there years ago. With the advent of encroaching civilization, the entrepreneurial spirit had entered them, and they had built the lodge. It wasn't easily accessible. The last five miles was 4-wheel drive only. For a few months even 4-wheelers had to chain up to get there and sometimes it could only be reached by snowmobile.

Hardy souls who ventured there were treated to the best down-home food and drink and most cordial hospitality in the whole world. Sundays meant smorgasbord and blue grass music played by other local homesteaders. It was an event worth crawling miles to get to.

We were some miles from Big Jack's but the sky was still clear and the moon still bright. In that cold the snow was crusted hard so I wouldn't have to wear my snowshoes. We would be able to make good time and get there around midnight or a little after. Jack and Irma's would still be open. The thought of sitting by their fire while Irma poured me a nice hot cup of strong black coffee and Jack stirred in a short pull of rotgut had been an enticing carrot dangling before my nose.

My clothes were nearly dry. The duration of one more short nap would finish the job.

I awakened again in fifteen or twenty minutes. I let my clothes have a few more minutes of drying time while I got camp packed. Then, after undressing, I redressed sliding into my warm underclothes and then into what would be necessary to meet the public at the lodge.

One last time I felt the warmth of the flames. I covered the fire with snow, shouldered my pack, pulled Blu to his feet, grabbed my rifle and off into the night. Downstream, homeward, we went with northern lights undulating overhead, the moon so bright that we cast shadows. Were things all the more beautiful because we had nearly perished, or were they so beautiful that thoughts of death were trivial in comparison?

I looked down at Blu and was grateful that he was still with me. As we hiked home I remember reflecting on how our relationship had begun six years before.

2. The Beginning

There had been some bad times, I suppose. But I can't remember any that amounted to anything. I'm sure I don't know of a time when I wished that he weren't mine, that maybe another dog would have been a better one. On the other hand I can't speak for him. There were plenty of times I gave him cause to wish for another owner.

I had grown up in a second floor, two-bedroom apartment in South Chicago. My brother and mother and father lived with me and downstairs lived my old country, grandparent landlords. They believed in an immaculate yard with perfectly manicured hedges and a lawn lacking only a hole and flag to rate with putting greens on the finest golf courses. Having a dog, therefore, had been out of the question. Nevertheless, boys want dogs.

I asked Santa for a dog every Christmas. After years of Santa not coming through, I drowned Mom and Dad with the same requests, but I would have had an easier time booking Tiffany's for a rodeo. I came to realize, though, that it wasn't me that they were trying to punish. On the contrary, it was the dog they were trying to protect. Perfect yard or not, the city was no place for the kind of dog I wanted.

The disappointment would be mine to bear until one day in January when I was attending college in Crete, Nebraska. A fraternity brother, Pete Danbeck, who was married to one of the prettiest girls in the school, said he was going down to the Crete Motel to look at a litter of Labrador pups. The owner of the motel, a fella by the name of Ragland, was also the owner of the bitch and her litter.

"If the blood-lines are respectable, I'm gonna get one," Pete told me. "I've heard Ragland's selling them at a mighty reasonable price." He knew I was crazy about dogs so he added, "You know, Tedd, if you get one too, we can build two kennels at my place and you can keep it there."

I didn't know what to say. After years of being told no and after an ill-fated attempt to adopt and raise a mistreated, worm-ridden pup that died within days, my conditioned response was, "I'll go see 'em with you. But how about I just play and hunt with yours after you buy one?"

Pete and Mary lived in a home they rented across the street from the campus. The next morning he picked me up at the dorm and we drove the short distance to the Crete Motel where Duchess had given birth to a litter of puppies sired by Doc's Del-Tone Blu. It was sunny but quite cold. Therefore I had expected to observe the pups indoors, but when we arrived Ragland took us to an outdoor kennel where Duchess was just finishing an afternoon shift at nursing.

Some of the fat, shaggy, jet black puppies were still hanging on in order to suck out the very last drop. Their patient mother was drained dry. Others were tumbling around barking and biting and pawing at each other using up what they'd just eaten.

"Well they seem to be healthy enough." Pete remarked raising his head to address Ragland, "What are their papers like? Do they have a pretty decent blood line?"

"They've got both bench and field-trial champions in their line that they can brag about when they grow up," he said. "Whenever you're done looking here, we can go in the office. I'll show you the AKC records."

Turning our attention back to the dogs we noticed that the stubbiest and homeliest was still attached to mamma. The little glutton was obviously intending to be the first in line when chow call sounded again.

"That one's the runt," Ragland said. "He goes for $50.00. The others'll cost $75.00."

By that time I'd already figured how I could ration out my spending money for the rest of the semester in order to have enough to purchase one of 'em. Ah, just idle, wishful thinking.

I reached down and picked up the runt, who by the way was still pulling on a nipple. The tug-of-war that ensued nearly pulled it off. The light smacking sound as her teat constricted back to its intended position was followed by an ever-so-slight whine from the mamma that I accepted as a thank you. Her eyes closed peacefully in relief.

I beheld this disgusting example of animal flesh as he was still struggling in the direction of the lost sucker and squealing like a pig. His face was wrinkled horribly, his fur covered him like a child's coat three sizes too large, his out-of-proportion feet gave him the appearance of wearing black snowshoes and his head seemed swollen to twice its normal size in proportion to his stunted but grotesquely fat little body. I fell in love.

"I'll take this one," I said. "I'll be back to pick him up after he's weaned."

What the heck, Pete and Mary had already said I could put a kennel next to theirs in their back yard. That was only a couple of blocks from the dorm. Pete had chosen his as well so we were off to break the news to Mary.

The week seemed to drag even with the added chores of pouring concrete for the kennel floors and erecting the chain link walls. When it came to concentrating on studies, well, that would just have to wait till I had my pup.

Toward the end of the week, Ragland called to inform us that the pups were ready to leave their mamma. Bright and early Saturday morning we arrived to find the little labs fighting for the possession of a rubber ball that was rolling and bouncing freely amongst them. The ball bounded loose and I recognized my new acquisition tearing across the garage driveway after it.

Now, the word "tearing" might be a bit much in this instance but, you see, it's used to describe his intent rather than his actual progress.

In his attempt to retrieve the escaping ball the exceptionally clumsy, poor excuse for a purebred retriever spent much of his energy in freeing his gargantuan webbed feet from the fur of his belly. So loose was his fur that one wondered if perchance his mother had forgotten to button his coat. His rotund little belly dragged so close to the ground that no more than a few inches rise of broken concrete in the driveway caused the pathetic pup to become rudely aware of the phenomenon known as high-centering. When this occurred all four legs flailed wildly in the air until one found a hold and valiantly pulled him free.

After a mighty struggle that seemed unworthy of just a ball, he finally caught up with it. Again I must explain that the use of the words "caught up" is probably somewhat abused in this case since their use implies that the ball was still moving away from the pursuer. Actually it had stopped rolling long before puppy's arrival and was just lying there waiting—no, begging—to be caught.

"If this is any indication of how he's gonna be when he's old enough to go get me a duck maybe I might do better to just find a long stick." My attempt at levity was unnecessary as Pete and Ragland were already nearly convulsing from my pup's display.

Anyway, the show wasn't over. The problem it seemed was that the over endowment of fur on the back of his neck prevented him from seeing the exact location of the ball. When he would lower his head to grab it the loose fur would fall forward over his eyes. After a few vain attempts on his part I reached down and picked up the pup with one hand and the ball with the other, leaned him back so his eyes were unobstructed and *put* the ball in his mouth. His eyes widened, his body stiffened and his head shook back and forth while a guttural noise emitted from his throat. A victory display, I suppose.

With the morning's entertainment concluded, Pete and I completed our transaction with Ragland. We stowed our new charges in Pete's Gremlin and as we drove away Ragland couldn't resist, "You make sure you keep that runt penned or leashed so's he doesn't hurt anybody you hear!?"

During those first few months, in particular the first weeks of ownership, I was at a great advantage having my place of residence in the dormitory. Pete and Mary, however, didn't fare as well. Those two took the full load of constant irritation produced by the separation pains of two vocally healthy puppies. My involvement, on the other hand, was only with regard to regular routines of feeding, watering, training, cleaning the kennels and enjoying the antics of a puppy that actually belonged to me—and I had the papers to prove it.

I did have one dilemma. Mary and Pete had quickly decided on the name of Luke for their pup but I couldn't come up with one for mine. All the names on his family tree seemed so elegant and proud. This weighed heavily on me, for I wanted something proper and fitting.

The task was quite a bit more difficult than it would seem it should be. You see, "proper" would have meant something like Duke or King or Black Marvel. "Fitting" on the other hand would have meant something like Clumsy or Ug or Big Foot or Misfit. The quandary was to find something between those two extremes. After days of frustrated deliberation the problem was solved simply and painlessly.

Pete and I went to visit the owner of the sire of our two pups to view the sire himself. Pete had previously seen him and had said that he was a magnificent animal. Doc's Del-Tone Blu, turned out to be the proudest most defiant looking dog I had ever seen. His stature was one that was bathed in self-esteem. The loyalty he possessed for his master was unexcelled. Combined with his impressive field record, it made me realize that such a dog needed a namesake and my pup was going to be it.

I would name him for what I hoped he would become. It might even be good psychology. If I called him something special, even with so many cards stacked against him, he might just turn out to be something special. Blu Magnum was it! Yep, that name would do just fine.

During his formative years it was not always easy keeping a positive attitude in regard to his envisioned future excellence. His feet, you see, seemed to grow at a more rapid rate than the rest of his body. His coat remained a few jumps ahead as well. And it seemed that if and when he ever filled in he would resemble a black rhino more than a black dog.

The thing that disturbed me most was that his attitude toward becoming a champion was still less than would have been desired. He made a game out of everything. He was more concerned with winning friends and having a good time than he was with the business of becoming a proud hunter showing undaunted loyalty to his master.

Then there were displays of unreserved and even out-of-key howling at the sound of a siren. Totally unbecoming a regal purebred.

Once he and Luke got loose. When Pete finally caught up with them they were in the yard of a bull terrier. Luke had had sense enough to remove himself from the other dog's territory but Blu just lay there while the terrier ripped open his nose and ear.

"If I'd been drinking I'd have thought I imagined it," Pete said when relating the incident. "Blu seemed to be trying to reason with that crazy terrier. He didn't care one bit about the extra holes that were openin' up in his body."

I wanted to paint a flower on his butt. He could have at least tried to whip that little dog or at least fight it to a standoff. It was getting embarrassing.

After a few weeks of training I felt that he was ready to put on a retrieving show for some of the guys at the dorm. He was still a pup, but he had been doing really well with dry retrieves of his training dummy. I assembled a bunch of the guys behind the dorm to show him off. Earlier that morning Pete and I had captured a live pigeon which I had tied up and stashed in my coat pocket. This was to be a surprise for Blu.

The demonstration began and young Blu was doing exceptionally well. He was retrieving his dummy like a champ. I was burning with pride, my chest about to split my coat wide open. Everybody was commenting on how good a trainer I must be to have such a young pup performing so admirably. He was ready. He had to be because I had already told everybody that he would retrieve anything.

Legs flying in all directions trying to control his oversized webbed feet, and joy beaming in his eyes, because he could sense how he was pleasing everyone, he came racing back with the dummy on his umpteenth retrieve. I commanded, "Give." He released the dummy into my hand. "Sit." and he sat head up chest out looking down-field. With his back turned away from me I switched the pigeon for the dummy and heaved it into the waiting arms of Pete standing down-field. Pete immediately set it on the lawn and stepped away. With a loud, "Hut." I sent Blu barreling across the grass intent on the object on the lawn.

He was at the pigeon in a flash. He picked it up deftly and turned on a dime all in one perfectly timed motion. But then instead of rushing straight back without breaking stride, he stopped abruptly.

I was momentarily stunned but then shrugged it off as being a normal reaction for he had just encountered a new feel, smell and taste. But when he did not instantly recover and come racing back, I began to panic.

Instead he laid the pigeon gently on the ground. Then he hooked his teeth in the string that bound it and carefully loosened the bonds with soft shakes and nods of his head, and with tender nudges of his nose roused it to flight.

"Hey, Tedd, you think maybe when we go duck huntin' we should paint a red cross on his back? Maybe hang a first aid kit around his neck?"

I could feel the blood swelling up in my face as my friends laughed and wisecracked.

"You think he'll get mad if we shoot shells with real shot in 'em?"

On sticks, socks and canvas dummies he was without equal but on real birds he was a canine Florence Nightingale. I wanted a hunter. It seemed I had a conscientious objector.

Well, who cares, right?! I didn't want him retrieving pigeons anyway. He knew that. He was only showing another fine example of his boundless knowledge. He was just very selective. I could believe that. So why couldn't anybody else?

The solution to his dove attitude was all too obvious. What he really needed was actual interaction with the objects of his future involvement. More simply put, he needed to see a duck. At least that was the sort of thing that was inferred in teachers' manuals in my education courses.

So Sunday morning, before the campus started swarming, Blu-dog and I made a bee-line for the pond below the men's dormitories. There we had a veritable gold mine in feathers. And those feathers were attached to the proper birds. At that hour of the morning Blu was nothing but spit and vinegar. Ears perked, tail curled up and over his back, eyes bright and inquisitive checking out everything, he was the picture of something that really wanted to learn. The anxiety he exhibited for the absorption of knowledge was a sight that would bring tears to the eyes of any loving parent. He had me in such a state of euphoria that it was hard to contain myself.

I was beginning to wish that I had waited till a weekday afternoon when the campus was really bustling. Who knows what inspiration, what greatness, he could have brought to those who would gaze upon him?

"Today is the day!" The experience would bring him to realize his true destiny. The greatest there ever was or ever would be. The retrieving champion of the world!

By the time we reached the pond I was stepping out proud as an elk in rut. I could see the ducks but Blu had not yet focused on anything further away than about two inches in front of his nose. A nose that was investigating everything.

In just a matter of seconds though he lifted his head from his sniffings and low and behold, there they were.

His head jerked up and back and a little to one side in a questioning posture. Then he looked up at me as if asking a question. With a nod from me and a "Yes, my boy, there they are." he made an uncontrolled dash for the water and, in his usual form, fell awkwardly in. That slight unbalance was not a major deterrent however. He surfaced stroking exuberantly in the direction of his quarry. Not too bad a form either. So long as his legs were underwater he almost looked coordinated.

Had I been aware of the ducks' reaction I probably would have been disheartened, but their unconcerned demeanor did not register with me until much later. They obviously knew something I didn't.

At Blu's approach the birds leisurely split off in all directions with not a single pair left in the bunch. There wasn't even one that lagged slightly behind the rest. It could have been choreographed. The fan they formed was perfect. All were equidistant from a center point which, it seemed, was occupied by Blu-dog.

It was inconsiderate, unfair and cruel and unusual punishment. I was sure those ducks could see that Blu was merely an inquisitive pup. Their professional maneuvers were inappropriate to say the least. They could have played along just a little. At least they could have acted distressed. But no, they had to put on a show that could have permanently damaged the emotional stability of a willing student during the time that the foundation was being laid for the rest of his life. It would be difficult for me to forgive them.

There he was in the middle of the pond treading water and swinging from one direction to another looking for some indication from one of the dozen or so birds that it was the most likely target. He had not even developed his swimming ability past a minnow yet. I wondered whether or not he would have sense enough to head for shore while he still had some strength? With so much preoccupying his little brain I doubted it. Off came my boots and jacket just in case.

Then suddenly to my surprise and approval he chose one

out of the crowd, homed in and stroked. What a will of iron and ability for making crucial decisions. And by golly, he was even gaining!

"Go get 'em, Bluper!"

The duck was swimming a staggered pattern but Blu was not baffled. His quarry was in his sights and it was full steam ahead. When he was almost within reach the steel-jawed trap opened wide ready to scoop up its prey and head victoriously home. But suddenly, with sweet victory almost in the bank, the unexpected happened. The dirty bird disappeared off the face of the pond.

That did it! The nerve. After all, my boy had passed his first test with flying colors even though it had posed problems I never would have held him responsible for. But now when he should have received a reward for his accomplishments he was hit with ploys, deceptions and even trick questions. I was sure that this new issue was beyond his power to cope. That unexpected dive caused utter confusion.

Tormented, Blu swished back and forth in random jerks with occasional dunkings of his head causing excessive choking and gagging. I knew he was getting tired but I also knew that he wanted a duck before returning to his master. The depression of coming home empty-handed would have been too much for him. Panic was setting in.

He now swam frantically in the direction of the rest of the flock that had regrouped to watch the comedy. Again they went in all directions but this time their escape was random.

Blu proceeded to pursue the nearest bird but when it sped up and outdistanced one of its comrades Blu would abruptly change course and attack the next nearest duck, and the next, and the next, and the next. Finally his panic became so pronounced that he was swimming a zigzag pattern that led nowhere. And then even that pattern ceased and he just spun back and forth in the water with ducks on all sides quacking jeers and insults.

It was then that he saw them. They were on the far bank just sitting there with their long necks curled back resting on their backs. Swans! OK, so they weren't ducks. But they had webbed feet. That was close enough. Besides, they were on dry land!

I didn't notice what he was after until the circle of ducks broke to let him pass and instead of pursuing ducks he was making haste for the far shore. My eyes outdistanced him searching for his new interest. When I spotted his objective my lungs filled with air and the words I produced frantically were, "Blu, no! Blu, come! Blu, no!!!" It was no use. The puppy who wanted so desperately to please his master, to be successful, to be victorious had become a berserker.

The poor guy. All his desperate little eyes could see was broad bills and webbed feet. And as trophies, man those new guys on shore were so big he might have to quarter 'em to get 'em home. What he didn't realize was that to an inexperienced pup of his present stature, these babies were classed in the Big and Dangerous Game category. He was way undergunned.

Since he was oblivious to my commands I was following the shore line making for the far bank as fast as my legs could carry me. I'd been injured in a football accident the year before and times like these, when my legs couldn't move me as fast as I once could go, were extremely frustrating. I knew that the bank I was heading for could at any moment turn into a bloody battlefield, the equivalent of the Battle of Dunkirk with the attacker being routed and pushed back into the sea.

I was still quite a distance away when the landing craft hit the beach. Blu came out of the water the picture of exhaustion. His head hung low. His tongue even lower. He clumsily loped up the bank.

The swans, unconcerned, were still nesting but their heads had now turned slightly to their left to watch Blu's progress. They sensed that he posed no real threat but they began making low guttural sounds professing their annoyance at maybe having to stand up.

Blu, with what energy he could still muster, approached to within about six or eight feet. At that point he noticed that his approach had produced little reaction so he stopped abruptly with his head cocked to one side and his ears at attention. I had hoped he would stay confused long enough for me to get there. Those hopes were soon dashed.

Taking the lack of concern on the part of the swans as an insult, he assumed the oafish posture of front legs extended in front of him, head also extended but low to the ground and rump raised as high as he could stretch it without it coming off. Then he began to bark incessantly. When he noticed that even this did not produce a suitable reaction he began to shuffle and bounce from side to side and forward and back shaking his head menacingly. Well, at least he thought it was menacing. Lord I was glad no one was up to witness that display. The picture was one of complete physical, mental and emotional imbalance.

Nevertheless, that finally did it. He got the response he so richly deserved. I knew the battle was just about over.

There were only three swans. But Blu might as well have been outnumbered one hundred to one. To their credit I must admit that they displayed incredible patience. A patience that had exhausted itself and I really couldn't blame them.

Rigidly and sternly they rose from their comfortable sitting positions. The sounds emanating from them had all but ceased and they stared ominously down at Blu. Their heads followed his antics and their eyes glared angrily.

Blu didn't see any of this. What he figured was that their reaction was a sign that he had intimidated them and that their fear of him would soon put them to flight, the chase being a grand one. He was sure that all he needed was to get just a little bit closer.

When Blu inched to within five feet his target swan froze. At four feet its neck slowly began to lift its head up and back. At three it set its feet and leaned slightly backward. At two the backward progress of the head was completed. And finally, when Blu was directly underneath and reaching out to grab hold, the swan pulled the trigger. The mainspring in its neck released, sending the hard, club-like bill down like a shot to strike squarely on top of Blu's head. The sound that reached my ears was most similar to that of a baseball bat hitting a tree. Immediately following came a muffled whine and Blu was flattened like a pancake.

Dazed, legs like rubber and head bobbing, Blu tried to rise like a valiant boxer before the referee counted ten. The swan had prepared himself and down came another shot as accurate as the one before. Predictably, Blu's reaction was the same as from the first strike. The only difference was that this time he didn't try to get up.

I got to the swans' playing field right then and even though I was putting on a defiant show of hollering and growling and waving my arms, the swans did not seem overly concerned and only backed off slightly. I got the impression that they were ready to do to me the same as they had done to Blu if I became overly aggressive.

What a sorry sight Blu was. He was laid out straight and soaking wet, with his back up, both hind legs to the same side and both front legs stretched out in front of him. There between his front legs was his oversized black head, chin flat on the ground. He was not unconscious but he might as well have been. His eyes were only three-quarters open—make that five-eighths—the pupils staring up at me and the lower whites bloodshot.

I figured that he had already learned that swans were off-limits so I deemed no lecture necessary. After a few gentle and reassuring strokes over his head and down his shoulders I picked up my black vegetable. Cradling him in my arms we headed for home.

3. Chicago

In just two short months it had become difficult to be without him. The fact that people can become so attached to dogs has always intrigued me. I mean, they don't look like us. They don't talk, so communication is difficult. They don't walk like us or eat like us or even sweat like us.

So it has to be the fact that a dog's only goal in life is to please and love his master. That they are only ninety percent successful at pleasing is not as important as having a perfect record at loving. The remarkable thing is that they do it without sending a single card or bouquet of flowers. They never remember an anniversary or a birthday or Valentine's Day but somehow they still manage.

Dogs don't have the superior intellect of people who had the foresight to set aside these special days to show their love. They're stuck with having to love three hundred sixty-five days a year. I'll bet that if we desire it the Good Lord has got a special place in Heaven for these crude, dirty, mangy, big-hearted beasts. And I'll bet it's at the side of the cream of mankind.

Although it was expressly forbidden, Blu was staying with me in the dormitory. It had become unnecessary for me to use an alarm clock. When Blu thought it time for me to rise, and it always seemed too early, he would jump onto my bed and plant his bottom on my neck and head. He'd remain there until the pressure won out over my will to sleep. I've always thanked my lucky stars that I wasn't one to sleep on my back.

One morning my furry, black alarm awakened me to find a late March blizzard covering the campus with sleet and snow. Marvelous! I've always been a sucker for weather when it's at its extreme (except for hot summer). I hurriedly dressed and we stepped out into the wet, bone-chilling high winds.

Nothing has ever been able to invigorate me more than some sort of violent storm. It gets my blood pumping and I get an adrenaline rush. At those times I can't seem to wipe the child-like, wide-eyed grin from my face. That particular storm was so intense that I'm sure I must have looked like a raving lunatic. Blu, on the other hand, never did seem to mirror this peculiarity of mine.

Last year's football mishap had temporarily paralyzed me from my neck down and had left me partially paralyzed on my right side. Though I had regained much mobility, my strength and balance after seven months in the hospital was far from being at its peak. Blu was learning at an early age that he was to be my support.

Every ten or twenty steps, the wind into which I was leaning would either gust or let-up, disturbing my delicate balance and sending me to the ground. Blu would think this meant wrestle time and he'd cover me with his cold, wet body pinning me to the slippery, wet ground. He'd rip off my hat, gloves, and be starting on my pants before I could roll myself over and make my reprimands heard over the high winds. Then, with his shoulders for support, I'd climb to a standing position and our adventure would resume into what I imagined to be an Arctic blizzard.

No one else was out and about and the visibility was so poor that campus landmarks were obscured till we would bump into one. The opportunity for my imagination to drift was limitless. It was as though we were alone in a vast wilderness.

There I was in the far north. My faithful dog was my only companion in a life and death struggle with nature.

The mining town of Chilcanuknuk was desperately holding on. Storms had cut them off from the rest of civilization for six weeks. The dreaded Mahaka disease was wreaking havoc among the populace. The malady explodes eyeballs and slowly swells the tongue until the mouth is filled breaking the jaw and pushing out the teeth. Eventually one chokes to death.

If the two of us couldn't get the vaccine to them in time every man, woman and child would…Well, let's just say they'd never see another spring.

We'd left the Yukon river about 200 miles back heading north, always north, right into this wall of ice and snow. The Arctic hurricane, like a jungle sniper, had eliminated my dog team one by one until only the two of us were left.

We had no supplies remaining. Only the white bag with the red cross on it containing the life-saving inoculate hung from my shoulder. We were tired…exhausted. With my uncanny ability to sense direction and distance I calculated that we were still 20 miles from Chilcanuknuk. Would we make it in time? Would we make it at all?! Or would we go the way of the rest of our team and freeze to death in this Godforsaken white hell, our bodies left to bloat in the spring thaw to be ravaged by hungry, wild…Heck I was gettin' cold. Time to get back to the dorm.

We returned to our room after nearly an hour and a half. I was drenched to the bone and an unknown number of falls and struggles to right myself had left me physically beaten, but all that fantasy time had rejuvenated my spirit.

Each outside door of the dormitory opened into a living room area. Surrounding each living room were five more doors. One opened into the restroom and the other four opened into bedrooms, each capable of housing two students. While we were away the rest of the guys had roused and were sitting in the living room, most still in their undershorts, reading the paper or watching Saturday morning cartoons. I had been lucky enough to have a room to myself so Blu's presence rarely inconvenienced anyone. This time, however, when Blu reached the center of the room he began shaking off the slush that drenched him.

Half-naked bodies were running, jumping and producing loud and obscene responses as virtually every square inch of that room was saturated. When those less inclined to appreciate the minor discomforts produced by such an invigorating act of nature had finished cursing the cold water, they continued piling on Blu with their oaths and then finished with me before they settled down.

I got a kick out of it but Blu, sensing that his action had caused his friends to be irritated with him, tried to make amends by rubbing his cold wet head against each warm dry leg. With that exercise the repeat show was almost an exact duplicate of the first all the way down to the final contortion. I hate reruns so I went to our room.

Two months later, the end of spring signaled the end of

the semester. We were on our way to Chicago. It was my home town but Blu had never seen a big city. I was concerned about how he'd handle it. We'd only be there for a couple of weeks though because having been away from school for a year recovering from my mishap I had some summer school make-up to do.

Blu and I car-pooled home with two other guys in a Volkswagen Beetle. I've had more comfortable journeys. We'd left in the early evening so the sun was just rising when we reached our South Chicago home. Without displaying any apprehension of any kind, Blu first watered one of the trees in the front yard and then sauntered up to the front door waiting for me to carry my luggage from the street. I stood for a moment searching my memory to see if I could find any recollection of him ever having been there before. Nope, he hadn't. Quite presumptuous of him I thought.

We woke Mom and Dad. Introductions were unnecessary. Naturally I'd written and called home many times since I'd acquired Blu so my folks knew all about him. Blu on the other hand knew nothing about them but it didn't matter. He always treated everyone like an old buddy. After a short greeting I retired for some sack time and Blu stayed up with Mom and Pop to get better acquainted.

I stumbled out of the bedroom a little past noon. Mom was reading a book in the living room. "Morning, Mom. How you?"

"Afternoon, son. I'm doing well thank you. I was getting ready to call the coroner for you though." I gave her a hug and kiss anyway.

"Where are Dad and Blu?" I asked.

"Oh, they left for a walk a couple of hours ago."

Mom wasn't too concerned. Neither was I. Dad loved to walk. "Hike" as he loved to call it. We both knew that he could be gone for hours. I just hoped he wouldn't exhaust my dog.

"What are you up to today?" Mom inquired without raising her head from her reading.

"Thought I'd pop down a donut and then hit the beaches and see if I can find any of the guys."

"Oh, no you don't." she said as she marked her place in the book before closing it and setting it on the lamp table along with her glasses. "You're having a good breakfast before you leave this house. It won't take me any time at all to fix it. You get yourself cleaned up and dressed and it will be ready for you."

That's what I'd counted on but I said, "Oh, Mom, you don't need to do that. Stick with your book. Donuts'll be fine." She just continued toward the kitchen without another word. Was I smooth or what?

After having the perfect breakfast Mom gave me the keys to the new Oldsmobile 88. Though brand spanking new, it was most familiar. Having since birth been accustomed to new cars every two or three years always in one shade of brown or another, the new brown one produced no excitement. My folks always seemed to be 180 degrees off the current fashions. In this case earth tones, or rather earth tone, weren't due to be popular till the late '70s. Personally I would have preferred a bright red one.

Oh well, it sure beat walking to the beach and besides, I could easily fit eleven of the guys and gals in that boat with two more in the trunk if required. When loaded, that old Olds may very well have been the first "low-rider".

Calumet Beach was the first stop or rather cruise. The park was every shade of green and alive with families, couples and other associated groups of people playing catch with frisbees, baseballs, softballs, footballs, beach balls, or picnicking or sunbathing or lounging in the shade of trees or strolling hand-in-hand or arm-around-shoulder, basically and simply enjoying a gorgeous summer day. Everything was just the way

I remembered it and loved it and the familiarity of it all was reassuring and comforting. It was a sanctuary of safety and peace and tranquillity.

But as my mind escaped to memories of my adolescence, I began to notice that although the setting and the activities were the same, the characters had changed. In the past I could have stood in one place and seen dozens of familiar faces and at least a couple of hands full that I could have called by name. Now even while driving only occasional familiar faces would appear. Most were older fathers and mothers, or younger adolescents I remembered as being behind me in school, but friends' faces were gone.

I was becoming aware of a new milestone in my life which I did not approve of nor was I ready for. Though inconsequential in the eyes of adults and certainly not a real earth shaker, it was another one of many stressful awakenings in the life of a young adult.

I wasn't to an age yet where I could rationalize and see how many new friends I had made away from home. All I saw was that all my old friends were gone. It wasn't as though they had died or left the country. I'd eventually find most of them and we'd still get together on occasion, but at that moment they were just *gone*.

In generations past, young adults were kept busy and at home so this revelation, if it even existed, didn't carry much weight. But I was entering the age of leisure. With fewer productive objectives occupying my mind, my thoughts were left to dwell on and exaggerate unimportant natural changes.

I'm sure all my friends didn't experience this particular development; at least not necessarily to my extreme. Many of them had full-time jobs that kept them occupied or had already started their own families or hadn't even come home from school yet, or like my brother, Sid, and closest friend, Wayne, were in Vietnam. Even I was heading back to summer school in just two weeks where this would be virtually forgotten. But right then all that filled me was a feeling of total loss, and a blind-side hit from an angry linebacker would have hurt far less.

I'm sure that Sid and Wayne, who were dodging bullets thousands of miles from home, would have really felt sorry for me had they known of my dilemma. Okay, I admit it was pretty trivial, but it hurt just the same and at the time that was all I could focus on.

A cruise through Rainbow Beach only added fuel to my depression. You know it was bad when girls in bikinis didn't snap me out of it.

After only two hours I arrived back home. Dad and Blu had arrived shortly before me. As I had anticipated Dad had outlasted Blu. My dog was on the floor in my bedroom taking a nap. It seemed like the thing to do so I joined him. It felt good to have finally found a friend. All I said when Mom and Dad inquired about my outing was, "Nobody's around yet". I'm sure they knew what the problem was because they didn't press me for a lengthy description, which was out of character for them.

Blu and I awakened an hour later. The folks were in the living room so we went and sat with them. They told me that while I slept one of my buddies had called to inform me of a party that night. It was just what the doctor ordered…snapped me out of my depression instantly. I sat there and filled the folks in on some of the goings on at school till dinner. Then I got ready to party. I've since discovered that I'm not really a party animal. It's just that that's what we did. There were few alternatives. Then again we didn't look real hard for any either.

The party lasted well into the wee hours of the next morning. Although Blu had enjoyed all the noise and commotion, he still wound up sacking out between a sofa and lamp table for the last few hours. I knew he was ready for the out-of-doors and by golly so was I. I wasn't the least bit sleepy so we headed back to the beach.

This time we weren't looking for anybody. In fact, I hoped there wouldn't be anybody. I just wanted to enjoy the sun rising up out of Lake Michigan while the cool morning breeze blew in my face and the waves lapped across my bare feet. I knew that Blu would eat it up too.

The eastern sky was barely showing some pink when we pulled into the parking lot at Calumet Park. In a few hours there would be thousands of people there, but right then there weren't more than a dozen other cars in sight. A few contained couples, lovers who would have this sunrise indelibly etched into their minds. A romantic memory that they could call up for solace for many years to come. The rest were most likely vehicles of fisherman that we would meet down on the wharves.

We stepped out of the car to meet the calm, cool, early morning air. The only sound was from birds beginning to awaken and of the waves slapping against the rocks and dikes and gently washing the beaches. There was the occasional sound of a boat whistle making its way through the stillness.

Thirty-five yards down an easy sloping grass hill were the large stone blocks that stepped down to the lake forming the barrier between water and earth. As the sky became brighter with every passing moment, I rested on a middle step while Blu ran back and forth stopping only to sniff or piddle. Looking down this stone barrier toward the beach, a couple of hundred yards away, I could see fisherman. Some were preparing there tackle and others, already with their lines in the water, were sitting drinking coffee and smoking cigarettes. The steam and smoke rose slowly straight up.

After a few quiet moments of observation and reflection I rose and stepped, almost climbed, up onto the next higher, gigantic stone block so that my ambling down the wharf would not disturb the fisherman. I knew that catching fish was not their only reason for being there on that gorgeous morning. Like me they were also looking for peace and quiet.

As I would walk behind each they would look up and nod a good morning. Blu in turn would wonder down to get a customary pat on the head and since he didn't make a nuisance of himself, none seemed to mind but rather seemed to appreciate the affable gesture.

I only saw one bobber rolling gently on the near calm surface of the lake. All the other fisherman were using heavily weighted lines that left in a straight line from the tips of their poles and entered sharply into the water. The entry point was evidenced by a small series of ripple rings that rolled at the same cadence as the lone bobber. The scene was hypnotic. Therapy for the soul.

As we neared the end of the stone blocks the top of the sun could be seen poking up out of the lake's horizon and at the same time a gentle wind picked up as though the sun itself were blowing at us. We could now see the beach where it cut a slight arch into the shore line but first we needed to pass a few boat slips at the end of a concrete launching ramp.

The beach was literally covered with gulls, ducks and geese. They were busily feeding on the treasures that the lake continually coughed up on the shore. Each wave that slowly rolled up unto the sand would carry with it a new assortment of tasty morsels. The wave would leave them in a neat row at the terminus of its progress inland while it returned to get another load.

From Blu's reaction when he spotted the many birds, I was afraid he was headed for another fiasco similar to the one on the college pond. Though he understood and responded to commands while in training sessions, he wasn't yet mature enough to hold them in priority over play. There was no stopping him as he bolted in the direction of the avian congregation.

I was relieved to see that he was not taking this adventure as seriously as his first encounter. All he did was bounce and dance up and down the beach and in the water, only toying with the birds. They seemed to sense that they weren't in danger for they only retreated leisurely to air or water at Blu's easy approach and would return to the beach behind him as he passed.

The complete ball of the sun was visible now, a striking bright red. The wisps of clouds and eastern haze were orange. I sat on the sand to watch the drama in the sky and the joy on the beach.

Blu traversed the full length of the beach at least a dozen times, interrupted by plunges into the lake before he tired, shook himself vigorously to shed water, and walked up to where I sat. We sat together observing the birds the water the sky.

For the remainder of our time in Chicago nearly every morning was spent on the lake shore at one location or another in all sorts of weather. Most afternoons were occupied by treks through the many forest preserves south of town. That dog was teaching me that the simpler things in life were far more enjoyable than what I was used to.

4. Bank Lines and Catfish

Before leaving for home, the apartment below Mary and Pete had become available so I had reserved it. Returning for the summer in the Chevy station wagon that Mom and Dad had given me, Blu and I moved right in. The two-flat was conveniently located across the street from campus and already had Blu's kennel installed behind it.

The first weekend back at school I decided we'd go on a campout. I chose a beautiful spot, just a short drive away, on the Big Blue River. I pitched our new 8x16, two-room tent, arranged camp and went fishing late Friday afternoon.

With twelve willow poles over my right shoulder and a steel minnow bucket filled with crawdads in my left hand we hiked about three quarters of a mile up stream. Each five to seven foot willow branch already had a length of eight to ten feet of heavy nylon fishing line attached and wrapped around it. Each line was dressed with a sinker and large hook.

Before I climbed and slid down the bank I tied the cord that was attached to the minnow bucket handle through a belt loop on the left side of my cut-off blue jeans. I had left the solid outer bucket of the minnow bucket combination back at camp. I carried only the perforated inner bucket containing the bait. After a dry quarter hour the crayfish were happy when, after wading out to thigh deep water, I lowered the bucket into the river.

I then tied the cord that was attached to the bundle of poles onto a belt loop on my right side. Floating the bundle out in front of me I walked down river looking for a good spot to sink the first pole into the bank.

I'd gone only a few yards when I found our first suitable fishing hole. As I got closer to the bank the bottom dropped off into a hole that put the water to chest level. Dynamite spot! I was sure that if I could find eleven more like that, come morning, I'd have some big catfish to play with.

I inched up stream to the leading edge of the hole, pulled the floating bundle to me, untied it removing one pole and then resecured the bundle. I unwrapped the line and jammed the butt end of the pole as deep as I could into the eroded, muddy bank. Then I reached into the minnow bucket and grabbed a crawdad, or rather took out the one that grabbed me. After sticking the hook through the underside of its tail I released it into the current that carried it into the waters of the hole. That completed I made a visual note of the location and continued downstream.

This was Blu's introduction to line setting. He was forever playful running up and down the steep banks and plunging recklessly into the river. Whenever I'd stop to set a line, however, he'd stop and cock his head in wonderment at what I was doing.

"You see, pup, you set this pole as deep into the mud as you can so it points slightly up from the river. That's so the fish just can't pull it straight out. See, now you know why I sharpened the butt ends after I cut 'em down. Why'd I pick this spot? Well because see here, on this outside bend, behind this snag the water's cut out a deep hole. The hole even goes under the bank where the big ones like to sit and wait for their dinner to float by."

I never would have imagined how much company a dog could be. And I never had to answer a question I didn't know the answer to.

We were only about a quarter of a mile from camp and on our sixth set when I saw the granddaddy of all catfish sanctuaries. The bank made a near 90 degree sweep to the left. Just past the corner, a large cottonwood had toppled into the river some years before. Its top was laying downstream and its large ball of roots had hung up on roots from other trees that were poking out from the mud bank.

Being that it was an outside bend, the current had carried many other logs, branches, large sections of bark and discarded and lost manmade articles into the cottonwoods root ball. All the debris presented a formidable barrier to the forward flow of the river. Upstream from the cottonwood's collection the water slowly swirled in an eddy.

This one had to be a shoulder, maybe neck-deeper for sure. And it extended a good twenty to twenty-five feet upstream and easily ten to twelve feet out from the bank. And who knows how far it cut under?!

"Blu-dog, if this one doesn't have a record breaker in it I'll eat the rest of these crawdads right out of the bucket!" I said as I pulled the bundle of poles toward me. "Man, Bluper, we're gonna get a monster out of here that's gonna make whatever else we catch look like bait! Maybe two!" I continued as I chose the two stoutest poles from those remaining. "I think we'll even come back and check this one a couple of times through the night!"

I waded closer to the eddy with the tied on bait bucket and pole bundle floating downstream to my left and a pole in each hand. The water had reached my waist. I was so excited I couldn't stop talking. "Hot dog, Blu, it's gonna take all that we've got to hoist this monst....woooahahahah!!!," I stepped on something hard and irregular sticking up from the bottom loosing my balance. The tug of the bucket and poles didn't help any as I stumbled in the direction they were pulling barely able to keep my feet.

"Whoa ho doggie, I almost lost it on that, heyyyawwww!!!....blubblubblubblub..." I had stepped off into that "shoulder, maybe neck-deeper" only the murky water was already over my head and the weight of the bait bucket was still pulling me down!

I struggled desperately for the surface but couldn't swim against the weight of the bucket. My feet finally touched bottom in what must have been at least ten feet of water. Pushing off I rocketed to the surface but the heavy bucket only allowed a quick breath before it dragged me back under.

At the surface I noticed that during my first decent I had drifted ten feet down stream. The bundle of poles had stopped in the snag but on my way back down I could feel the taut cord, that was connected to the bundle, swinging me even further downstream. I was afraid that I might be under the snag.

My fears were confirmed when upon touching bottom, although too dark to see, I could feel sticks, roots and other debris brushing against my bare chest and legs.

I fumbled with the knot on my belt loop that retained the bait bucket. No success. I quickly reached into my pocket, pulled out and opened my knife and cut both that cord and the one attached to the poles. I could feel the deep currents swirling and tugging me further into the snag so this time when I pushed off for the surface, I angled my assent upstream. When I burst through the surface I gasped a long drag of air.

My eyes closed in relief but I couldn't get too complacent. The currents were forcing me back into the snag. Swimming away from the root ball I gained the bank in short order and pulled myself unto the mud to rest.

Blu was there and ready to play. He thought I'd been recreating and now it was his turn. It hurt his feelings but I put a stop to that real quick.

I sat on the bank five or ten minutes catching breath and thanking God. Time to get back to business.

"I've got to get back down there, boy, and get the bait bucket." It was a two dollar bucket. Enough for a movie, popcorn and pop. No way I was going to let the river keep it.

I didn't figure it had moved very much being water filled and sitting on the bottom so I was sure it would be easy to locate. About twenty feet upstream from the ball of roots I pushed off into the eddy, took a few deep breaths, held the last one and headed for the bottom and the invisible bait bucket.

Within seconds of feeling around the bottom, I located it and pulled it toward the shallower middle of the river. As I began to feel the gentle current of the river proper, the bottom rose quickly and I pulled my way along it with my left hand, the bait bucket in my right. Soon, I reached waist deep water.

"Got it, Bluper," I shouted as I stood up. He was happy. He probably didn't know why, except that my present tone was welcomed after my last reprimand had sent him into a pout.

I made my way upstream around and above the deep hole and onto the bank. Setting down the bait bucket in a couple of inches of water to keep my crawdads wet, I walked down the bank and out onto the log snag. Then I ventured onto its root system, reaching down through its maze to retrieve my bundle of poles and the two singles that had drifted and lodged there.

Arriving back at the bucket I sank the two stout willows into the bank so that their baits drifted into the hole. Then, after tying the bucket and bundle back onto my belt loops, we continued downstream. This time I had with me a walking stick. It was a sturdy, straight branch broken from a tree. I was still in the process of discovering what I could and could not do with my newly acquired handicap.

"Well, Blu, looks as though a little support's gonna be needed for walking sometimes. Quite typical, don't you think, that I had to be nearly killed to figure that out?" At that he wagged his tail vigorously looking at me with big eyes and hanging tongue. I thought it rude of him to so joyously agree that I was an idiot.

By the time we had finished setting our remaining five lines the sun had disappeared but we easily reached camp before dark. The last set was less than half a mile below our campsite.

I got a fire going, had dinner and then, leaning against a large maple, sat and played some tunes on my harmonica. Blu sat next to me and howled along. Lousy harmony, but we weren't trying to impress anybody.

Ten minutes or so of the jam and Blu tired of it. He opted instead to go swimming. I played on.

An hour later I felt tired and decided to turn in early. "Yo, Blu! Hey boy, let's go check those two lines before we turn in." Blu loped up over the edge of the bank responding to my call and we started upstream. When we reach the bank opposite the prime spot we had to slide down the bank to get closer because, in the dark, even with a flashlight, we couldn't see that far.

At water level I shined the light across the gently flowing river. "No action yet, fella. Bet ya there'll be something tuggin' at those poles in the morning though." We went back to camp and I turned in to the enclosed cabin portion of the tent. Blu was in the screened in room with the door opened so he could come and go as he pleased.

The last few months he had spent with me in the dormitory. At my folks' home in Chicago, where they had no outside facility for a dog, he had slept at the foot of my bed. At least in those locations, though, I had slept in a bed while he on the floor. The situation was altogether different while camping.

He seemed to feel that he had just as much right to the ground as I did. I probably would have let him sleep in the enclosed portion with me had it not been for the fact that he was soaked in river water and his coat was heavily impregnated with sand and silt. Besides, I thought he'd be happier with his own room. Most children would.

For about fifteen minutes after I zipped him out he whined and continually rubbed against the canvas wall separating us. Occasionally he would scratch at the zipper and I would respond with a scolding. The commotion finally ceased and seconds later I heard splashing in the river while he, obviously conceding his defeat, took a swim.

I never noticed when the splashing stopped. However, the unsyncopated, rapid thudding of clumsy feet roused me to a sitting position in my sleeping bag just in time to see in the moonlit tent a large bulge develop in the wall, the zipper split, and a sixty pound, flailing, sopping wet animal come flying through the air to rest heavily in my lap.

Dazed, his head bobbed around rapidly while he tried to gain his bearings. Finally, looking up at me, he remembered the situation. His eyes brightened, his tongue flopped out of an open mouth, and his tail started leading the orchestra in a show of victory.

The tent was ripped and the blanket was soaked. Even then it was difficult to be angry with the possessor of a love that strong. I rolled him off to the side, patted him goodnight and together we slept out the night.

I awakened shortly before sunrise to a face full of mosquito bites. The little devils had easily found their feeding ground through the torn zipper. Blu was still sleeping but as I arose he lifted his head to see what was going on. It dawned on me that I had never checked the two poles through the night so I hurriedly pulled on my still-wet cut-offs in anticipation. While pulling up the fly I heard a not so distant meowing coming from outside. Blu heard it too and raised his head, perkier this time.

At six months, Blu had only a few growing months of any consequence left but, needless to say, there were still a great number of attitude adjustment months for which to make allowances. Blu, as was his custom with all living things, except other male dogs, tried ever so hard to make friends with any new animal that crossed his path. The meowing told us that there was a brand new potential friend somewhere outside. Before I could pull on my sweatshirt he had darted past me, through the hole in the tent and out of sight. I pulled on and tied my tennis shoes and headed for the encounter that Blu had undoubtedly already made.

Fifteen yards to the side of the tent was a tree with three trunks coming out of the ground. Presumably the trunks had a common root system. They broke ground in such a way that the area between them left just enough room for a cat to defend. And just then there happened to be a cat defending it. It looked to be a pure bred Siamese. An adolescent.

Blu had become quite a bit larger than I had expected having been the runt of the litter and all. Though I was pleased at this growth it did pose a bit of a problem in that he was growing in size so fast that his coordination was not able to keep pace. In situations like this his clumsiness was atrocious. Though he became somewhat more graceful in his later years, this fall-all-over-himself awkwardness would always exhibit itself when he became happily excited.

Blu was bouncing around like an oaf trying in every way he new to make apparent his intent to play. Any normal animal the age of that cat would have been ninety-nine percent inclined to do the same, especially a cat. After all the saying, "playful as a kitten" has its sound base in fact. Granted Blu's size would be intimidating at first but kittens or puppies get over that deterrent quickly when the urge to play kicks in.

He was trying really hard. He'd even control himself and lay down still, except for his wagging tail, for ten or fifteen seconds at a time. He'd then get back up dancing and if he'd get too close and the kitten would hiss in anger he'd back off gently, respectfully, before resuming the bounce. That cat even hissed at me when I tried to approach once. Once was enough for me but Blu kept trying exceptionally hard to be a friend.

That kitten sure had a lot of nerve. After all, if it didn't want attention it should have kept its mouth shut. It could have slipped away unnoticed.

Finally Blu must have decided to just go for broke. He lay down with his front paws outstretched, chin to the ground, butt up and tail wagging so fast it was in danger of shaking something loose and inched his way toward the crabby little feline.

The inevitable happened. Heck, I saw it coming and could have dodged it. That's how perceptible it was. But not Blu. That tiny paw came out from between those trunks with claws extended and took him right in the nose. The audacity!

That did it. After all the time he had spent bending over backwards to be nice—and to a cat no less. No one would have thought the lesser of him had he taken after her from the start with murder on his mind. Instead he had actually attempted to bury the hatchet and begin an equal, give and take, relationship. He had the cat outgunned from the start. He didn't have to be nice. It was all out of the goodness of his heart, nothing more. And what does he get in return? The proverbial slap in the face. Well, that was the last straw.

With unusual sternness, Blu stood straight up looking straight down on the pussy cat still coiled with ears flat, hissing. I was shocked. I had never seen him express such anger. I didn't blame him—I had just never seen it. He stood there motionless for another few moments seemingly giving it one last chance for an apology. It never came and with calculated accuracy he lifted his right paw and planted it firmly between the shoulder blades of the obnoxious feline and pinned it helplessly to the ground.

Except for her hind legs, which dug frantically at the dirt, she was unable to move and Blu, who was intent on making perfectly clear his total superiority, was unwilling to permit her to do so. I was taking all this in approvingly feeling it was about time but after a while thought she had had enough. After all it couldn't breath, so I called Blu off.

He acknowledged my command with a dignified and defiant glance in my direction disagreeing with me on the duration of punishment. He then returned his gaze to the helpless animal underfoot. I thought about this for a moment and figured he was right so I gave him until the cat's struggles were weakening.

A short while later I said, "How 'bout now, guy? You don't wanna croak 'er do ya?" With reluctance and one last push and twist he released it, sending it staggering off meowing wildly.

Unhappy that he had had to resort to violence, he walked somberly back to the tent and lay down contemplating his conduct.

I was more anxious than ever to check my lines, especially the two hummers, but this experience had been quite traumatic for Blu. I gave him a few more minutes to meditate.

Finally I didn't call to him but only started walking upstream along the high bank. I hadn't gone far before I heard him coming up behind me. He passed me at a gentle trot rather than his usual break-neck gallop. "Good boy." I said, "Stay busy. Keep your mind off it. This too shall pass."

High on the bank I could see that the willow pole closest the snag was bent and bobbing and weaving slightly. It wasn't displaying the action that I would have liked, but that didn't always mean that the fish was smaller than desired.

"Maybe it's our monster but he's just been on all night. Even Moby Dick got tired ya know," I said to Blu as though he possessed my same disappointment in the fight displayed and he responded with a little more dance to his step. Actually he hadn't even recognized the motion in the pole yet.

We crossed the river well above the hole not wanting to scare the fish into desperation before we could get hold of the pole. When we were almost within reach of it my puppy finally noticed the unnatural movement and stared at it quizzically not knowing exactly what he should do about it. I'd had him fishing before but always then I'd had a rod and reel.

It wasn't till after slowly sliding the butt end of the willow from the bank and the fish renewing its fight, at the added resistance I presented, that Blu recognized what was happening and began to bound and whine excitedly.

It was a big fish. Maybe not the one I had dreamed of, but certainly no slouch. It didn't flip-flop back and forth in a jerking, quick fashion but rather pulled strong, steady and deep, methodically swishing. When I'd pull upwards, rather than coming to the surface, it would simply roll while still out of sight in the murky water causing a rolling turbulation of suspended bottom muck.

Certain that I'd never be able to just lift this one from the river without breaking the line or the pole I inched sideways along the steep part of the bank targeting the beach-like area fifty feet upstream. Besides having his own weight and strength in his favor, he was also aided by the rivers current as he swam downstream.

Minutes later I reached the beach and slowly backed away from the water in an attempt to beach it. As it sensed itself being pulled closer to the surface and the bank he mustered added power. With the increased thrashing I feared a broken line or straightened hook.

I slowly moved forward allowing the fish to reach deeper water but not before I was able to get my first glimpse of my catch. My level of excitement increased dramatically when I saw its upwards of three foot length and its wide, flat head. It wasn't the sea monster I'd dreamed of last night, but if I could land him, he'd make a fine dinner for a lot of people.

"I'm gonna have to drain him a lot more before he'll drag easy without breakin' my line, Bluper." Blu liked it when he was made a part of the action. He was at the waters' edge with his tail going and his neck stretched in the direction of the spot where the line entered the water. When I'd speak to him his tail would add a few miles an hour and his ears would go up.

"We'll just have to walk him up and down the beach a bit. But when the time comes be ready cause it's going to take both of us to keep him on dry land." When I'd add enough excitement to my voice it'd transfer over to Blu and he'd lapse into a tizzy.

At a pace intended to tire rather than frighten the fish we made our way up and back along the beach. Occasionally we'd venture slightly inland to test the fish's remaining strength without getting it too excited. It took nearly fifteen minutes of this before our fish moved like dead weight.

When he was in that state I was easily able to beach it alone. Keeping up my frenzied, one-sided conversation with Blu made him feel a part of the drama and every now and then, when he could control himself, he'd take a swat at the fish with his paw in an attempt to do his part to push it further up onto shore.

Our catch was an easy forty-two maybe forty-six inches and must have weighted in at thirty pounds or more. After unhooking it I ran one end of the quarter-inch cord I carried as a stringer through the mouth of the fish and out through a gill. I then ran the end through a loop made at the other end of the same cord and tied it to a live bush growing from the bank. I pushed the fish back into the river so it would stay alive and fresh and we headed upstream to check our other lines.

We returned in half an hour with two other catfish. One about a pound and a half, the other near four pounds. Another of our lines had had a large carp on it but not being partial to that particular species I had released it. Blu wasn't very happy about me doing that and chased after it until it disappeared in the opaque water.

I'd strung them both on a branch so when we reached our "catch of the day" I restrung them on the cord stringer and we headed for camp. That was a long quarter-mile walk carrying nearly thirty-five pounds of squirming animals.

At camp I put the fish back into the water before going to check our remaining lines. "I'm gettin' mighty hungry. You?" Blu got attentive, acknowledging the sound of my voice as I rose from the river. God, how I loved how he was agreeable with almost every spoken word. "My stomach's grumblin'. Sure hope we don't have any problems with the rest of our sets."

We promptly made way to our furthest set downstream. Our final checkpoint would place us only yards from our camp and fresh fish for breakfast.

We returned in three quarters of an hour. Our downstream lines were barren except for the head of a small carp. A snapping turtle had gotten to that line before I did. One other hook was without bait but the other three hadn't been touched.

At camp I set in to preparing breakfast. First I got a fire going. Then I removed our midsized fish from the stringer. An hour ago I would have chosen the small one but now I was ravenous and I was certain Blu was as well.

I dispatched it quickly with a thwack from the blunt end of my hatchet. Slitting it from vent to whiskers I removed its innards and then began the dislikeable chore of skinning it. Like peeling an apple only the catfish's hide wasn't as inclined to let loose. The next step was to slice off the thick, firm fillets. I much preferred river to lake or pond cats. The meat always seemed so much more mushy on the latter.

The procedure was interrupted frequently in order to continue feeding the fire with more and more and larger and larger dry hardwoods. The fire was leaping and crackling to a height of three or more feet. Just anticipating the smell of fresh-caught catfish sizzling as it broiled over hot coals got my stomach to grumbling even more. So much so that it would have been embarrassing had there been company present.

The fish was finally ready to flop onto the foil-covered grill. All that was required was for the flame to reduce itself to red, glowing coals. While we waited I got the coffeepot ready, opened a can of beans and placed them both near the fire. This way they'd have a head start. Then I went into the tent to get my blanket and put it to air in the morning breeze and sunshine. It would still be some minutes yet so I went to the river to clean up.

When Blu and I returned to the fire pit the flames were only slightly dancing above the extremely hot remnants of wood so I sat to rest and stare into there mystical depths as they died completely.

In short order my broiling fire was ready. I oiled the foil, poked a few holes through it, laid the fillets and bony portions of the carcass on it and set it all over the pit. In only seconds the aroma had me in a state of euphoria. I was certain that people back in town were wondering what the grumbling noise was.

Having been preheated, the coffee was done first and a hot black cup as an appetizer was splendid.

The fish and beans were done quickly. Blu was beside himself. He was springing around like a bucking bronco sometimes doing complete 360's without touching the ground. I took one of the fillets and, after pouring Blu's dry dogfood unto a cleared spot on the ground, broke it into small pieces and mixed it into the dry chunks. He had his nose buried in it before I could pull away. Now it was time to bury myself in my share.

I have since had dinners preceded by a cocktail. Then escargot, or smoked salmon on bread squares covered with capers. Followed by crisp salad with blue cheese and fresh ground pepper. And then Chateaubriand smothered in Béarnaise sauce, topping everything off with ameretto cheesecake and a brandy Alexander. What I had along the banks of the Big Blue river that summer morning was coffee, pork and beans, and catfish. I recommend the former menu as a superb substitute if the latter is not available.

Nap time!

5. His First Season

The time I had waited anxiously for was upon us. Blu's first hunting season. He was nine months old, nearly full grown, just some filling out to do. Boy, was I proud of him.

For some reason he had blossomed into a fine looking animal. A massive, well-shaped head, thick neck, strong shoulders and back, large chest, small waist, and firm hind quarters. And he carried it all properly too. Head up and alert, body straight, and tail stiffly curled forward. He was beautiful…until he got excited.

Yep, he had grown so fast from the runt to the giant that his coordination hadn't had a chance to catch up. When in a joyous mood his contortions were most unusual to watch.

Being so large and strong, they could be quite damaging to himself and to those around him, animate and inanimate.

When he was set free from his kennel, for instance, the lives of one and all were in his hands until he settled down. All those unaccustomed to him were warned accordingly. It was much like turning on a bulldozer, putting it in gear, and then jumping off to let it go its own way until it ran out of gas. The fact that he possessed a tail surely as devastating as any crocodile's made him all the more perilous.

His lack of coordination occasionally became apparent in other instances as well. Once he nearly rendered himself senseless while performing a common sneeze. I noticed the beginning of a real zinger coming on, oh, say, nearly a minute before the explosion.

His eyes half closed as he stood still concentrating. The right side of his lip raised just enough to show a little white. The right nostril and eye quivered ever so slightly. Then they all returned to normal for a few seconds. Then they repeated the same procedure again. This time though his mouth slightly opened and his head barely raised, but again everything returned to normal. After a few more seconds it happened again but the mouth opened a little wider and the head raised a little higher and the eyes closed completely.

These symptoms recurred at least a half dozen times. Each time the telltale signs became more pronounced and the air intake to his lungs increased to a point where the pressure within must have been sufficient to inflate a tractor tire. Then it happened.

I looked around quickly to be sure nothing of value was near and returned my gaze to see an inflation that, until that time, had only been achieved by a pregnant buffalo. His jaws opened to near dislocation and his neck raised to near breaking point while his head swayed slowly from side to side. His eyes shut so tightly that I feared they'd never again be capable of opening and his whole frame quivered with such force from tension that I thought every muscle would be torn.

With a blast that could be heard across town a minute's worth of built-up pressure was released in a fraction of a second bringing his chin down fast and hard to kiss the concrete floor. The impact was sufficient to split his chin, cause his gums and nose to bleed and send him dazed and staggering off into la la land.

One fine morning, exceptionally suited for hunting, we left the house very early planning on making a whole day of it. In readiness were packed lunch, a thermos of coffee, a canteen of water, bow and arrows for an early morning deer hunt, .22 rifle for mid-morning bunnies, and shotgun for afternoon pond-hopping for ducks. We were adequately equipped for a month of survival training, an invasion of aliens, or one day of leisure hunting.

It had rained hard all night, making everything water-logged and muddy. Still, heavily overcast, it made for cold and uncomfortable conditions. It was ideally suited for a hunt.

We arrived at our destination an hour before day-light and peered down the long, rolling dirt road that led to the small wooded area I would be treed in while waiting for deer to leave their feeding grounds. In the ambient light of the full moon, that shown through the cloud cover, the road looked surprisingly good for having withstood an all night downpour.

"By golly, Bluper, the rain must have hit so hard that it just ran right off instead of soaking in." Blu just sat on the passenger seat staring straight ahead with no response. That should have told me something.

"Here we go!"

If only I had taken the time to get out of the station wagon and set foot on that road. The instant the wagon left the security of the gravel I felt it lower a few inches.

Anticipating clear sailing I had hit the road at a good clip. Therefore, stopping at the edge and pushing it back the few feet to the county road was out of the question.

Having eliminated the more cautious course of action, I proceeded onward to keep up momentum, hoping to reach the end and the security of a grass patch. There I might be able to turn around for a straight shot back. This was Blu's first taste of back-road driving. Through the coming years he would learn to detest it.

He was immediately slammed into the door as we fishtailed from the brink of one ditch to the other. He jumped over both seats into the cargo area hoping for more protection, but the poor guy, having no hands with which to grasp hold, was bounced about like a pinball.

To this day, after years more experience on bad roads, I'm still amazed that we made it to the end of that one. Our grass patch was no help. Having to stop to turn around, valuable momentum was lost, so the mud received its just reward swallowing us axle deep.

I was thoroughly dismayed. How was I to get this vehicle back down that half-mile gauntlet? It was nothing short of a miracle that we had made it all the way in. And that was after gaining required force on a firm gravel road. Even if I were successful in digging and rocking and lifting our way out of this present dilemma there was no way to regain any momentum.

Blu thought our present motionless state was the best thing since beefsteak. He had no desire whatever to go back down that road after his ride of terror. Where we were was just fine with him and he was doing his best to convince me of the same.

He had plunged headlong into the front seat ricocheting off the dash and onto the floor. Without a lag he had sprung onto the seat, spun in place two or three times rejoicing, then lit in my lap with his left paw over my right shoulder and his slobbering tongue flapping a mile-a-minute up the side of my face.

Needless to say this was neither the time nor the place for such a show of happiness and affection. Most human beings are devoid of such emotions in times of duress and I removed him from the front of the vehicle quickly and rudely.

I fought the unrelenting mud with shovel and branches and grasses for nearly two hours and moved about ten feet. The sun was up by then. It was nearly eight o'clock. We only had about three thousand feet to go. A few quick calculations made me realize that at our present rate spring flowers would be blooming before we reached the county road. I concluded it was time to summon help.

After a cross-country trek of thirty minutes we arrived wet and muddy in the farmyard of one of the locals. At the end of my pitiful story, a hearty chuckle and a "Hop on" were the responses from the understanding farmer who had mounted his tractor and was ready for the rescue mission. Had our roles been reversed I probably would have spent an hour lecturing but being older and wiser he realized that what I had just been through was equal to a semester's worth of lectures. Boy was he right. What is it about all but the most wise, that they refuse to believe all but their own mistakes?

As I reflected on the morning's adventure I realized that there was a lesson to be learned from my pup. Having had no place to go and all the time in the world to get there, I should have calmed down, regrouped my thoughts, taken Blu's lead returning some of his affection, and then spent the morning hunting. Afterwards I could have gone in search of a tow and still had plenty of time. Maybe I would have even bagged something.

In the years that followed, whenever an emergency has abruptly developed, I have remembered that morning in the mud and have always tried to play down the problem's seriousness with levity or a pleasing thought or word. Sure enough, those few moments are usually enough for me to become objective. Usually the situation isn't nearly as hazardous or depressing or destructive as first thought.

We were grateful to be back on gravel by ten o'clock. After a sincere thank you and a vain attempt to offer money for our rescue, we were headed home. But we couldn't go home. Not empty handed. We had been gone nearly six hours and had enough armament to annihilate a small army. We had to bag something.

Still wet and muddy and now also cold and tired we reversed direction and made way for a series of area ponds that harbored transient ducks. Even one duck would reduce the ridicule to a minimum. Who was I kidding? Even one empty shell casing would have satisfied me. I remember praying that the first pond, about a mile and a half down the road, would yield up just one swimming bird. Even a scrawny teal would have filled the bill…or a coot!

Then it happened. Temptation flew before my eyes. If even an insignificant teal or coot would satisfy the hunter, how much more the monarch of the fall skies? The Canada goose.

A flock of about forty flew at about two hundred feet altitude. "Hot dog Bluper! If they're that low they've gotta be lookin' for somewhere to land and feed. We're gonna tail 'em till they come down and then pop one." My depression disappeared, which was good. But so did my recollection of the morning's events, which was bad.

Keeping up with a flock of anything was no easy task on the county roads that formed one mile squares on the ground. I was making way at a good clip with only occasional glances at the road. Most of the time my eyes were glued to that flight of honking birds.

With so little time for watching the road. I certainly had

no time at all for looking along the side of it. Therefore it should come as no surprise that the sign that read "GRAVEL ENDS 1/2 MILE" went unobserved. So did the ever-so-subtle line in the road meaning the end of security and the beginning of misery—until it was too late to stop. I saw it with only enough time to mumble something vulgar and then we again became an integral part of our earth. Blu immediately jumped over the seats into the back of the wagon.

Our only hope was to keep up speed and somehow stay in the middle of the road until we hit the next intersection where we would again find gravel. The attempt was a valiant one with Blu again ricocheting around the back of the station wagon as we fish-tailed for a few hundred yards.

Suddenly the vehicle ceased to respond to the steering wheel. We were helpless. We slid quickly to the left and assumed a position in the adjacent road ditch. Mud came up over the hood and nearly covered the windshield. The sudden halt also catapulted Blu, and all his mud from our previous episode, into the front seat. The car was buried, but good, in knee-deep goo.

We weren't a dozen miles from where we had spent the morning like hogs in slop and here we were rootin' around again.

I just sat there, eyes closed, my chin on my chest, and my hands in my lap feeling sorry for myself. I wished I had just gone straight home and faced the music. That would have been far better than the three-quarter-mile slog we had ahead of us back to the farmstead at the beginning of the section. With my troublesome leg, mud was not my favorite medium in which to walk.

It would be a while before we got to the house and then back again so I remained in the car long enough to share a sandwich with my fellow mud-wrestler.

The door opened hard against the mud. Actually, there

should be a word in the English language to describe this stuff other than "mud". Mud's thicker. Water's thinner. This stuff, on the other hand, couldn't be shoveled and a fish couldn't quite swim in it. I think I'll call it "wud".

The door opened just wide enough for us to escape while the wud oozed in behind us. Blu immediately high-centered. Pushing and pulling each other we were able to get out of the ditch and onto the road that was only ankle deep with wud.

Having reached higher ground I surveyed the situation and saw that the far lip of the ditch on the other side of the road was thick with grass and therefore seemed to afford a more suitable surface for my tired legs. We crossed the road. In an attempt to cross the ditch on the other side my feet slipped out from under me and I reached the bottom on the seat of my pants and the back of my jacket.

Being at Blu's level, naturally he thought it play time so within seconds the two of us blended in beautifully with our surroundings. Fending him off, I regained an upright position only to have to fall back to hands and knees to climb the other bank.

The narrow lip of grass was like a cold drink on a hot day. I pulled a handful and used it to wipe away some of the wud that covered me, then headed south toward the house.

Winter wheat fields on both sides of the road were almost entirely underwater. Only on an occasional high spot appeared the telltale green that would grow into an ocean of amber waves on the plains by late next spring.

Blu was about fifty yards ahead of me when I heard high-pitched barking. The distance between us prevented me from seeing exactly what was taking place. I could only make out a tiny speck in the middle of a water puddle that seemed to hold my pup's fascination. Blu was in the throes of his clumsy dance.

As I drew closer the scene became clear. The speck in the

middle of the puddle was the mound of dirt that surrounded a pocket gopher hole and it included Mr. Pocket Gopher himself. The hole in the middle was brim full of water. The gopher had apparently been forced to retreat from his home due to the flood. With nowhere to go he was desperately defending himself and his home from an intruder one hundred times his size.

Unbeknownst to the terrified rodent, Blu possessed no harmful intentions. Blu was interested only in play but the gopher, ready to strike in defense, was following his every move and barking loudly and rapidly as a warning.

He showed no added alarm when I arrived on the scene as if to express the notion that he would take care of me when he finished with the first intruder. The comedy show lightened my spirits somewhat so I just watched without interference for a minute or two.

After a time I felt empathy for the gopher that had enough on its mind without the added harassment of a black giant. I was just about to call Blu off, to be on our way, when he inadvertently got just a hair too close to the angry rodent. With lightening speed gopher sprang forward and with its half-inch buck teeth latched onto the nose of my unsuspecting puppy-dog.

The howl that ensued was an unmistakable "ouch" that continued like a hound on a hot trail. The whole while Blu spun around in rapid circles trying in vain to shed the berserker on the end of his nose. The gopher was hanging on for dear life while Blu continued to spin. Centrifugal force caused the gopher to stick straight out from the end of Blu's snout.

Finally it could hold on no longer and came sailing through the air to land in a splash at my feet. He righted himself instantly but groggily and turned my way as if to say "Okay, you're next."

Before he could regain his balance from his dizzying spin I raised my foot and brought the heel down on the back of its neck ending its struggles quickly. I felt sad having to snuff out the life of one so valiant but then again it beat getting bit and I was sure, in its state of rage, that that was exactly what it would have done.

"How's the shnoz, Bluper?" He was still whimpering and rubbing his nose vigorously into the cool, soothing wud. I went to examine the wound.

"Whoa. He got you a pretty good pop there, boy." He had been bleeding profusely from the deep gash as evidenced by the red wud and water in the vicinity. The flow was lessening though as it clotted and as he packed more and more wud on it by rootin'. He stared at me with sad eyes.

"You sure paint a pathetic picture with that swollen, wudy nose." I kidded. "You just don't understand why he got so rough do you? Well, I'll tell you, boy. You'll have to learn to be a little less trusting. At least stay on your guard. There's always gonna be someone out there who'll take a piece of you if they can."

Trudging onward we finally reached the farmhouse. Inside was another savior. We must have been quite a sight, covered with wud from head to foot. I wouldn't have blamed the farmer in the least if he got himself a good chuckle out of us. Being a gentleman, though, he did his level best to hold back the laughter. His efforts were commendable until I answered his inquiry about Blu's swollen nose.

The tale of our encounter with the pocket gopher pushed him to his breaking point. Gentleman or not he burst into uproarious laughter that brought his wife to the back door to see what was the matter. The farmer was unable to speak so I had to relate the story again to the lady while her husband got even louder with every word. When I finished, she joined him.

I glanced down at Bluper. Seeing him sitting there in the

wud that he looked so much a part of, with a nose almost the size of a man's fist I couldn't contain myself either. The three of us lurched with unrestrained laughter at Blu's expense.

Each time the laughter began to subside all that was necessary was a glance down at the pathetic wud-puppy to get it started all over again.

Finally, while the farmer got himself bundled up and the tractor warmed up, his wife was kind enough to let me get warm on the back porch with a cup of fresh coffee. "Thanks. I wouldn't trade this cup for a hundred dollar bill," I told her. Which was easy for me to say since I'd never had a hundred dollar bill.

Pulling the car, that had sunk below its front bumper, out of a five foot deep road ditch was no easy matter even for a tractor. However, the task was finally accomplished and the farmer returned to his home. As I got into the station wagon I could still hear him laughing down the road.

I'd had enough. It was only 2:30 in the afternoon. I had no game in the bag. I wanted only to go home.

Thank God no one was depending on my day's hunt to stay alive. One pocket gopher does not many feed. The worst that happened was that Blu and I were the brunt of ridicule from Pete and Mary. Mary was nicer about it, being the lady that she is. I mean she held it back till it hurt. But she didn't quite achieve sainthood. Then there were only the other five hundred people that Pete blabbed to.

It wound up to be a story about me, the great hunter who spent a whole day out with enough fire power to bring down a herd of elephants. After never firing a shot I had returned cold, wet, wuddy, exhausted, and with a pocket gopher killed by a size eleven. A gopher, mind you, that had held me at bay and had whooped my dog. It was a while before that story died.

A couple of weeks later we tried again. This time we narrowed down our prey to just ducks. And this time Pete came along. "I've just got to see this team with my own two eyes," he quipped. The remark was not appreciated.

We left Luke home so that the two young dogs would not be continually trying to out perform each other, mutilating ducks. We left well before sunrise and got set up in a blind on the west bank of Olive Creek Lake. It was a state owned lake not far from home.

The morning was a gorgeous one. Not many mornings are otherwise to my way of thinking. It was still and quiet except for the night sounds of the outdoors, an owl here a raccoon there, and refreshingly but not bitterly cold. Decoys had been set and Pete and I were sitting back in the blind waiting for shooting time and sipping hot coffee. Blu was nervous with anticipation, his tail slapping furiously at the reed walls of the blind.

If hunting did not have these quiet, lonesome times, it would hold little fascination for me.

Gradually the sky became brighter. Finally a glance at my watch showed it was legal to shoot. Now all we needed was something to shoot at. We scanned the skies searching for a flock close enough to call into our decoys. Within minutes we discovered one.

Pete produced his duck call and began quacking so admirably that I was tempted to shoot him and let Blu drag him to the car. Sweet revenge for two weeks of taunting. I was sure Mary would have understood. And if I could have loaded the jury at my trial with duck hunters they'd have come in with a verdict of innocent by reason of an honest mistake.

"I can hear 'em answering, Pete. Keep quakin'. A little softer now. They're circlin' down. Gettin' ready to land." Boom, boom!

As we had raised and fired the birds had broken formation and headed every which way. One duck had sputtered and fallen about forty yards out.

Over-anxious, and still actually a puppy, Blu made for the lake and his quarry without orders. No harm done. There was still plenty of time to teach him the finer points of retrieving. What counted was desire and he certainly did not lack that.

He bounded through the shallows for thirty or forty feet and hit deep water strokin'. He reached the wounded bird, gently cradled it in his jaws, performed a one hundred and eighty degree turn and headed for shore. Wow! Was I proud of my runt!

He tiptoed through the shallows. It seemed that he was trying not to cause additional discomfort to the already injured and shocked duck. Returning to the blind he laid the animal down gently, licked it a couple of times and left the rest to us.

"Gee, you think he knows it's his job to retrieve it? Or do you figure maybe he thinks he's supposed to rescue it?" Pete fancied himself a comedian. "Your dog a hunter or a lifeguard?" The blind resounded with the sound of a man laughing at his own joke.

"It don't really matter now! Does it? The bird's here! Ain't it? Blu just knows a bruised bird tastes bad." You didn't expect me to add credence to Pete's tasteless barbs did you?

A stiff breeze had begun to blow. Blu, now soaking wet, was shivering miserably as ice formed on his winter coat. It was some time before we got a chance at another flock so without the opportunity to exert himself he was mighty cold. When we did shoot it was almost directly overhead.

One bird dropped on the bank about fifty feet down the bank, south. Another made it out over open water about a hundred yards before it came down.

Stiffly and reluctantly Blu left the blind and returned with the dead duck that had fallen on the bank. He made no attempt to hit the water after the other. "Bet ya he didn't even see that other quacker," Pete said in unexpected defense of my pup.

"Ya, his eyes stayed on that first bird all the way. No way he could have guessed the other one was even hit."

Pete and I could just barely see the carcass of the bird in the choppy water. Blu had not yet learned hand signals so If he couldn't see it he couldn't retrieve it. "That north wind is pushing it to the bank." Pete said. "Let's just sit here and see if we get some more shots. When the duck gets closer to shore I'll take your dog and go get it."

Twenty minutes later the wind had done its job sailing the duck's body into some dead trees fallen into the south end of the lake. "Sure you don't want me and Blu to go get it?"

"No." Pete answered. "I'd kinda like to see how well he handles commands from me."

"Sounds like a winner to me. I'll just sit here and drink coffee. It's cold out there."

I sat huddled up watching the sky for ducks, drinking warm coffee and following their progress down and around the shore. Blu showed little enthusiasm in that cold wind. After a bit he loosened up some, but the gung-ho attitude was gone.

They finally reached the area where the duck had come to rest. I couldn't see it, but from Pete's audible commands it was apparent that the bird was found. It also seemed that it was out of Pete's reach, hung up on the branches of one of the downed trees stretched out into the lake. Blu was not overzealous about plunging into the icy water. In fact, I could make him out ignoring Pete's every command.

The quarter mile of water separating us seemed to magnify each word. Blu was sitting ten feet from Pete and looking around innocently as though he heard or understood nothing. From Pete's tone and eloquence, I surmised that he was becoming frustrated and peeved. The further out into the branches Pete climbed trying to coax Bluper to do the same, the louder and more profound he became. "Blu, you get your

_____ _____ _____ out here and get this _____ _____ _____ duck or I'm gonna _____ _____ _____ wop the livin' _____ _____ _____ out of you with a _____ _____ _____!!!" You get the picture.

Finally he got so loud I nearly had to cover my ears. There was also, shall we say, a certain impiety in his choice of words. But he was even able to surpass that when, precariously reaching for the duck, he lost his balance on the ice covered tree trunk and his grasp on the branches and plunged chest deep into the home of the fishes. I actually expected to see the lake begin to boil.

"Blub blub, you _____ _____ _____ blub blub, poor excuse for a, blub blub, _____ _____ blub blub, retriever. When I, blub blub, get my, blub blub, _____ _____ _____ out of this, blub blub, _____ _____ _____ lake, you're gonna wish, blub blub that the _____ _____ _____ _____ blub blub and a ton of _____ _____ _____ bricks fell on your, blub blub _____ _____ _____ _____ head!!!"

Pete grabbed the duck and briskly bulleted it at Blu, striking him solidly in the rib cage. The hollow slap carried across the lake. That, I'm relatively certain, made quite clear to Blu the role he was supposed to have played in that fiasco. And that Pete was quite perplexed that he had not.

The impact knocked Blu back a step or two. Instantly his tail found a place between his legs to hide. His head lowered, his ears glued themselves to his cheeks and he slowly sank to the shore awaiting the wrath of Pete…that is if Pete could pull himself out of the drink.

His waders had filled with water adding considerable weight and the ever-so-thin coating of ice on the tree made his attempts to extricate himself look like something staged in a slapstick comedy. Extreme anger and the shock of cold water, however, have the ability to produce enough adrenaline to do almost anything. With a mighty pull Pete finally sprang from the water as though he had bounced off of a trampoline.

He stormed through the branches making a beeline for Blu. All the while came a steady flow of seldom heard words that would have melted the ears of a salty old sailor.

When he reached Blu he made even more manifest, and rightfully so, his feeling of disgust. The walk back cooled him though and Pete began to experience Blu's side of the story. By the time they reached the blind Pete was shivering out of control.

"Pete, you take your butt straight to the car. We'll pack up the gear." By then he couldn't even answer me but turned and led out toward where the car was parked.

Blu had thawed out completely from exertion and fear and, not wanting from me the same medicine he'd had to swallow from Pete, he was more than willing to lend a hand. One by one he retrieved the two dozen decoys Pete had set before sunrise while I stowed them in the duffel bags.

Two short round trips had all our gear stuffed in Pete's Gremlin. Back home Pete got properly cooked in a nice hot bath.

Chalk up another hard lesson for Blu-dog.

6. Movin' to the Country

Aside from hunting it became a ritual for Blu and me to take regular walks through the many wooded areas on campus. Those times reminded me of my high school days when my dad and I would go to the park and practice throwing and kicking a football. It meant a lot to me back then and it drew Dad and me closer together. I'm sure it had a lot to do with the relationship Blu and I developed as well. Time spent like that is only good.

Because of our strong bond we could sense each other's feelings. It wasn't a matter of his merely obeying my commands. I could talk to him and he would understand from my mood, tone, actions. I would sense his wants and needs in the same way. It was rapport achieved only through close, constant contact.

You can train a champion with fifteen or twenty minute training sessions each day. A dog like that will obey each and every familiar command. But don't expect any more from him, like when you need him to talk to and understand, or to stay out of the way and know why, or when you want him to just be there. He can sense the need.

One day we were returning home from a walk on campus. Blu was running free, playing, observing, learning. I had crossed the street that separated the campus from our yard and was heading toward the house when I turned to notice that a squirrel scolding Blu from a low branch had kept Blu from crossing with me. Nothing to arouse great concern.

I checked the street both ways for cars and seeing only one, still a few blocks distant, I called for him to "Come". But the squirrel told him to stay. Being a little put out that a squirrel took precedence over me, I shouted "Come" a little louder and a little sterner.

Blu took a step in my direction but when he did the rodent increased its tempo and Blu stayed under the tree. I bellowed "Come" even louder, knowing that if he came immediately he could still make it across without waiting for the car to pass. Still the squirrel had him mesmerized and Blu stayed under that tree.

A few seconds later, however, the squirrel made a dash up the tree and disappeared in a hole. There being nothing left to whet his curiosity, and knowing that I was becoming quite perturbed, he turned and, at top speed, made for the house caring about nothing except getting there as fast as possible. He'd waited too long.

"Blu, no! Stay! No, Blu, no! Stop! No!" I shouted hysterically but he was intent on granting my first wish and kept coming. He reached a point in the street at the same time the car did. I watched in horror as the car struck him broadside, drove over him, and, as the car continued on its way with no attempt whatever to stop, left Blu's body to roll after it.

I stood in shock, helpless. I felt the same sick feeling in the pit of my stomach I'd felt a few years before when a doctor had told me that I would remain paralyzed from the neck down. I had lost consciousness of everything but that black bundle rolling and bouncing violently along the asphalt. In my stupor I hallucinated the body coming to an abrupt halt, springing to its feet and running as though nothing had happened toward the house.

When my hallucination ran past me, eliminating from my sight the object that my stunned mind was focused on, I was jolted back into awareness. I turned quickly in amazement to see Blu making for the front porch at break-neck speed.

I shook my head hard and looked back into the street. It was empty except for the vehicle that had caused all the confusion going out of sight over a slight rise. Turning back toward the house Blu was there sitting, staring, panting.

Still a bit groggy and unsure of reality I staggered, rubber-kneed, to the porch.

He had been hit! There were a few patches of skin gone and mentally he was in another world. "Bluper, how can this be?! I saw it! I saw you get broadsided. I saw you run over!"

I gave him a big hug but released quickly when I realized that there might be some hidden damage. Blu was still unaware of my presence. He panted and stared into nowhere. I had regained my composure and began a closer examination.

There seemed to be no broken bones and, from the lack of bleeding from mouth or nose, no internal injuries. No immediately visible pain came from poking around his torso either. After the exam I tried to get him to lie down by pushing down on his shoulders but it was like pushing on a cement statue. He wouldn't budge. He sat, panted, stared. I sat next to him and waited.

It was sometime before he slurped in his tongue swallowing a few times, rolled his head around and lay down. "Are you back with me, Blu?" He turned his head toward me at my words. Wonderment was in his gaze, but the shock was gone. I examined him again, poking and prodding.

The only times he'd wince or twitch was when I'd touch a bared muscle where he'd been skinned. Now that he could again feel pain I was more satisfied with the diagnosis but was sure to keep a close eye on him for the next few hours. I treated his bare spots and cuts and wrapped some.

The Lord had smiled down on both of us that day. An accident that should have killed him had only left him with scrapes and cuts. There was also a fear of moving vehicles that would send him into a road ditch at the first sound of rolling tires for the rest of his life.

Blu was a year and eight months old when I graduated from college that summer. I got a job with the Water Pollution Control Division of the Nebraska State Department of Environmental Control. Took me two weeks just to remember the name of the outfit I worked for. Now that I was making the big bucks we could afford to move up from the fifty-five dollars a month I paid for the small apartment.

With the help of friends I located a vacant farmhouse three miles outside of town. Looking over my budget I calculated that I could afford to spend $125.00 a month for the place. The owner of the vacant acreage lived fifteen miles away.

Pete went with me to see him. He drove. During the ride I practiced over and over the exact words I would use to get the farmer/landlord to come down to $125.00. We arrived at the farmer's home and made contact. Let me tell you, I was ready to haggle.

I told him of my desire to rent and waited while he

determined whether or not he wanted me as a tenant. All the while my spiel was on the tip of my tongue just itching to deal out those convincing, memorized lines.

My mind was still practicing when the farmer said suddenly, "Well, I suppose I'd have to have $75.00 a month. Do you think you can afford it, boy?"

I hadn't been paying attention. All that was going through my head were my lines so I wouldn't forget them. I just about blurted out "Sorry sir, what I can afford is $125.00. Take it or leave it." But just as my mouth opened nearly wide enough to get my foot in it, what he said registered. My mind blew from overload, so what came out sounded something like, "Aaarrugghhhuuaalllaa." And Pete said, "He'll take it!"

While the farmer gave me the terms of payment and told me some other things I would need to know about the place he kept glancing at me from the corner of his eye as though he figured I was some sort of idiot. Had I said what I almost did, there'd have been no doubt in my mind that what he thought was true. He reluctantly handed me the key.

The move to the country was wonderful. But since the place had been vacant for quite some time it needed a lot of work. It was a two-story, three-bedroom, semi-Victorian white house with a fenced yard and a full front porch. The view from the porch and across the lane was that of a one hundred fifty- by seventy-five-foot garden patch and beyond that a tall grassed and sparsely treed pasture.

The house and farmyard consisted of a large barn, garage, vehicle shed, grain bin, and chicken house. It sat in about the middle of a hundred and sixty acres about a quarter of a mile from the gravel county road. The pasture, complete with black angus cattle, and the fields were rented to another farmer. About a hundred acres was in wheat and milo and the rest was prairie, trees, pasture and farmyard. The eastern boundary was forested. The north and west were county roads. The south was, for the most part, plum thicket that would yield the juiciest wild plums ever put into a pie.

Just north of the house was a thickly wooded area running one hundred yards east and west and forty yards deep north and south. The trees had been planted many years before to protect the house from winter winds.

Standing halfway down the lane looking at our new home, I saw a picture postcard. A perfect setting for living and raising a hunting dog.

Blu's doghouse was moved in next to the chicken house in the southeast area of the farmyard. That way he'd be able to watch over the chickens I planned to have that next spring, and still be able to see anyone coming down our lane. The kennel was left in town. I had decided that a long chain would give him more freedom to play and guard.

When I would drive in the lane returning from work, Blu would recognize it and he'd begin his antics. He knew that within minutes he would gain his freedom and be able to explore the one hundred sixty acres at his leisure. He'd tug and pull and jerk at that chain as though he were a trapped grizzly. He went through a lot of chains and collars that way.

Each time he would snap one I would have to make a trip to the Western Auto hardware store and get a set one strength greater. Eventually I had to go to log chain for his lead, and a short piece of log chain as a collar. The runt had grown to be quite powerful.

I'd park the car alongside the house and the ritual would commence. I would walk over to Blu, who was still in the midst of his seizure, and release him. He'd instantly recover from his fit and be at full speed within three or four strides heading straight for the barn at the opposite end of the yard. Twenty feet from the barn and still at full speed he would make a one hundred and eighty degree turn rolling in the process, sometimes slamming into the door of the barn. Gaining his feet like a gymnast he would rush straight back at me. When the range narrowed to ten or twelve feet he would leave the ground barreling directly at my chest.

I'd simply step aside and watch him fly past, legs flailing. Identical performances transpired each and every work day if I wasn't out overnight with a crew or Blu and I weren't on the road together. He never did catch on to my dodge. Or more correctly he didn't care.

He'd then follow me into the house where I'd change clothes and we would go for a hike around the farm. He investigated every burrow and track and pile of spoor, and wasn't bored by checking the same ones everyday and acting as though each time was the first.

From out of the "come-home-from-work, let-Blu-off-his-chain, one-hundred-yard-dash, near-head-on-collision ritual" developed a sport that I called "puppy-dog football". Actually I'm surprised that it didn't become popular across the nation. If *Wide World of Sports* had had the opportunity to film a game I'm certain it would have. But they never showed.

The object of the game was simple. There were no rules. And there was no way to keep score. So even those confused by games like football and hockey would have enjoyed watching puppy-dog football.

It could be played indoors or out. Any area eight feet by eight feet or larger would suffice. Any type playing surface was suitable. And all that was needed to play was one large gung-ho dog, one immature-matured human and one inanimate object large enough to be seen at six feet and small enough to fit in the participants mouth or hand. So you see, all the criteria necessary for a popular sport were applied to the development of this game. I'd even wager it was Olympic material.

The opponents faced each other with from two to six feet between them. The immature-matured human would need to be on his hands and knees with the inanimate object in one hand. The large, gung-ho dog needed to be in a sitting position. Helmet and shoulder pads are recommended for the immature-matured human but, being immature, they will probably never be worn.

When the human feels sufficiently capable of taking a beating he throws the object over his shoulder so that it lands from two to ten feet directly behind him. This places the human between the object and the large dog. The human then gives the dog the command to retrieve and the match commences.

The large and gung-ho dog is to do anything to get to that inanimate object. The immature-matured, and now also simple-minded, human is to do anything to keep the dog from reaching it. Duration of the match depends entirely on the aggressiveness of the large and gung-ho dog, and the thickness of the immature-matured human's head. Blu and I would play this game until I was exhausted or one or the other of us sustained debilitating injury.

His favorite tactic was to come straight on into my shoulder a few times to tire me. Then he would come in low and when I'd lower to meet him, he would suddenly rise up and try to jump over my back. Sometimes this produced good results for him. Sometimes, though, I'd make him believe I was falling for his deception and as he'd make his dive over my back, I'd come up quickly into his underside and he'd crumple back to his side of the playing field to try again. Once, however, the trick backfired on us both.

I had been weakened by a half dozen or so matches. During the execution of my counter to his dive ploy my timing had been off. I was just a little late coming up with my head into his underside. I missed solar plexus. I missed stomach. The last thing I remember was hearing air escaping in a sudden burst from Blu's mouth.

Where I hit him caused immediate involuntary constriction of every muscle in his body, including his hind legs. At that particular point in time they happened to be directly in front of my face.

The impact of his right knee against my forehead and his left against my right cheek bone put me out for at least a full ten-count. When I came to, Blu had ceased writhing and was lying on his side next to me panting. I was doing same. That match had ended in an undisputed tie. Neither of us was in the least bit interested in a sudden death overtime.

The game was over for that day but its devastating outcome did not result in the banning of the sport. For many years to come puppy-dog football would be played despite the bruises, bloody mouths and noses and sore muscles.

Time sped by. Fall was upon us again bringing with it another hunting season. We hunted weekends and checked traps mornings and evenings everyday. Blu had become quite adept at retrieving and retrieved for me everything from pheasants to squirrels, ducks to rabbits. The furry creatures were not his favorite, however. He'd be spittin' hairs all day.

I had lost much of my coordination due to my paralysis. Therefore, when shooting, I'd generally miss a great deal more than I'd hit. Don't misunderstand. I'm mighty grateful for the recovery I received. It was Blu who would get irritated with my condition.

He would be virtually quivering with excitement and anticipation when a rooster pheasant would rise or a flock of ducks flew within range. Then, when I'd shoot and miss, you just wouldn't have believed the look I'd get. Straight into my eyes he'd stare as if to say, "Great, I go to all this trouble. And for what?" He would slowly turn away trying ever so hard to overcome his disappointment in me. I knew he wanted to get his paws on my shotgun. But I wouldn't give it to him. I was afraid he'd wind up being a better shot, and then I'd have to retrieve.

Occasionally, though, I'd score a hit and he'd show off admirably, knowing it might be some time before my abilities would allow him another opportunity.

Blu came to love trapping too. Not because he had any special responsibilities. On the contrary, he had none. He was free to run for the sake of running and explore all the new smells that were endless sources of learning and amusement for him. All I required of him was to stay clear of the traps for his own safety's sake and so that his scent was not left or the camouflaged traps disturbed.

Almost always we trapped alone. I was able to pay close attention to Blu's whereabouts. One cold winter's morning, however, Dad accompanied us. He and Mom had come to spend Christmas on the farm. Dad loved the outdoors. He loved hiking even more.

I rose early and dressed. I went to knock on my folks bedroom door to rouse Dad. As I raised my hand to knock, the door opened and Pop was standing there dressed and ready to go. "Wondered if you were ever going to drag it out." He said. "If I'd known where your traps were set I'd have run 'em and been back." Dad was a funny guy.

It was a bone chiller, but we kept warm trudging through deep snow and catching up on what had been happening in our lives while we'd been apart. We were so engrossed in each other that I had lost track of Blu. As I opened my mouth to call him a blood curdling howl pierced our ears.

It came from the ditch fifty yards ahead of us where the next set was located. I'd either just caught Big Foot, or my inquisitive dog had capitalized on my lack of awareness and had snuck ahead to see for himself what one of those things, he was never allowed to go near was. He'd found out.

We pushed ahead through the snow as quickly as we could. All the while Blu howled in the pain produced by a #3 steel-jaw trap. If he was trying to tell me how much it hurt he didn't have to. I'd got my hand caught in one once and the initial smack had stung miserably.

Reaching the edge of the ditch we saw Blu tugging viciously at the trap that was secured by a short length of chain attached to two feet of pipe. The pipe was hammered all the way down into the frozen ground.

His eyes were flaming and his lips were curled back over his teeth. He looked meaner than I would have ever thought possible. I handed Dad the .22 rifle I was carrying and rushed to the aid of my pooch. I failed to realize that Blu was unaware of who he was, who we were, or what was happening. He was shocked into a frenzied rage. He was no more than a cornered, wounded wolf.

When I reached in to release the jaws of the trap he was on me quicker than a heartbeat. He bit down on my good leg so hard that it went numb and I collapsed to the ground. He pulled me in closer with a tremendous jerk and with his strong jaws worked his way up my leg, then to my wrist and up my arm, and it was not till he was at my shoulder with his next stop my throat that I was able to summon the strength to start rolling. I kept rolling until I was beyond his reach.

Except at my wrist, in the gap between mitten and coat, there was no blood visible due to the many layers of clothes I wore.

"Dad, you're gonna have to walk to the farm and get the wagon. I can't put weight on my leg."

"You think it's broken, son?"

"I don't know for sure right now. But I don't think so. I never heard anything pop. I think it's just kinda in shock."

"What about Blu?" Dad questioned as he handed me back the rifle with a look in his eye that asked a different question.

"Oh, no, Pop." I answered shaking my head and smiling. "I'm just gonna let him settle down a while. I should'a done that in the first place. Just wasn't thinking I guess. Hearing him yelpin' like that had me in as much shock as he was in. He'll be fine though when that paw goes numb."

"Sure you don't want me to stay with you a while? At least till your feeling comes back?" I know Dad was still concerned about what Blu might do to me.

"No, thanks, Pop. I'll be all right. I'll just sit here and talk to Bluper while I'm waitin' for this thing to wake up." I slapped the side of my leg. "That'll calm Blu down too. He'll be fine, really. He was just out of it there for a while."

Dad reluctantly left in the direction of the farm. Till he was out of sight I think he looked over his shoulder at us on every other step. You know, I think he might have shot Blu if he hadn't have been in as much shock as Blu and me at the time.

"Well, Blu-dog, you got me a couple good ones. Sure glad you don't get this testy when were playin' puppy-dog football. You feelin' any better yet?" From the look in his eyes I knew he was coming back. He was almost my dog again, but I waited a little while longer.

My leg and arm were responsive again, though far from peak performance, so I made a quick feel to check and see if, in fact, anything was broken. "Ooo, pretty sore, Blu, but it doesn't look like you popped any of my bones." I attempted to right myself.

"Kinda wobbly here, boy, but I think we'll make it fine." Stumbling a few steps up, and few steps back, a dozen or so times to loosen up, I noticed only passivity from Blu who was whining softly. I thought it safe to step back into the ring again.

"You're gonna be just fine, Blu boy." I said as I stroked his head and shoulders. "You'll see. You're gonna be sore a while. No doubt about that. Just like me. But you're gonna be just fine." The stroking had proceeded down his trapped leg to his paw where I massaged gently. The whimpering increased but the look in his eyes was the Blu I knew.

As I righted the trap Blu hobbled on three legs to keep with it. I laid the trap flat on the ground putting a foot on each spring. "You still takin' this okay boy? Or do you want me to stop?" He kept whimpering but showed no signs of increased pain. I proceeded.

I pressed weight on both springs releasing them and spread the jaws with my hands. Blu raised his paw from the jaws quickly and I let the trap slam back shut. We sat back in the snow together I rubbing my leg and arm and Blu licking his paw.

A few more minutes and we were ready to go.

The walk to the road helped work out some of the kinks, but we were grateful when Dad pulled up alongside and gave us a ride the rest of the way home. In a couple of days we were both back to normal.

7. Country Livin'

Our first spring on the farm was wondrous for all of us. I say us because the family had grown. The zoo included one hundred baby chicks, six ducklings, a shetland pony that had wandered in, and only the good Lord knows how many cats.

Used to be I could easily sleep till noon or one o'clock. On the farm, sleep was reduced to a necessary chore. Before leaving for work I'd feed the chicks and ducks and do a little weed pulling in the garden.

Oh, the garden. Certain smells, sights, or feels drift me off to those memories even today. Cool and still mornings with a freshness in the air that was intoxicating. The aroma of new growth all around, bare feet wet from heavy dew, the melodies of song birds waking joyously, that of the owls going to sleep, and the chickens and ducks chirping and quacking in the new day gave new meaning to the word happiness.

What could be more perfect except to add a loyal dog that actually belonged to me? Not just because the papers and bill of sale said so, but he said so too. His unfettered joy told me that there was no person in the whole world that he would rather belong to than me. That made me proud and glad that I belonged to him.

How had I managed to live so long without a companion such as he? How had I lived so long without this mansion with a roof of sky? Only ignorance of it had kept it from me.

When they were large enough to get out of their box on their own, Blu would guard our brood of chicks all day. They roamed freely through the yard a-peckin' and a-scratchin'. In the evening, just before sunset, we would round them up and herd them back into the chicken house for the night. Coyotes and other various critters were always looking for a chicken dinner.

The weeds near the chicken house were thick and deep and could therefore hide any particularly adventurous chick that may have decided to stay out past curfew. After the bulk of the flock had been herded indoors it was Blu's job to round up those intent on going AWOL. Time and again Blu would return to the door carrying very aggravated little birds who felt cheated for not being allowed a night out.

The ducks were another story. They refused to be herded. They all had to be caught. And they weren't as passive about it as the chicks. They would go tearing off in all directions quacking wildly with Blu in hot pursuit and put up quite a tussle when caught.

Once, in order to subdue one, Blu bit down just a little too hard accidentally, producing a dead duck. From that time forward I deemed it prudent to let the ducks fend for themselves. Sadly, by the time they had reached adulthood, only two remained, Ned and Pearl. Those two had learned the survival ropes so well that they stayed healthy for some time thereafter.

One early Saturday morning while hanging out laundry, Blu and I discovered yet another farmyard inhabitant.

I first noticed Blu sniffing and scratching at the door of the old, dilapidated shed that bordered the back yard. Nine times out of ten this meant a new experience for both of us, be it rewarding or otherwise, so I went to investigate. At the shed, which was probably the original chicken house, I lifted and pulled the door open wide enough to see inside.

There in the back, dark corner, hunched up in anger and fear was what I personally believe to be the ugliest of all God's creatures. An opossum. Though most fearful in countenance, the opossum is a docile creature that rarely uses its teeth for anything but eating.

I tugged the door open wide enough for both of us to squeeze in. Blu approached slowly and cautiously, like a pointer approaching a covey of quail. Just one mechanical step before another was begun. The closer he got the uglier the opossum became. Its lips were curled far back over its teeth and its mouth was wide open. It seemed ready and able to repel any attack on its privacy.

What a sight. Coarse, scraggly hair, a rat-like tail, a bald face with beady eyes and a pink nose, gums and palate. Nothing but ugly there. Certainly not the kind of pet you would want to cuddle with or take for walks through the neighborhood expecting admiring glances.

When opossum realized that his fierce looks and hisses were not going to intimidate this black giant, whose head alone was nearly as big as the whole bundle of ugliness, it closed its eyes, flopped on its side, and fainted. Or so Blu thought.

Blu jerked his head back, cocked it to one side questioningly, and looked back to me for an answer. "What you looking at me for? I didn't do it." I said as I shook my head and shrugged my shoulders. I was curious to see how he'd unravel this paradox.

He turned back to the ball of fur, deliberating. I could tell when the lightbulb went on in his head. He looked back at me with a wide-eyed gaze, almost a smile on his face. I knew what he was thinking. He figured that just his presence had been enough to subdue this fierce creature. His pride was showing, and it was a little disgusting. Bluper was actually believing that he was such a mean dude that merely his gaze would turn his enemies to putty.

He began strutting around the shed. All he needed was a cape, a loincloth, and maybe a mask and a headdress, and he would have looked just like one of those professional wrestlers. Bluper pranced back over to where the opossum lay and nudged it rudely with his nose. The exercise conveyed, "You may rise and remove yourself now."

Continuing to strut he looked back over his shoulder, smugly, to watch his defeated foe make a submissive retreat. Opossum still didn't move a muscle.

Losing some arrogance and taking on some humility, his questioning look reappeared. He walked back over to the lifeless animal and nudged it again. This time more gently. What was wrong? He couldn't fathom it. He looked at me again and then back at the opossum. This time he gave it a series of gentle pushes with his nose and whimpered slightly.

Victory had suddenly turned to sorrow and regret. He now assumed that he'd not simply caused his opponent to surrender but rather had caused its demise. It was time I stepped in before he started blubbering.

I had let the situation get out of hand. We couldn't just leave and shut the door. With his own eyes, Blu had to see that the opossum was all right. I strode to where it lay and lifted it gently with both hands and turned and walked out into the backyard. Blu followed, whimpering.

In the freshly mown grass I laid the faker down and walked toward a hidden vantage point around the corner of the house. Blu wouldn't leave the opossum's side. He felt responsible and wouldn't leave without first doing everything in his power to correct his wrong.

He picked the animal up in his mouth and paced back and forth. Then he ever-so-gently shook it. Then he lifted it up in the air and shook it some more. When none of this worked he held it a few inches from the ground and dropped it. He picked it up and dropped it again and picked it up and dropped it again and again and again. He probably would have gone on doing that all day had I not forcibly pulled him away.

I dragged Blu around the corner of the house. At our hiding place I lowered myself to one knee and put my arm around my grieving boy. We watched together.

In a few moments we saw movement in the body. Blu stopped bellyaching and his head lifted in amazement. Only the opossum's head moved as he looked from side to side to see if it was safe to rise. Perceiving no enemies he rose and waddled off into the grove of trees behind the shed.

Blu was himself again. I'm certain that he was fighting at my hold on him in order that he might go over and apologize blubberingly for what he had done. I refused to let him make a spectacle of himself. The poor opossum had had enough for one day.

By late summer our first garden was progressing beautifully. I'd planted every vegetable, herb and weed known to modern man. The money I spent on seeds could have kept us in store bought vegetables for at least ten years.

There were corn, tomatoes and all the other veggies found commonly in any self-respecting truck patch. But then there were also peanuts, salsify (what in the heck was salsify?), all types of melons, asparagus, raspberry and huckleberry bushes, strawberries, and even tobacco. The tobacco was the most amazing of all.

I'd started growing it from seed in the house in February. By early June the growth had only progressed two inches. Nothing promising. I transplanted them into the garden anyway. They'd either make it or become part of the compost.

Their first two days looked like curtains for the tiny tobacco seedlings. But on that third morning, miraculously, they were all standing straight. From that morning on all they did was grow. And I mean grow. It seemed that on hot, still days you could actually see them get taller. When standing amongst them you could hear it. So much so that by late July they were upwards of seven feet tall, still growing, and producing beautiful leaves which I'd hang to dry in the rafters of the garage.

When dry, ground, rolled in cigarette paper and lit, they smelled fabulously and tasted like no other smoke I'd ever had. But when inhaled I'd swear that smoke was taking big bites out of my throat and lungs. I guess unblended, unaged burly tobacco was not meant for ordinary cigarettes. I have since quit the habit and that had to be one of the reasons why.

That summer we were visited by my cousins Wilma and Herbert. They had with them a beautiful female Irish Setter named Kelly. Blu and she became instant best friends. Kelly had an excellent pedigree, and Wilma and Herbert intended to show her in competition. That is until Blu stepped in.

There was one other thing I have failed to mention, besides other male dogs, that tended to get Blu's dander up. His stick. Or his ball, or training dummy, or rock, or whatever it was that he was retrieving at the time.

I was made aware of this peculiarity one day when I happened to throw a stick for him to retrieve into the pasture where the black angus cattle were grazing. I thought nothing of it. Blu never troubled the large beasts.

I had thrown it well away from the small herd but just close enough, it seemed, to spur the curiosity of one of the bulls. The bull sauntered over to it before I gave Blu the retrieve command of "Hut", and innocently started sniffing Blu's stick.

Seeing this, Blu didn't wait for the command. He bulleted toward the stick without uttering a sound. Ten feet from the bull he leaped forward ferociously and up onto its back. The bull spooked and bucked throwing Blu and making a hasty retreat to the rest of the herd with Blu growling alongside for twenty or thirty feet.

When Blu saw that the bull was convinced that it had had no business with that particular stick, he trotted leisurely back to where the stick lay, gingerly picked it up and trotted back to me. The attack astonished me. I simply remained wide-eyed with my jaws ajar. All that for a stick. I was glad for the bull's sake that that piece of wood hadn't been a piece of meat.

Anyway, Wilma and Herbert, and Kelly and Blu and I were out in the farmyard one day just killing time and throwing a stick for the dogs. First Kelly then Blu, but never both at the same time. I was sure to hold on to Blu when it was Kelly's turn. Kelly was substantially more graceful than Blu, her long, beautiful, red hair waving in the breeze as she'd run.

Herbert wanted to find out which dog was the fastest. I advised against it, relating the story of the angus bull. Herbert understood, but I could see that he was still itching to see which would win a race. We continued throwing the stick alternating dogs until my cousin's curiosity got the better of him.

The stick was thrown for Blu's turn and I released him to retrieve. But as I did so, Herbie also released Kelly. I'm sure he reasoned that Kelly was not just any bull out in the pasture. After all, Kelly and Blu were such good friends. To be honest,

I was startled for an instant but I really wasn't too concerned either.

The sleek Kelly outdistanced the bulky, lumbering Blu with ease. Kelly was faster. Poor thing.

Kelly picked up the stick and as she turned to race back Blu educated her. He hit her head-on at full speed, effortlessly knocking her over onto her back. Standing over her he reached down and clamped his strong jaws onto her nose until she released the stick. Actually he held on just a while longer to be certain that the lesson was cemented in her memory. (Heck of a teacher.) Then he picked up the stick and returned it to Herbie.

Oops. The whole fracas had only taken a few seconds, but that was more than enough time to put an end to Kelly's showgirl days. A cute little scar would forever be visible across the bridge of her nose. Wilma, on the other hand, didn't think it so cute.

The incident meant nothing to either Kelly or Blu. They still had an extremely friendly and affectionate relationship. I must confess that it was an exceedingly tactless way to treat a lady. I could imagine what might happen if I tried to bite one on the nose.

Late that summer my job changed somewhat. Instead of going out with two other guys to test treatment plants and their effluents, I was assigned the monitoring of stream quality in various river basins statewide. A fellow by the name of Jim Tebs and I split up the basins between us. Separately we covered the state once each month.

Jim and his wife Helen became close friends and godparents to Blu. They both loved Blu and he returned their love without reservation. He always looked forward to the visits to Helen and Jimmy's house for treats and playtime.

Now that I traveled alone there was plenty of room for Blu to go with me. Whenever I'd stop to take samples, be it from the Niobrara, Platte, Republican, or just a small tributary, Blu would explore the territory. Before he'd start, though, he would do one other thing. Intentionally, he would trot onto the bridge, lift his leg and add some flow to the river below.

It seemed he had set a goal of being the first dog to wee off of every bridge in Nebraska. Though it never quite came to that, I am confident that he did attain the profound distinction of having weed off of more Nebraska bridges than any other dog. Now there's a bit of trivia that you won't find in any history books.

Motel owners, where we spent nights, and other folks, especially children, along our regular routes got to know him better than they knew me. I was just his driver. I'd fill out all the forms. I'd pay all the bills. I'd get all the samples. I'd carry everything into the motel at night. I'd run all the tests. I'd feed him before I'd feed myself. I'd take him out for walks. He'd socialize, play, eat and sleep.

I was the master?!

One very early morning we were on our scheduled run of the Elkhorn River basin. We had traveled over a hundred miles and it was still before eight o'clock. We were on a winding section of road near St. Paul when I had to swerve to miss the body of a black Labrador.

I didn't like seeing the bodies of animals mutilated by being continually run over, so when I could I'd pull over and carry or drag it onto the shoulder. There was no traffic so I pulled over and backed up to where the lab lay. I got out, walked over, grabbed it by the hind legs and was starting to drag it off the road when I heard a faint whine from what I had assumed was a dead animal.

Blu heard it too and, answering the whine with one of his own, tried desperately to squeeze through the partially opened window.

"Okay, okay, don't worry, boy, I won't just leave her here."

My reassurance didn't settle him at all. I looked up and down the road. "Great, not a house in sight. Now what?" Then remembering, "Oh, heck, I don't even have my .22! Well, we can't leave her here, Bluper."

I gently carried her to the car and laid her on the back seat. Blu was heartbroken. From the way he looked and sounded you'd think he was the one that was hurt. He jumped into the back seat and began licking her wounds. He did it with such care and tenderness that he must have sensed the seriousness.

I still had a job to do so instead of backtracking I continued toward St. Paul. At sight of the first house, I pulled into its yard. The dog was not theirs. In fact they had no recollection of any of their neighbors having a lab either. I asked for directions to the vet in St. Paul.

After a short ride I carried her into the vet's office. I wanted Blu to stay in the car but he'd have none of that. He stayed right with me all the way into the examining room.

The vet had me lay her on the examining table. She was still unconscious but the noises she was making were louder and steadier. He found a lot of hide gone from her hind quarters.

"She's not mine but my dog here wouldn't have any part of leaving her out on the road. So I brought her to you. Think you can do anything?"

"She's in deep shock," he said. "It'll be a while before I can tell exactly what's wrong. Don't worry, I'll take care of doing whatever needs to be done."

I thanked him and literally dragged Blu back to the car. "Blu, there's absolutely nothing else we can do. The doc'll take care of her." I'm afraid that that wasn't a good enough answer for Bluper but we still had a schedule to keep and were running a little behind.

We never did find out how that female lab fared. Blu was deeply depressed the rest of that day and that night at the motel.

8. Pheasant Huntin'

Falling leaves ushered in another fall. Blu's third hunting season. Ultra-hot and humid Nebraska summers made fall a welcome relief. Summer to me has always brought to mind visions of sweat, clinging dirt, rashes, hay fever, prickly and irritating plants, and blood-thirsty parasitic crawling things. I suppose Blu, with his heavy black coat, had even more hellacious visualizations. Though we rarely let the horrid summer season crimp our fun loving style, fall really let the good times role.

I was never sure what it was that let him know it was time. Whatever primitive instinct was responsible, it was never wrong. His exceptional jubilation would signal that the flocks of migrators were beginning to vacation in the deep south. From then on the sky would be filled with the joyous noise of those gypsy vagabonds flying the same routes their ancestors have flown for countless ages.

I have to admit that at times I'd be envious of his natural instincts. The ones that man has long since lost, if, in fact, man ever really possessed them in the first place. Thanks to Blu though, I was acquiring secondary instincts. Ones that were triggered by the natural ones alive in him. Through him, not a calendar, I knew when our season had arrived.

In contrast to the lazy and dreary summer days of having to invent things to do, we again had a purpose. The summer's labors were finally realized from the garden. Wild things had matured and were taking their places as self-sufficient individuals. Others were preparing to plant the seed necessary to produce new life next spring. And Blu and I were making ready to thoroughly enjoy the pleasures and excitement that fall invariably brings.

Blu was in his prime that year. He had accepted his calling as a hunter. He thrived on it. He lived for it. He would go all day and not understand why we ceased at dark.

We were much alike in our attitudes toward the hunt. I have come to classify hunters in four categories. First is the "out-hunter." He gets the urge to provide something that modern society doesn't sell retail. He'll hunt anything, anytime, anywhere. Not simply for the kill, but for the joys that the chase and merely being "out" bring.

Next is the "trophy-hunter." He'll certainly take the meat but his primary concern is an exceptional mount for his home.

Then we have the "meat-hunter," who's strictly interested in filling the freezer. Anything legal will suffice. It doesn't have to be pretty.

Any of these three types, singly or in combination, are

normal, healthy human beings who are filling an inner need that has been fostered for thousands of years. I believe that if this need ever totally dies out from our species, so will go the viability of the whole human race.

The forth type of hunter is the one that concerns me. He's been around as long as the others and will always be with us, but he's dangerous to himself and everyone around him.

Fortunately, although the stereotype, he is the least common of the four. He is the "killer". The one who slaughters, caring only as an afterthought for meat or trophy. He is usually seen hunting side by side, in a pack, with more of his kind. Each one trying to outdo and impress the other.

I've met a few of these. They are barely able to make it to the next hunting season, if indeed they do, without killing something. Sadly, if not able to mutilate animals, they would more than likely begin on the human race.

Blu and I were out-hunters. We'd not only go out to hunt but would also hunt in order to get out. Satisfaction was in the stalk and the beauty and unsophisticated nobility of wild things. There's a lot to be said for a tasty meal too.

One Friday afternoon before leaving the office, Jimmy Tebs, George Sudwik and I made arrangements to meet the next day. Opening day it was of pheasant season.

The two men arrived early enough for a friendly cup of coffee at the kitchen table while I described where we might flush up a rooster or two. I had acquired permission from my neighbor to hunt the quarter section across the county road to the west. With that quarter and the one I lived on, we had a few enjoyable hours ahead of us.

I was certain that Blu would flush enough birds to give each of us a couple of exciting moments. But we were intcrested more in good company and exercise than we were in filling bag limits. Obviously three out-hunters.

We were getting pretty engrossed in our "I remember the

time when" session when I noticed that it was only minutes till shootin' time. We sucked up the last of the coffee, loaded our shotguns and headed for the fields. Anticipation and spirits were high.

The fence row running north and south along the east side of the pasture ran down a twelve foot wide weed strip that was an ideal shelter for early rising pheasants. We were to work it south to the plum thicket, the plum thicket east to the trees, and the trees north to their terminus at the county road.

I figured by the time we finished that march the birds would have left cover heading for feeding grounds. We would backtrack a little, then head west through the milo field, across the pasture, another thin strip of milo, and cross the road to hunt my neighbor's property.

Down that first fence row Blu and I worked one side of the fence while Jimmy and George worked the other. I sent Blu right through the weed patch hoping he'd raise a bird or two that we might otherwise walk right past. Birds that haven't been shot at will usually hang pretty tight to cover. Blu worked systematically, covering nearly every square inch of ground in that patch.

Blu was like a young child on Christmas morning. It was the first day of pheasant season. A beautiful, clear, crisp autumn morning. His master was alongside and two good buddies were just inches away. He had not a care in the world and his only desire was to please his companions. How could there be a more perfect occasion for him to strut his stuff? Inexperience causing a tad too much over exuberance happened, in this case, to be the major contributing factor to Blu's blunder.

Blu was performing marvelously. He was staying well within gun range and had been successful in flushing a number of birds. All but two had been hens and the three of us had missed the roosters, but that was no fault of Blu's. Unaffected by our lack of perfection he was still going about his assigned task.

The barbed wire fence running through the weed patch did not run directly down the center. On the milo side of the fence, the side Blu and I were on, were eleven of the twelve feet of weeds. We had taken that side in hopes that Blu's expertise would produce sufficient birds for all of us to shoot at. At the same time the grazed pasture afforded more comfortable walking for my guests.

The fence was not only of barbed wire. About two and a half feet off the ground ran a smooth strand of wire that had a bite every bit as sharp as its barbed cousin. It was deceptive, for to the naked eye its danger was invisible. Running through the wire was a charge of electricity that would cause Hercules to crumple to his knees and the most intimidating of bulls to bellow and run in fear.

Blu's meandering sweeps of the weed patch had brought him dangerously close to the devious wire. When he'd successfully flush a bird, and the "Good boy" praises would come from the other side of the fence, he'd rush to the other side for pats on the head and scratching on the back. In doing so he would cross under the fence coming within inches of the sadistic strand of steel.

His back would clear with room to spare. It was his tail that dazzled me. With the first of the praises it would begin wagging joyously. By the time he passed under the fence it looked like a solid Japanese fan rather than a thin, short-haired tail. I'd cringe.

The only thing that saved him was that he was moving so fast that it would wag to the right and down while he passed under the fence. Before it could come back up and then down to the left he had already reached the other side clear of the wire. I couldn't believe how long his luck had held.

We had nearly reached the end of the fence row. Blu had

ventured a little out of gun range heading toward the plum thicket and had somehow managed to get himself onto the pasture side of the fence.

The simple command, "Come" reversed his direction and he came prancing back toward us excitedly. His tail wagged in unison with his step. Lord, he stayed close to that wire. He was so close that when his tail wagged to his right it would stretch well over it.

I'm not sure which it was. Either Blu stepped into a minor depression in the ground, or the wire raised ever so slightly between posts. No matter, it was just enough to put the tip of his tail at the same level as that infernal wire. His luck had played out.

The next right wag brought wire and tail into direct contact. The response was a loud and piercing "Aahhuuu!" At the same instant all four feet seemed to bite into the dirt as one, propelling the body that they were supporting at such a horrendous rate that the corners of Blu's mouth were pulled back and flapping.

A rocket sled would have been left in the dust. Anything or anyone that would have been standing in front of him would have been vaporized. His mind was focused on getting as far away from the devilish spot as fast as he could. I cannot conceive of any vehicle that could have produced more efficient results.

As all four legs completed their first stride they left in their wake a wall of earth and torn grass. While clear of the ground they stretched to their farthest limits to take another large bite of the pasture.

Luckily, none of us were near his direct line of departure. We were all nearly destroyed, nevertheless, by what might be termed the aftershock. The two roosters that had flushed at Blu's yelp probably went home wondering if it truly was opening day. They were well within range, but not a one of us was remotely capable of lifting gun to shoulder.

I was laughing terribly hard. Jimmy was on his knees with George about to take the plunge. They were holding their bellies in hopes of averting hernias. Their laughter was so intense that I was genuinely concerned for their health. I was unable, however, to lift a finger to aid them.

Blu was a good fifty yards away and still smoking real estate. In another fifty he settled down some. He stopped, turned, and, quivering sheepishly, almost belly-crawled all the way back. By the time he reached us we were relatively capable of bringing oxygen back to our blue faces. But when we looked down at that frightened pooch whose eyes begged for help and understanding, his desperately needed help and understanding had to wait until we were again capable of self-control. Lord, how cruel can man be?

Rest assured we more than made up for our sadistic behavior once we composed ourselves. But when any one of us would break into sudden, uncontrolled laughter at the most inopportune time during the rest of that day, the other two would know exactly what vision had reappeared in his mind.

Finally we crossed the road to hunt the less cultivated, heavier covered quarter section of my neighbor. By this time the shooting had intensified across the countryside. We fostered hopes of the heavier cover harboring birds that were hiding from what they probably thought was World War III.

Jimmy, so far, was the only one who had successfully bagged his dinner, and he took great pleasure in reminding George and me of that fact about every three minutes.

Shortly after Blu and I started stirring up a tall thicket a group of a dozen or so birds took to the air out the other side where the two men waited. George dropped his first while Jimmy downed his second. Being the host, I was glad that both of my guests had been successful.

As the day progressed, and shooting around about increased, the birds got spookier and would flush from cover long before they were within range. It became less likely that any of us would get another bird. That wasn't important though. Friends were together and we were having an enjoyable time in the out-of-doors.

Most men aren't poets, easily capable of putting simple things into words without some spark to motivate them. Most men need something, at least a fired shot or two, or an accident-prone dog, to keep the words flowing. They can talk about their prowess as a hunter if they scored a hit, or blame the wind or a bush or the dog if they missed. That's what it's all about. Profound conceptions could be conjured up later. This was time for mindless, undemanding, revitalizing recreation.

Blu, still young and exuberant, soon forgot his encounter with the live wire, or rather filed it away. The consequence of being young is inexperience. And inexperience always breeds mistakes. Blu was to make his share of them while waiting to become old and wise. And like all of us as we age, we make fewer mistakes partially due to wisdom but mostly because there are fewer to make.

The day progressed perfectly. It was early afternoon and we were ready to call it a day. Our stomachs said it was time to eat. We headed home. We'd go south following a slight ridge to where we'd cross the dam at the north end of a pond. Then we'd turn east for the house. Halfway to the dam we needed to cross a steep dry wash that cut the ridge west to east. The three of us disappeared into the wash already discussing the day's hunt. Jimmy bragging and George and I naturally reaching for every reason imaginable to excuse our second and third place status.

We temporarily postponed the palaver while we negotiated a jumble of old hog wire that laid rusting in the bottom of the wash. It wasn't long though before we emerged up the other side. In another fifty yards we all realized that we'd lost track of Blu.

We had called an end to the hunt. We just assumed Blu had too. While engrossed in our idle chatter we had forgotten him. He was still zig-zagging in the area where we had given up the hunt.

He was trying to pick up one last scent trail, refusing to the last, as usual, to say the hunt was through. We marveled at his perseverance. I shouted to him, over the hundred yards of terrain we had covered, to "Come".

That was all the grandstander was waiting for. The zig-zag display had been meaningless, except of course for showing off. The instant he heard my voice he was streaking along the same path we had just followed. There had been no hesitating for even one last sniff as if to say, "I thought they'd never turn around and watch me perform. Now I can finally end this foolishness and get back with the boys." In just moments he'd pay for his vanity.

At the rate he was traveling there was no possibility of him negotiating the jumble of hog wire at the bottom of the wash. He wouldn't even see it until it was too late. I tried to warn him but, running through eighteen- to twenty-four-inch dried weeds and grasses, he didn't hear me.

He plunged headlong into the ravine. A fraction of a second after he disappeared we heard the sound of air suddenly escaping from healthy lungs. When he should have been cresting on our side of the dry wash, he didn't show. I started back.

I hadn't taken more than a dozen steps when he appeared, still running, but at only half speed, and floundering. Commendable...had he not been going in the wrong direction.

He was headed back the way he had come. Semi-conscious, his fortitude had driven him onward. He went about twenty yards before collapsing. His effort was laudable, but he'd just scored a touchdown for the other team.

When I reached him, "Wrong-way Blu", was on another of his many voyages through la la land. He had learned two valuable lessons that day. But I wondered how much more of that schooling he could take.

9. Eatin' Machines

December 3rd was Blu's third birthday. Birthdays were gala occasions. His closest friends would be there. A half dozen cats, all in party hats made from note paper, scotch tape and rubber band, and Helen and Jimmy bearing gifts.

On the evening of the 3rd I would arrive home with the largest roundsteak I could find, a gallon of ice cream, a birthday cake, and toys and treats for the birthday boy as well as some incidentals for his guests.

From the instant meal preparations began there was no holding Blu down. His enthusiasm was overwhelming. His nose was everywhere pulsating at such a rate that it would have certainly developed severe cramps had the meal not been served up quickly.

When the guests had all arrived dinner would be served. The four legged guests feasted on milk and tuna while Blu's birthday special consisted of eight cups of dry dog food covered with the cut up round steak and a half dozen raw eggs.

Without exception, the eating of such a meal amazed all newcomers to the festivities. Actually, it never ceased to amaze me. How he could pack away that much food in just a few minutes and bounce up ready for more is beyond my comprehension.

Cake and ice cream would come. But first the guests. Most had cringed in various corners of the house after seeing Blu tearing into his dinner, fearing that they would be next on the menu. They would be given a chance to pick at their bowls.

Then gifts would be exchanged and opened. There were always birthday cards from Helen and Jimmy and Mom and Dad wishing him a joyous day and many happy returns. One by one he would gingerly open his gifts and personally thank the giver.

Ninety percent were dog treats of which fifty percent were devoured on the spot. The "eating machine" would have consumed everything had it not been removed forcibly to save some for later, and leave room for dessert.

When all gifts were opened and all torn paper and pieces of shredded boxes picked up it was time for cake and ice cream. Two-leggeds received a piece of cake and scoop of ice cream each. The four-legged guests shared one scoop of ice cream. What remained was placed before the excited Blu-dog who buried his face in it and didn't come out till it was all gone.

That was the coup de grace. The look of contentment on his face was that of a junkie. While he went from guest to guest expressing his gratitude he'd walk very tenderly so as not to burst the over inflated balloon that he had somehow swallowed.

He would tread softly into the living room and lie down

on his side with his legs straight out, looking the part of a dead, bloated horse, and snore himself into oblivion.

Thank God birthdays only come once a year. A greater frequency would have caused his rapturous suicide.

Blu loved parties. It seemed the louder the party and larger the crowd the better he liked it. That's where he and I never quite saw eye to eye. He could never get enough, and as a mixer he had no equal. To him, civilization was a blessing. He definitely enjoyed the out-of-doors, but at the end of the day he liked nothing better than having scores of people around.

On many occasions he'd even sneak away from the farm and make the three mile trek into town. Whenever this occurred there were three places I needed to look in order to find him.

Closest to the farm was Doane Drive. It was a street at the east edge of town crawling with children. He would stop there first to play with his little friends.

When he tired of that diversion or if the children were called home he made his way to the college campus. There he was well known and accepted and he would visit. Anytime, day or night, the campus was usually good for someone on whom he could impose himself. Those new to the campus were at first frightened by his advances. But that emotion was replaced by a gentler one in short order.

When he was certain he had not neglected anyone he would continue on to his last, and favorite place, Jimmy and Helen's. They lived all the way in the southwest corner of town.

If his absence from the farm had gone undetected for two or three hours I'd go straight there. Either Jimmy would be spoiling him or, if no one was home, Blu would be waiting patiently at the back door.

Ah, there was one other place I could look if he didn't turn up at one of the other three. If any of the men or women on the town's police force intercepted him on his sojourn they would hold him in protective custody till I arrived.

Only once that I can remember had he even been the least bit annoyed at having people around. Even that time turned out to be my fault.

The boys in the fraternity had asked if I would allow them the use of my house for a fraternity/sorority pre-rush-week mixer. After receiving their assurance that the house would still be standing when the party was over I granted their request. Ostensibly, all I need supply was the house. The frat would furnish beverages and eats.

From the moment the first guest arrived Blu was jubilant. The party progressed successfully and was quite orderly. More so than I had expected. Late in the evening, however, when the adult beverages were still flowing strong, the food played out.

For a fraternity of hogs, the situation had become dangerous. I had become desperate. Sure, I had a box of crackers here and a package of cookies there. But I didn't have anything in great enough quantity to satisfy a bunch of guys who, if they were not enrolled in college, would probably be penned in a feedlot somewhere...or did I?

My head swiveled on my neck to perceive a fifty pound solution to my problem propped up in the corner of the kitchen. How else could I ever hope to satisfy so many guests at so little cost? With all the beer that had passed through their gullets they couldn't tell prime rib from horse droppings anyway. Somehow, though, I had to make it look inviting.

I got a big pot out of the cupboard and started scooping in Blu's dog food. All the while Blu stood with his nose inches away from the top of the bag his tail wagging thinking that I was preparing a meal for him.

I would have to let it all soak for five minutes or so before I could serve it. I feared that I didn't even have that much time before they started eating my furniture. With time in such short supply I wished that Blu would stay out of my way. After all, he had eaten only a few bites from his own bowl that sat on the floor just a few feet away. There was still enough left in there to feed an army. So why was he so…?…?…?…To feed an army—that was it!

With gratitude I patted Blu on the head. I picked up his bowl, spilled the contents onto a large tray, separated the individual soggy pieces discarding those that were half eaten, put tooth picks in each of those remaining, and proudly entered the living room with my tray of hors d'oeuvres.

While in the kitchen preparing this feast, a crowd of those not so full of spirits had gathered to watch. When I had entered the living room they had followed, performing as though nothing was out of the ordinary.

When the "wild bunch" saw the new eats coming they rushed over like so many bears at a picnic and plunged in gobbling.

Blu was beside himself. He frantically strutted around growling deeply in his throat. He was incensed at having so many eating of his own dinner without so much as a thank you.

Finally though, the fellows started feeding him a piece every now and then and that seemed to satisfy him. It was ironic. Blu was feeding them *his* table scraps.

It didn't take long for the tray of goodies to disappear. One of the guys in particular was robustly demanding more of what he thought to be one of the best snacks he had ever had with beer.

Being the generous fellow that I am, I was more than happy to oblige. After all, I had a whole pot of them soaking in the kitchen. I was certain they were ready to take a tooth pick. In short order I had another tray being served.

The connoisseur descended upon this one as hungrily as he had the first. This time though he complained that, though passable, that batch wasn't nearly as good as the first.

I explained that the first serving had had a chance to marinate longer. He nodded in understanding but suggested that from then on I should let it set overnight in whatever special marinate that was. Then he asked if it was hard to make. I looked over at Blu for a contemplative moment. He was drooling profusely. Then I looked back at my inquiring guest and said, "No, actually it's easy as spit."

Had Blu still been put out by the free distribution of his food, he would have rejoiced after the third or forth serving. It was then that the gluttons discovered what they were eating. Running into the yard, they gave nearly all of it back.

To my readers I say: Don't try this at home.

Soon winter was behind us and spring brought with it a time of rebirth. No guns or traps this time. Cameras or just eyes and ears were our tools. Blu was as inquisitive as I, maybe more. When required he could keep a low profile. He was keen on observing and understanding.

On one particularly ill-behaved occasion, however, he was unable to contain his enthusiasm. He disturbed everything he could get his nose into and chased everything that ran from him. He totally upset the serenity of an otherwise ideal day, interfering with all the little animals busy rebuilding what the winter had destroyed. All this he had accomplished while rebelling against my every command.

Granted, since we lived virtually on an equal basis, I had been responsible for spoiling him somewhat. Actually "civilizing" may be a better choice of words. We had reached a happy medium between each other's worlds. When one or the other of us would cross over a bit too far into the other's territory, however, it did cause a problem on occasion.

Now and then stringent disciplinary tactics needed to be applied. When Blu knew that what he had done was wrong he would unobjectionably take a just and proper amount of punishment. If, however, in his opinion, the punishment was more severe than what was required, a battle might ensue if I persisted.

He might attack me with teeth bared, snapping. If this reminder brought me to the realization that I had overreached necessity I'd stop and apologize. However if I disagreed, I would meet his attack in like manner and we'd role in the mud for a while. Mostly these encounters were no more than a lot of shouting and growling and pushing and shoving with only an occasional meaningful bite or knuckle-sandwich. In most instances my judgment prevailed.

Whackings were seldom necessary. Most situations called for only a sound scolding. In fact, if I kept my temper under control, displays of disappointment or depriving him of some usual form of enjoyment were more apt to produce a satisfactory result.

That day punishment was definitely required and more than a simple reprimand or even swats on the butt were necessary. Even an all out brawl seemed inadequate. It had been such an utter display of rudeness, tomfoolery and disrespect.

He had disturbed much that day so only that which would be most disturbing to him would suffice. It was a difficult problem to resolve. While traversing the milo field and then the pasture on the way back to the house the wheels in my head kept turning doing their utmost to concoct appropriate punishment. It had to be something that he would remember. Something that would ask him the question, "How do *you* like it?" My mind had drawn a blank. The animals he had harassed were powerless in exacting any type of retribution.

While walking across the pasture the cows had begun to saunter over to us, as was their custom, in hopes of a special handful of something good to eat. The same grass that they could easily extract from the ground seemed to taste better to them if I pulled it and hand fed it. Their annoying persistence did not make it any easier for me to think.

Wait, just a minute. The answer to my problem stood all around me. How often have we heard the saying, "can't see the forest for the trees" and still we tend to ignore what is right before our eyes? In that case I couldn't see the potential of those forcefully persistent brutes because of their forceful persistence.

These cows had a one track mind when it came to eats. One can see the similarities here between them and my fraternity brothers. They would unrelentingly annoy a potential benefactor until such time that that benefactor delivered up a morsel or two. The perfect solution.

We continued across the pasture. All the while I, in no uncertain terms, verbally let Blu know that I had been extremely unhappy with his conduct. By the time we reached the fence separating the pasture from the farm yard Blu was quite dejected and willing to do anything to make amends. The stage was set. I told him to sit while I crossed into the yard.

When I had removed myself from Blu and the half-ton beggars I followed up the sit command with "Stay!" Blu's eyes and the eyes of a dozen head of cattle watched as I crossed the yard to the house and disappeared through the back door. I stood out of sight by the back porch window to observe Blu's, "Abuse 101", class.

The cattle were behind and on both sides of Blu. They continued to watch the back door hoping that I would reappear. Within seconds, though, they lost interest in what was not and rekindled interest in what was. They began milling anxiously around Blu. Except for his eyes, that would slowly look up to the left and then to the right, he sat motionlessly. He knew and dreaded what was about to transpire.

The friendly milling had not produced a single mouthful

of grass so the tormentors deemed further action necessary. A bull began by lowering his head and gently, but firmly, pushing Blu over onto his right side. Blu responded by slowly and timidly rising back up to a sitting position. A cow then pushed him over from the other side.

This time Blu tried, on his belly, to slowly inch his way under the fence to safety. Without showing myself I opened the back door and hollered out, "Sit! Stay!" With that he stopped abruptly and crawled back those few inches rising again to a sitting position. Blu looked up at his tormentors sheepishly expressing, "Come on, guys, be nice." There was a "pleeease" in there somewhere.

Most of the brutes had their noses only inches away from Blu. They would nudge him from side to side without any sincere attempt at being gentle. After a few more rude pushes Blu realized that all the pleading he could muster only fell on deaf ears so his anxious gaze moved from the surrounding herd to the back door of the house. He had hoped that I would appear and deliver him from the abuse.

The herd began to get more and more intense with their intimidations. They wanted their customary peace offerings even if they had to squash it out of him.

By then I felt that Blu had learned his lesson about bullying those of a lessor stature. Also fearing that at any moment the herd would loose patience and become dangerous, I stepped outside and shouted "Come".

Without so much as a parting glance, Blu removed himself from his place of torment and burned a perfectly straight line across the yard from the herd to my waiting arms. His joy was overwhelming. I'd been on one knee to greet him. His lunge knocked me flat on the ground. He proceeded to paw and lick me in sheer delight of having been mercifully delivered from what he thought would have been certain agonizing death.

10. Life After Death

Not long after Blu's encounter with our resident herd of black angus cattle, Pearl, our hen mallard, became the proud layer of thirteen beautiful eggs. Except for the usual stream of kittens, those were to be the first animals born since we made our move to the country. The chickens had already been butchered and packed away in the freezer without having multiplied. The morning the eggs were discovered began a day of boarding up windows and holes in the old shed in order to keep everything out but oxygen.

I awaited their arrival with fatherly expectation. Each day before going to and after coming from work, Blu and I would make an inspection of the nest and the building to be sure all was secure. In time, Blu picked up on my concern and excitement and waited anxiously for the two daily inspections.

After what seemed ages, I arrived home one day to find thirteen healthy ducklings cheeping up a storm while their mother tried to keep a handle on the situation. I was so proud and excited that Blu and I drove to the Western Auto store and bought one of those kiddy wadding pools. We sped back to the farm where we filled the pool with water and plopped in thirteen happy little ducks.

All the while Pearl was quacking joyously in thanks that someone had finally succeeded in corralling her eager-to-experience-the-world brood. I was amazed to see that the hours-old ducklings were already proficient at swimming. Even with a big black brute like Blu pushing them around the pool with his nose as though they were bathtub toys.

For the next two days I made especially sure that all the quackers were rounded up by hand before bedtime and placed in their predator-proof home. I just couldn't wait for the time when they would be old enough to follow me single file, parade style, around the yard quacking up a symphony while I played my harmonica and Blu howled.

How had I ever lived so long in Chicago without these simple joys? Okay, so maybe I did go a little overboard. But I was making up for a lot of lost time. I wanted to experience all those things I had been deprived of by asphalt and concrete.

On the fourth day after the hatch I drove down the lane in anticipation of that being the day I would be the grand master of the parade. I went directly to the shed. As I entered the dilapidated building I heard Pearl quacking loudly fifty yards away by the stock watering trough. Her quacking meant nothing to me. She always quacked. The ducklings weren't in the shed nor anywhere within close proximity outside.

Still Pearl's loud quacking had registered no alarm within me. I kept searching the yard until, out of annoyance more than anything else, I acknowledged Pearl's boisterousness and started toward the trough.

The trough was a concrete structure close to the front of the barn, about seven feet long, five feet wide and three feet deep. The cattle weren't in that section of pasture so it was empty except for eight or ten inches of rain water. It wasn't much to be concerned about.

The closer I got to the trough the louder and more frantic were Pearl's cries. It finally penetrated that something was terribly wrong.

I kept kicking around in the tall weeds hoping to turn up some evidence of Pearl's and my ducklings. I still didn't realize that the trough was the object of Pearl's concern. My shuffling brought me close to the edge of the trough where, out of the corner of my eye, I could see inside. What I saw drove needles into my heart. Though Pearl was waddling and quacking hysterically only five or six feet from me, she seemed distant. Almost a dream.

All that filled my world at that moment was the sight of thirteen ducklings floating limply on the stagnant water. Their heads out of sight beneath the surface. They had drowned.

Their mother must have led them in for a swim. When swim time was over, mamma had jumped and flown up over the two-foot walls of the trough expecting her young to follow. The little ones, unable to fly, were not capable of getting up and over the perpendicular walls of the concrete structure.

It must have been horrible for Pearl. She had watched helplessly and uncomprehendingly as her offspring swam around chirping in panic until their strength played out. No longer being able to support the weight of their heads they had collapsed into that few inches of water.

Pearl was never quite right after the mass death of her

babies. She spent most of her time quacking constantly and never straying far from the trough that had claimed them. She would not let me nor Blu go near her, wanting no comforting.

The constant quacking, even through the night, became quite annoying. The logical, rational me was tempted on many occasions to have her for dinner. But my emotional side couldn't find the courage to do the necessary preliminaries. I guess even a duck can be allowed the courtesy to mourn.

Her refusal to leave the area of the disaster and her constant noise left her vulnerable to attack from predators. It was not long before Pearl, like her ducklings, ceased to exist. One morning, hearing no quacking, I went to find her remains. There was no more than a handful of feathers, and entrails.

Ned, the drake mallard, who had removed himself from much of the goings on, likewise met his end only days later. Events such as these led me to appreciate life but to realize that an end to it is an inevitability that must be come to terms with. I was shattered by the realization that even an Eden like the farm could manifest a cruel and destructive side.

That same summer Blu and I acquired an additional family member that helped fill the part of our hearts left empty by the deaths of our ducks.

I had just dropped off some water samples at the laboratory in Lincoln. Blu and I were headed home after three days on the road. About the middle of a ten mile stretch of highway called the Denton road I noticed a spot on the asphalt a few hundred yards ahead. As we drew nearer I perceived it as some form of life. I began to slow down in order to give it ample time to remove itself from our path.

The closer we got the more apparent it became that that small living object was a kitten. It appeared to have little, if any, intention of getting out of the way. I, on the other hand, had no desire to stop and just assumed that when we got close enough it would scamper off. Nevertheless, I slowed a bit more to give the inexperienced kitten plenty of maneuvering space.

Finally we were close enough to see its mouth opening and shutting in a perpetual meow. Still it sat in the middle of the road staring at the two-ton station wagon bearing down on it. We were at a distance that, if the kitten did not move immediately or I did not slam on the brakes, it would be curtains for kitty.

I stepped hard on the brake. When the vehicle came to a full stop the vision of the kitten was obscured by the hood of the car. I felt as though I had been in a game of chicken and lost. Better that, though, than making the kitten one of many semi-permanent grease spots on the Denton road.

Blu followed me out the driver's side and around the front of the car. I had to meet this gutsy little feline. It was still sitting, still meowing, and still staring up at the bumper of its adversary, daring it to come closer.

Kitty had won decisively and earned the right to ride in its defeated opponent. We proceeded to check at the farms a mile in either direction to see where the kitten belonged. We found no one that was familiar with him. The farmers offered to keep him; cats were welcome on farms to keep the rodent populations down, but I had decided that another cat wouldn't hurt us so if the true owner could not be found we'd take him home. After all, he had won us fair and square.

The last farm within reasonable distance had been checked. All the while the brave and belligerent warrior had not shut up for a moment. Once he even connected a right cross to Blu's nose when Blu's curiosity brought him within range. We just had to understand that the vanquished foe has no rights when in the presence of the victor.

The rest of the way home Blu sat near the window. His head was bent down staring questioningly, but respectfully, at the kitten who stared back...but with no respect at all.

When we reached home I picked him up in one hand, fumbling for the back door key with the other. He squirmed all the way from the car to the door. He didn't fight frantically like most unfamiliar cats would but only squirmed uneasily as if to say, "Hey, man, put me down!" So when I reached the back door step, I did. Then I opened the door.

Instead of scampering off and hiding under the porch like I was certain he would, he pranced right through the opened door as if he owned the joint. Not even a cautious look or sniff first. I knew then that that runt was going to need watching.

I left Blu to keep an eye on him while I went back to the car to fetch my gear. When I returned I discovered that Bluper was doing a good job of it. The kitten was balanced on the edge of the toilet bowl reaching as far over as he could in order to get a drink. Blu was right there with him, his nose only inches away. No telling how long the kitten had been out on the road before we came along. It was obvious that it had been long enough for him to develop quite a thirst.

When Blu heard me enter he looked over at me with a quick jerk of his head as if he had been caught in the act of doing something naughty. I couldn't understand why. As far as I was concerned he was doing exactly what I wanted. He was keeping an eye on the kitten. An instant later, though, I understood the reason for his guilt.

Blu's intentions, though not brutal, were not entirely honorable either. My boy hesitated a moment thinking, "Should I or shouldn't I?" Then I guess he figured he should and gave the kitten a firm nudge. After all, he owed him one for the smack on the nose. It was enough to send kitty over the edge, splashing into the water below.

For the first time the little kitten showed some panic. He splashed around wildly, cat-screaming with all he had. With great displeasure I reached into the toilet, pulled him out and placed him in the sink where I could dry him off.

I didn't scold Blu. He was just returning a favor. Besides what he had done saved me hours of deliberation over a suitable name for the new member of the family. The kittens name would be T.W.—short for "Toilet Water".

T.W. wound up to be the most unlike-a-cat cat I had ever known. He was not your typical sly, sometimes underhanded, timid, but, at the same time, arrogantly independent feline. Of those traits he held dearly to only the arrogant independence. And he was inherently curious and mischievous, but in no respect was he timid, underhanded, or sly about it. His most astounding trait was one that proved most dangerous to his well-being. He feared nothing and no one.

He was continually playing with whomever and whatever he pleased. He had no regard for the intended playmate's or, more appropriately put, intended victim's privacy, comfort, or its size and strength in relation to his own.

One evening I was reading a good book while relaxing on the sofa. Blu was stretched out inches from my feet sound asleep on the shag carpet. T.W. was in the doorway between the living and dining rooms playing with the cap of a pen he had found somewhere.

Every now and then I would look up from my reading to watch and marvel at his antics. I would smile in wonderment at the ease with which a kitten can find amusement. For half an hour this went on without interruption. Then something strange suddenly happened. He stopped.

It was the sort of rousing you get when after falling asleep in front of a blaring TV someone shuts it off. You abruptly awaken to the startling quiet. I looked up to see him rigid, motionless, in the attack posture. He stared intently at something close to the ground between him and me.

All I could see between the two of us was Blu sleeping soundly and comfortably. Except for the gentle, methodical heaving of Blu's chest there was nothing to attract attention, I thought. For the life of me I could not see what it was about Blu-dog that so mesmerized T.W., although I knew it didn't take much. But what I was sure of was that something significant was going to transpire.

In preparation for the assault the "jungle cat" rolled his shoulders slowly and deliberately while remaining otherwise immobile. Then his paws, stretched out before him, lifted at their first joint and just as slowly and deliberately he stretched and curled the toes in ritual loosening before the kill.

Following that he lay still, awaiting the right moment. That moment when his prey would be most vulnerable. That moment when the intended victim least expected the razor-sharp claws and powerful jaws that would most certainly mean the end of life.

Actually, that moment had been available to T.W. for the better part of an hour. Blu, snoring like an old wino, was oblivious to all around him. My kitten was undoubtedly caught up in a fantasy. He was preparing an ambush on a rogue black rhino, the biggest and baddest animal in the jungle.

He began his stalk. Inching ahead, while never raising shoulders or haunches more than a fraction higher than when at rest, he lessened the distance between himself and his prey.

I still couldn't see what had "Zimba" so enthralled. I only knew how rude this invasion of Blu's privacy would be. I thought of stopping this spectacle. But I didn't dwell on it too long. Poor Blu; the brunt of yet another bad joke. If only he hadn't of taken them so well.

Then I saw it. The object of T.W.'s rear attack. As T.W. stalked nearer and nearer I could see that he was heading up the area contained between Blu's limp tail and his hind legs. There in the box canyon where they meet to form rear of dog was that which is common to male animals, if not previously made eunuch. That part of the anatomy, not being as generously coated with hair, posed a striking contrast to the otherwise jet black body. The proverbial "sore thumb", so to speak, was what had distracted T.W. from his pen cap.

In all fairness to my more humane side I must admit that at that discovery I did start to think more strongly of aborting the invasion. The problem was that I thought about it a little too long. My indecisiveness proved me a poor field general, and thus proved sorely painful to Blu.

Before I could make up my mind, T.W. had made up his. The moment had arrived. The distance had been narrowed to striking range. The victim could not escape. The predatory machine sprang forward. With two perfectly calculated bounds it was looking directly into the face, sort of, of the victim.

An instant later a paw producing four tiny switchblades shot out and connected brutally with the target. With the joining of claws and flesh came an uncanny, high pitched, sharp, "Aaaooooo!" from the unsuspecting prey.

Blu shot up quickly with the awkwardness of having been roused precipitously from sound sleep. Swishing his head left to right he looked for that which had caused his crude discomfort. He was certain that only a foe of great stature could have inflicted such pain. His bewildered gaze was looking too high.

Seeing nothing formidable to left, front or right, and concluding that I was at too great a distance to be suspect, he spun expertly, poised for retaliation to his rear. He was still looking too high.

He perceived nothing at which he could direct a counter-attack and was conspicuously perplexed. Suddenly he detected movement directly beneath him. Looking down with a quick jerk that sent slaver sailing from his jowls back between his front legs, he finally came upon his vicious assailant.

Blu was paralyzed with frustration. There was nothing he could do to vent his anger that would not thoroughly obliterate that little twerp. The realization that he had to restrain himself was killing him. Adding insult to injury, T.W. just stood there arrogantly. He was extremely proud of his successful, undetected assault.

The two of them faced off. Blu's head was straight down so that his ears hung down the sides of his snout. His mouth was slightly opened allowing his fluid tongue to drop unencumbered. T.W. looked straight up directly into Blu's nostrils and past them, haughtily into Blu's eyes.

After T.W. was sufficiently reassured that his victory was to go unchallenged, he turned smartly and pranced triumphantly out of the room. He played well the part of the conquering hero.

Blu followed him out with only his eyes, wishing that the lofty little midget was a hundred pounds heavier.

A few days later, Blu unintentionally got revenge. He was never one to deprive another of a meal. In fact any animal, be it cat, dog, or even mouse could eat from his bowl so long as Blu himself was not there first. Even if, while during the course of eating his dinner, he would leave it to get a drink and return to find another indulging in his meal, he would simply wait patiently for his turn. This trait I have never seen exhibited by any other dog.

However, if another happened to poke its nose into Blu's bowl while Blu's nose was already there, without hesitation, Blu would pick up the interloper by its head and fling it unceremoniously across the room. In that way he left no question as to the master of the bowl.

T.W., being T.W., had to sooner or later fall into this situation. The inevitability of such an occurrence was never anything to fret about. Many a kitten and puppy-dog had received their solo flying lessons over my kitchen floor. A lot of little animals, scampering and screaming in panic had been the only result. They had all learned a valuable lesson and not one had ever needed further instruction.

I was eating dinner one evening and Blu was eating his when T.W. came strutting in from his bed on the sofa pillow. The beggar came directly over to me, climbed up my pant leg, sat on my lap, and began meowing for a hand-out. I brushed him off, not being the least bit inclined to share my vittles that particular evening.

He remained on the floor staring up at me and never stopping the meow. I ignored him successfully. Realizing that he was wasting his energy on me he turned and headed for Blu. I stopped eating to watch the professor expertly educate another pupil. I never ceased to marvel at his masterful teaching ability.

As usual, T.W. discourteously poked in under Blu's chin. Blu hesitated between swallows only long enough to growl deeply, latch onto T.W.'s noggin, and air mail him into the wall on the other side of the kitchen. Without further adieu Blu continued eating while T.W. staggered awkwardly, but quickly, out of the room, screaming in panic all the way.

I had seen the same show many times so I continued eating as well. The only thing different about this rerun was that T.W. continued screaming for quite some time after most of the other students would have already ceased and been just quivering in shock in some corner of the house. I attributed this peculiarity to it being T.W. and finished my meal, as did Blu his.

When the screaming was still going on even after I had put my dishes to soak, I decided to give the kitten the once over. Finding him under the living room sofa I knelt down and pulled him out from under. To my dismay I discovered that Blu had accidentally punctured T.W.'s eye. It's fluids were streaming over T.W.'s face and chest.

I sopped up the mess and applied ointment to help guard against infection. After a long period of consoling, T.W.

finally quieted down and went to sleep in my lap. That night he slept curled up beneath my armpit where I could keep watch over him in case of any complications.

I lay awake for a while musing over a slight problem. The next morning Blu and I had to leave for three days on the road all the way to the southwest corner of the state. What was I to do with T.W.? In his condition I was concerned about leaving him home alone. A complication might mean a rush to the vet.

I had never taken one of my cats while working statewide before. But along with camping gear, food, change of cloths and Blu, T.W. was loaded up early the next morning and we were off to the Republican river basin.

To my relief, T.W. was feeling much better. As usual, he wouldn't shut up. It was not the panicked meowing of yesterday but rather his usual meow of idle chatter. He walked around the inside of the station wagon seemingly without pain. Had it not been for the large, gray, pupilless globe taking the place of a seeing eye, I would have thought that nothing at all had happened. That, and the fact that, being unaccustomed to the blind spot, he would occasionally walk into something.

T.W. seemed to take to riding very well. He sat either on the dash or the back of the front seat and was very attentive of all that went by.

Though it was unfortunate that he had lost his eye, he had learned to respect his betters, or at least his biggers. Since he exhibited that respect, he and Blu got along well. T.W. tagged along behind Blu-dog as though Blu were his big brother. Blu, playing the part, kept him under his wing, protecting him from all harm.

While T.W. was a kitten we kept him with us while traveling, even after he was out of danger from his wounded eye. But as he grew older he became more of a problem, always running off, so we began leaving him home with the rest of the family of cats. His absence was missed, but Blu and I managed.

Another year had passed and we enjoyed our life in the country as much as ever. Something, however, was missing. The move from Chicago to the community of Crete had been like being let out of a cage, but I soon tired of life even in that small town. That's when we moved to the country. I then thought for a while that country living was the ultimate. But that was not the case either. It seemed the added stomping ground and laid back lifestyle wasn't sufficient. I wasn't ready to retire. I needed some excitement.

Nebraska is beautiful with farm and pasture land stretching as far as the eye can see with an occasional forest, pond or river bottom to break the monotony. For a real change of pace there are the sand hills and pine ridge areas to the northwest. I venture to say, however, that you could walk all the way across the state without your heart ever racing in excitement, or seeing anything that hasn't already been written about, photographed, or abused a thousand times over.

Hunting, fishing and trapping were aging rapidly. I wanted more. I needed a change of scene, a change of climate, a change of life style. Blu, like it or not, was going to experience the change with me. He made friends easily anyway, so wherever we went he'd still always have his party time. Routines are necessary, but it does good to change even them once in a while.

It seemed like the right time. My perpetual dream since childhood was to come true. We were going to Alaska.

Blu and I had spent the last Christmas with family in Chicago. My cousin Bill was also visiting, but from Alaska. He'd lived and worked up there in the forest service for a number of years. The stories he told made me drool. It was then that I made up my mind to leave the following June.

There wasn't much time to dispose of a house full of stuff

and I knew that Blu would be of no help, especially after he found out where we were going.

The job would have been even more difficult had we remained in the country, so Blu and I and the cats (regular domesticated ones only, I'm afraid) made our way to a small house in town.

It was difficult leaving the farm that had been the major contributing factor to my revelation of life, but it had to be. Actually Blu thought it a piece of heaven having all the new people around.

Time passed quickly having so much to do. It wasn't long before we were on our way north to new things, new places, and new people.

11. The Road to Alaska

Everything would have been perfect if I had not had to give up T.W. It was hard enough to part with my other cats, but T.W. had really become a part of me. I had every intention of taking him, but as I was filling our new Jeep with gas just as we were leaving, he jumped out and ran under a pile of tires. It took me the better part of half an hour to coax him out from under.

I knew then that that same predicament would occur every time we stopped unless I penned or tied him up in some way. For a cat, the worst possible torture is to be penned or tied. Nebraska was his home. Tied up anywhere else would be exile, not an adventure.

Tears welled as I gave him one last smooch between his ears and handed him to his new owner. Blu and I mounted up and headed west never to see T.W. again.

It was early in the morning, the tenth of June. Our first stop was to be in Wind Cave National Park situated in the southwest corner of South Dakota's Black Hills. In the sand hills of western Nebraska the thermometer in the jeep read one hundred five degrees. I felt as though we were to be someone's dinner. Cooking slowly, we'd remain tender. The unseasonable heat persisted all that day and even into the night. The next day was slightly cooler as we drove the winding roads through those magnificent hills.

"Boy, I can't hardly imagine Alaska being any prettier than this." Blu continued to stare out the window intently taking in the scenery. "You'd make this place home with me wouldn't ya, Bluper?" It didn't matter that he wouldn't respond. It was only important that I had a live body to talk to. I felt that one degree saner than talking to the dashboard.

"Ya know though, I said the same thing back in the sand hills didn't I? Chances are there's gonna be a whole lot more tempting places between here and Alaska. Let's just make up our minds that we're going all the way. After we check out that place, if it ain't the best, we can always come back. Right?"

Blu just looked out the window. In his wisdom, he knew that if I asked and answered enough of my own questions I'd come up with the right answer without him having to put his two cents in.

I had feared that leaving home would depress Blu. I was relieved to see that he was instead perpetually excited. The adventure bug had apparently bitten him too. He knew that this was more than just another two or three day road trip. He never slept while we drove, which was his normal way to pass time between stops. He maintained constant wide-eyed vigil on our surroundings.

When we'd pull over, for whatever reason, he would clamber over my lap almost before we had rolled to a complete stop and be out the door investigating with fervor. He kept a full social calendar as well. Cordially he would acquaint himself with everyone we met along the way, typically, whether they liked it or not.

Leaving the deep, mystifying splendor of the Black Hills we ventured next into the vastness of the Wyoming sage prairie. Antelope were everywhere. They were even in amongst the domestic cattle. We saw many deer as well, but all of them were dead along the roadside. With antelope outnumbering the deer in this particular locality, the disproportionate number of road-killed deer to antelope amazed me. Were the antelope so much smarter, or the deer that much more stupid?

That afternoon was made somewhat uncomfortable by a bee deciding to be violent right smack dab in the middle of my armpit. My reflexes slammed my arm down hard against my ribs putting an end to its obnoxiously rude life. Justice was served, easing the pain somewhat. Actually, though, if Blu had not chased it all over the Jeep snapping at it, it probably would not have been quite so irritated when it happened on my pit.

I tried desperately to explain that fact of nature to Blu, while digging at my armpit in pain, but he seemed to think that he had just been doing his part to rid our property of an intruder. If I was dumb enough to get in the way, then he certainly could not be held responsible.

The night before, we had fried in South Dakota. The next we were freeze-dried on top of the Continental Divide just east of Butte, Montana.

Next morning we passed through Butte, Missoula, and were heading north toward Kalispell when we happened on a puppy wandering along the highway. She was the spitting image of Benjie, the movie dog. A pup that adorable had to belong to someone but this stretch of highway was devoid of habitation. Blu and I pulled over to see if she was wearing tags.

I had the fabric door on the driver's side removed and stored between the roll bar and fabric roof. When the Jeep stopped the puppy turned, walked directly to the vehicle and jumped right in at my feet as though she had been a hitchhiker, or more appropriately, a fare waiting for a taxi.

I expected her at any moment to sit back comfortably and incidentally tell me her destination, referring to me as "James". There was no fear in her. She wasn't even the least bit concerned about her present dilemma of being stranded in the middle of nowhere.

She gave the impression that she had always been on her own but I knew that could not be true. A little puppy-dog such as she would be meat for some coyote, or a big cat, or even a large bird, her first night out. Her attitude sure made me lonesome for T.W.

As thoughts of my kitten were meandering through my mind, Blu's curiosity put his nose against the nape of the North Country Wanderer. In the next second he nearly lost a piece of it. The little mutt attacked with the ferocity of a wolverine.

She was attempting to climb up Blu's chest to reach his throat and head which he had pulled back immediately at the first onslaught. He had only received a slight nick on the tip of his nose. Blu never rose from a sitting position but merely bobbed and weaved like an expert boxer dodging the punches of an amateur.

He was as astonished as I at the tenacity of this tiny ball of fur. She didn't cease her efforts to mangle Blu until, fearing for his life, or at least his pride, I reached down, grasped her between the ears and lifted her to my lap.

Upon my thighs she calmed down immediately. She placed her paws on my chest and licked my nose. Now that she had taught Blu who was boss she didn't even mind his final inspection of her.

I no longer feared for her life in the wilderness. I decided that if the wildlife in this vicinity were to be safe from extinction, a home would have to be found for the terror on Highway #93.

As Blu and I had taken in many a stray in the past, I would have kept her myself, but we would be crossing the border soon. Without required immunizations she would not be allowed into Canada. Besides, Canada does not take kindly to having its grizzly population threatened.

We stopped at the next three ranches on our way north. No one had ever seen her before nor had they heard of a neighbor with such an animal. The couple at the third ranch fell in love with her and said that she would be perfect for their grandchildren. They were pleasant folks and I felt that they would make a good home for the pup. I only hoped that the pup would leave them a grandchild or two.

As we pulled away from the ranch I said, "You know, Blu-dog, she's only been sittin' in here thirty minutes but I kinda' miss her already. Aw, it's only 'cause she's a T.W. clone." Blu looked over seeming to nod in agreement and then stared north.

We reached Glacier National Park. Next stop the Canadian border. We drove through the park slowly, stopping often to enjoy its many natural wonders.

A short distance up the Going to the Sun Highway, long before we hit the heavy snows, Blu and I pulled off at a scenic overlook to take in the surrounding beauty. We were sitting on a rock ledge above a rock slide area when, suddenly, out from under nearly every rock, little rodents emerged and began scurrying up toward us. They weren't chipmunks but a rather larger member of the rodent family.

Blu saw them. His head jerked alert and his tail began wagging in anticipation of good sport. Before he got started on what I knew would take me a long time to stop I told him "No!" and "Sit!" He did both reluctantly.

The squirrels continued their assault up the rocks until they were within striking range. There battle was fought with such conviction and determination that I had no choice but to retreat to the Jeep for a jar of peanuts.

Returning to the rock ledge I found a dozen or more sitting waiting for me. Another dozen surrounded Blu wondering why he had not offered them anything. Blu was dumbfounded. He had remained seated but looked around with quick jerks of his head at the little beggars who were, in some cases, no more than a foot from him.

They expected the usual treats that were the toll paid for the use of such a splendid road. Blu couldn't understand why his size alone didn't instigate panic in these tiny creatures. Neither could I. I think that their lack of fear bruised his pride some.

His depression did not last long, however. After I had fed peanuts to them, and of course him, for a while, he decided that "if you can't beat 'em join 'em". He lay down on his belly to let his new found friends examine him more closely. At times, Blu and a squirrel would be nose to nose in their get-acquainted sniffings.

Occurrences like those, that defied nature, made me all the more grateful that that dog belonged to me.

We both had an enjoyable time. We could have remained there all day but we knew we had to push on. A storm was raging above us.

I said good-bys, spilled out another jar of peanuts on a large flat rock, and continued onward and upward. Blu sat in the back of the Jeep watching his new friends fade into the distance until a curve in the road obscured the hungry squirrels from view.

As we ascended the Going to the Sun Highway, the

contrast between its heavily snow-packed roadside and the scorching plains of Nebraska made me feel that we had slept through two seasons. Experiencing that much climactic change in just two days was shocking.

When we reached the top we were in the midst of a blizzard. We got out and stood in the parking lot of the large tourist lodge absorbing the splendor of the late spring snow storm. There really wasn't anything to see except for the snow itself since it cut visibility to about a hundred feet. I was just feeding my addiction to violent storms.

We were well out of the storm by the time we reached Canada but we could still see it raging in the mountains behind us.

The guards at the border gates were cordial and helpful, not at all what I had expected. Actually, I'm not sure what I expected except maybe to feel like a foreigner, whatever that means. I didn't feel any different than I would have had I gone through a toll gate on the Skyway in South Chicago.

Of course they asked some questions and told me what was expected in their country and I had to stop and seal the firing mechanisms on my rifles, but it was all done in such a pleasant way that they made me feel right at home.

A short distance from the border station, Blu and I made camp in Waterton Lakes Provincial Park. Glacier in the U.S.A. and Waterton in Canada combined to be called Waterton-Glacier International Peace Park is a fine example of how two separate nations can coexist in peace, sharing their God-given treasures.

We did not eat dinner till 10:30 that night. Even this far south of Alaska, the Land of the Midnight Sun, it was light enough to see our cooking. One of the fascinations of Alaska that I was anxious to see was a sun that circled overhead rather than rose in the east and set in the west.

While a boy in grade school I had seen this phenomenon

demonstrated many times using a world globe and a beach ball to represent the sun. Even so, it was still difficult for my feeble mind to comprehend it fully without seeing it for myself. As light in the west went out, stars began to appear and it became evident that the North Star was no longer all that far north.

We were camped along an enticing stream so at 5:00 A.M. I was up to try my hand at fly-fishing. I had heard that that method of fishing was fun, so before we had left Nebraska I had bought a fly-fishing rig.

The thermometer in the Jeep read thirty-five degrees. I brewed a pot of coffee and had a couple of cups to take out the chill while sitting at the fire. Then, with pole in hand, we went to the river.

We were back at the fire cooking breakfast within twenty minutes. I'd succeeded in loosing my net, three spinners, twenty yards of line, and my temper. Still, I was able to see through that ugly mood to a sport that could be fun if I was not always loosing something. Someone would have to teach me to fly-fish the proper way.

Before I had finished cooking, snow appeared in large flakes that drifted down like ultra light down feathers through a breathlessly calm atmosphere. They sizzled as they hit the small flames and hot coals.

As I ate from a plate in my lap, large wet flakes landed on the back of my neck and hands. In such splendor my ugly mood disappeared.

After breakfast and breakfast dishes I decided to hole up in my sleeping bag under my lean-to and take full advantage of the gentle, peaceful, pristine snowfall. The hypnotic effect of watching individual flakes slowly fall to the ground undisturbed by even the slightest of breezes soon put me to sleep.

My rest persisted until 1:30 that afternoon. When I awoke the snow was still falling and had accumulated to five or more inches. The temperature was still barely above freezing and the humidity was high. Those factors made for an uncomfortable condition. Snow had not made its way under my lean-to, but my sleeping bag and every other piece of equipment I possessed was damp. The beautiful scene was becoming annoying.

According to my booklet of the park, the Kilmorey Motor Lodge was only miles from our present location. The description pictured it as a pleasantly quaint and homey place of rest. Sounded like a winner to me.

With camp broken we left our temporary home and made for the Kilmorey. After a hot bath, some dry duds, and a full belly, we rested in the Kilmorey's lounge/library with a good book. I hoped that we would be able to partake of the view that the lodge boasted of before leaving the next morning. We needed the low-hanging clouds to cooperate.

At 7:00 the following morning, Blu and I were packed to go. It was still cold but the bright sunshine made the chill easily bearable. A cloudless sky revealed a spectacular view. No explanation could do it justice. Go see it.

That part of Alberta through which we next passed looked much like Nebraska plains, except for the purple line that ran along the western horizon...the Continental Divide, the Rocky Mountains.

It was in that stretch of highway that I stopped to read a historical marker commemorating Fort Spitzee. The fort was built by John Johnson for the purpose of trading with the Indians. Movie goers and Robert Redford fans know him as Jeremiah Johnson.

He had been called Liver Eatin' Johnson. It was said that, while carrying out a vendetta against the Crow Indian Nation, his calling card had been that he would remove the livers of his slain foes and, from them, take a bite or two. In this way he was sure to identify himself as the slayer. This act was said to have elicited great fear and respect from his enemy. I know it would have from me.

It had been a time and he a breed of man that the world may never experience again. They were men so adept at wilderness living that they were more at home and better fit to cope with the hardships of an unforgiving land than even many of the Indians, or, for that matter, the animals that had called the wilderness home for untold ages.

To have been even close to a spot where a man such as he had crossed was an honor to me. Even with traffic whizzing by I could see him clearly. He rode tall in his saddle. His red beard flowed as he looked with disgust and pity upon those of us who dared invade and blemish his home and way of life. Even though his way was cruel, harsh and dangerous, he took pride in his self-sufficiency. He might err, but he held no one responsible for his actions but himself. He liked it that way. He was an American man.

That had been a good day. Blu and I had been permitted the privilege of crossing the path of Mr. Johnson. Later we had seen our first moose in Banff Provincial Park, and, just before making camp in Jasper Provincial Park, we were afforded our first opportunity to see a grizzly bear.

We pitched our lean-to in Kerkeslin River campground at 11:00 that night. I was able to make entries into my log without the aid of artificial light. A mule deer browsed only yards behind our shelter.

We would have had a much earlier start the next morning had Blu not decided it was play time while I was squatted on a rock in the river washing breakfast dishes. He came from behind, lodged his nose under my armpit, and lifted.

Boy, that water was cold. A forty degree air temperature didn't help. It had been frustrating trying to make my point with Blu while trying not to awaken the whole campground.

After drying out, most of the rest of that day was spent sightseeing in Jasper. What a gorgeous piece of real estate.

The sun was quite low when we crossed the Continental Divide into British Columbia.

The sun had set before we were subjected to a queer and frightening experience. It was that period of the evening that only lasts a half hour or so, when dim light and the lack of shadows makes perceiving reality a challenge, when car headlights or the lack of them make little difference in your ability to see clearly.

We were on paved but extremely poor road. The winter had left numerous chuck holes and frost heaves. In order to thread our way through these obstructions we were moving at only a moderate speed. We had not met another car for quite some time.

The landscape consisted of extremely tall, dark evergreens growing very close together. It seemed that when the road had been built the bulldozers had left no margin for error. The trees came almost to the very edge of the highway going up the mountain to our left and down to our right.

Only an intermittent wisp of a breeze sang mournfully from the tree tops. It was the type of evening I normally relish. And I did then. At least for a while.

There was nothing particularly menacing about the area. But the right combination of dark and light, the ominous appearance of the forest, the stillness, the ever-so-slight moaning of the wind, and the lack of other human life gave an eerie feel that chilled me.

"This is neat, uh, Bluper?!" Blu stared, cautiously.

Then, as I habitually glanced into my rear view mirror, a form appeared at the side of the road about seventy-five yards behind us. I lifted my foot from the gas and coasted.

While I watched, it crossed the highway at a quick pace but not a run. At that distance and in that light I couldn't tell if it was on all fours or merely crouching. It disappeared into the forest up the mountain.

"Did you see that, Blu?!" He did. He was quivering with excitement looking back over the seat. At least I had thought it was excitement.

"What the heck was that?! A moose? Grizzly? This crazy light's playing tricks. If it was on four legs it sure was low to the back side. But if it wasn't… We're goin' back!"

I chose a landmark. A tree at the point where the creature had disappeared into the deep woods. I executed a U-turn and made for that tree with all haste.

I could only pull a few feet off the road. We walked briskly to the other side to see if we could pick up a track. I needed to identify that thing.

In the coarse stone of the shoulder we could only see where it had disturbed some of it. There was no definite outline to give away its identity. Blu had identified something though. Something he didn't like. As he sniffed the tracks the hair rose on his neck and shoulders.

My excitement overwhelmed me. I was tempted to break the seal on my .50 caliber rifle and push down a load. I thought better of it though. We still had a lot of driving to do in Canada. An extended vacation in a Canadian village jail had not seemed appealing.

Blu and I made haste to the other side of the road and began our ascent of the mountain through a thick forest littered with deadfalls. My eyes were on the ground in front of us or the forest in front of and above us. I strained in the dim light for some sign of our quarry.

The going was extremely difficult, having to crawl over or under a myriad of dead trees littering the understory. From occasional fresh scratches or disturbed undergrowth it seemed that the creature had gone straight up the mountainside.

We had progressed only three or four hundred yards. Without warning, for no apparent reason, my breathing became labored, my body covered itself with goosebumps, and my heart, already going double time, pounded even more rapidly. It had seemed that at any moment it would beat its way right through my breastbone.

We froze in our tracks. My fear was fed a steak dinner, almost to panic, when I looked down and saw that Blu felt the same way. His legs were braced ready to do battle, the hair on the back of his neck and shoulders was at attention, and his lips were curled back up and over his fangs. His eyes glared in fear and anger as he turned his head slowly from side to side searching for a cause…something or someone to blame and vent his anger upon.

The breeze had ceased. All that could be heard was the beating of my heart and the barely audible whispered growl emitting from Blu's clenched teeth.

Blu's fear had him ready to fight. Mine had me ready to run. But which way? Blu had not yet concentrated his glance in any one direction. I had not seen nor had I heard anything that might give away the hiding place of whatever was there. Never before had I experienced such a feeling. To this day I have never experienced it again.

The urge to run was overwhelming. The problem was I'd not been able to run a step since I had broken my neck. It was either stand and fight or turn and walk out. Neither option overwhelmed me with delight but the first seemed utterly ridiculous. I had no idea what it was that I would be fighting except that it outweighed me by at least a few hundred pounds. Not having even one hand grenade in my possession I had nothing that I considered adequate with which to fight.

Senses were at peak performance. Eyes strained for even the slightest glimpse. Ears, for the slightest sound. Even my nose labored for some unusual scent. My tongue tasted only sweat. I felt nothing but my own body shaking out of control. Only one sense registered that something lurked there…my sixth one.

Without doubt I knew that it was watching my every move. Only, where was it, what was it, and what were its intentions?

The situation had been almost more than I could handle. Had I been capable of running I would have headed down the hill as fast as my legs could have carried me. Each panicked step would have magnified the fear until I would have been running in blind terror. I would have reached the road at full speed continuing past the Jeep and down the mountain in a straight line until I ran into a tree or my lungs burst. Or, more likely, till my running triggered the hunter instinct in my adversary and it would chase, catch and destroy.

My physical deterrent, however, forced me to keep my head somewhat. If my feet could not run away with me, my mind would not. I turned slowly, picked up the largest stick within reach, and made a controlled but shaky descent toward my vehicle.

The forest was nearly pitch black. Every muscle was tense and every sense still worked overtime. Blu, being more physically capable than I, was ahead of me out of sight and sound. I was alone in an unfamiliar and unfriendly forest.

The feeling of something watching me was with me all the way to the Jeep. As we pulled away I stared into the rear view mirror. All the while I felt something was returning my gaze.

Safely away from "terror mountain" I looked down between the seats to see the stick I had carried. It sure didn't look like much. I wondered what good it would have done me had I been attacked. Maybe I could have used it to brain myself to save me from the agony of a torturous mauling.

Then I looked over at Blu. "Youuuu dirty pile of mange. Youuuu actually left me up there all alone holdin' the bag. What am I sayin'? I was holdin' a lousy stick. Heck, I was barely holdin' my own water!"

Blu was sitting on the passenger seat and in response

momentarily looked over at me, and then turned to resume his gaze out the windshield. I unmistakingly sensed, "Hey, you got us up there. I didn't." It's frustrating to loose an argument to a dog!

That day's sightseeing in Jasper coupled with our experience in the deep woods of eastern British Columbia made for a long day but few miles. The tenseness of the circumstances, and the stark fear that had kept me going subsided. I was drained. Exhausted. A lodge or campground were not necessary. About fifteen miles from our bout with the unknown I found a pull-off area that more than suited our needs.

Blu was already asleep when I turned off the ignition. I had to disturb him to retrieve my sleeping bag from under the gear he was bedded on.

It was no easy task shutting my eyes that night. The woods around us might have been infested with those things. The little bit of sleep that I did get was in a sitting position in the driver's seat.

The next day I was only capable of one hundred fifty miles or so before I petered out. We stopped for a bite and called it a day at Fort McLeod. We met some nice folks there, did some fishing, and got some rest.

Our stay at Fort McLeod was enjoyable. Our leaving regrettable. The following morning we drove into beautiful fifty degree sunshine.

A few hours later we arrived at Dawson Creek, the beginning of the AlCan Highway. I pulled over and checked the tune of the engine, changed the oil, and even bought little plastic shields for my headlights. It had been warned that the next thousand miles of rock road was grueling on vehicles and their occupants.

As we said good by to pavement I noticed the shields down between the seats. "Oh, for Pete's sake, Blu, I forgot to mount those darn things. Well, we're not stopping now. I'll put 'em on when we stop for gas."

At the next gas stop I bought gas and two new headlights. Not even an hour out of Dawson Creek a truck had come baring down on us heading south. It had spit up enough rock to break both headlights, the windshield in three places, and ding up the hood and driver's side of the Jeep. Had the window not been zipped shut to keep out the dust, the side of my head would have been dinged up as well.

Oh, that dust! When we started at Dawson Creek a sign had read, "HEADLIGHTS TO REMAIN ON AT ALL TIMES WHILE DRIVING." I couldn't understand it. In a country that stayed light well into the night hours, I thought that a ridiculous law.

At this time I would like to publicly apologize to the lawmakers who enacted that particular law for the names I called them before I discovered the wisdom of their ruling. The white dust would become so thick at times that it was impossible to read a license plate just a few car lengths ahead. Even with lights on, there would be barely enough time to react to oncoming vehicles or those slow moving ones approached from the rear.

Going was slow over most of the narrow, dusty, potholed, rocky AlCan. Large freight and lumber trucks acted as cattle prods pushing the reluctant traffic. Drivers from all over the world obeyed the trucks in fear of being pressed into the stone if they tarried too long.

The trucks had ceased being machines. Their drivers went unnoticed. It seemed they were alive with minds of their own. Minds focused on getting from one point on the AlCan to another and letting nothing interfere with that goal.

There was no worse feeling than being a few feet off the rear bumper of a large, slow moving recreational vehicle with a logging truck a few feet off mine. I would be unable to pass because of the cloud of visually impenetrable dust created by the RV. It had to be like what a fly feels just before the swatter smears him on the window pane.

Then the truck would decide to pass and he'd get so close that I could have stuck out my tongue and, with it, touched his tires that were at eye level. I didn't, though, because the dust would have choked me to death. Or if my tongue had got caught in one of the treads it would have yanked me out through the window.

There were many stretches so narrow that I had to pull over to let an oncoming truck pass. But it was outside curves that were most dreaded. If I happened to be in one while a truck was on the inside, the trucks gargantuan, spinning wheels would spit up pounds of road stone seemingly trying to bury us alive.

When they were alongside like that the towering cargo of logs would blot out the little sunshine that made it through the dust. It was like driving blind through a tunnel. The only way I could know that I was still on the road was by watching the wheels of the truck and making sure that I never let them get more than two or three feet away. All the while my ears would ring with the sound of rocks bouncing off of the body of my Jeep.

In all the excitement my nose wasn't big enough to handle the intake of oxygen required by my over-worked lungs to supply the blood pumped by my panic-stricken heart. I'd have to open my mouth to draw more from wherever it could be found. By the time an ordeal like that was over, my lips, tongue, gums, and teeth would be caked with white dust that hardened like plaster. There would even be a coating on the walls of my lungs that needed to be coughed up. By the end of a day, face, hair and clothes were all white as well.

Towards the end of the first day we were both tired, dirty and thirsty. According to some folks to whom I'd spoken earlier that day, there was a nice campsite far enough off the highway to be clean and quiet somewhere in our vicinity.

The first road we tried led only to a gravel pit. We wound up getting bogged down in marshy tussocks on a slightly visible path that led into the woods. Ten or fifteen minutes of winching was required to get us to dry ground. We went back to the main highway and proceeded to search up and down it for about five miles. We found nothing.

I decided to keep driving north till we found the next possible place to throw out a sleeping bag. Little did either of us know that it would be four more hours before we would be laying our weary, and dirty, heads to rest.

Temptation struck me. Off to the left ran the most enticing firebreak I had ever seen. It ran down into a heavily and darkly forested valley with, according to the map, a river running through it.

The possibility loomed before us of having our own private campsite on a north country river. Even though the break was bedded with the same type of tussocks we had only moments ago been stuck in, I could not resist. Besides, we had been successful in winching out of the last bog. So, we would just winch our way out of the next if it became necessary.

It was only two miles to the river, but it took us an hour to get there. Fortunately we never got stuck but on many occasions I had to get out to move deadfalls that were obstructing our path or fill in some exceptionally sloppy areas with logs and sticks.

In doing so I got my first taste of north country mosquitoes. Each time I'd exit the Jeep and take a step into the soggy forest floor a cloud of the little blood suckers would rise to the occasion and begin their feast. I would get the outside work done as quickly as possible and hustle back into the safety of the Jeep. Inside I would spend a minute or two finishing off the critters that had followed me, say a few teasing words to those buzzing outside seeking entrance, and then continue on toward the river.

Opening before us when we reached the river was a scene from my dreams. Between steep banks bordered by magnificent forest rushed crystal clear water. It wound its way around countless gravel bars and boulders.

What had really caught my eye though was a small clearing on the edge of the river. It rose only slightly out of the tussocks. Just enough to be dry. A perfect place for a campsite.

It was the kind of spot where one would want to spend a couple of days, at least, if not a lifetime. The problem was that right where our shelter would need to sit there stood four seven-foot poles staked deep into the ground. They formed a perfect square with nine or ten foot sides. At their tops the corners were joined together with four more poles lashed in place with rawhide strips.

Hanging from the cross poles were the feet and feathers of a number of birds of prey. Talons glittered in the red light of a late night sunset. On the ground in the center of the poles was a low rock altar. Bones were littered on and around it. Within the confines of the poles, but mostly outside it, were numerous footprints.

Camping was out of the question. The only suitable site was already spoken for. Obviously it was used by locals for some type of ceremony. I doubted strongly if my presence would have been accepted with any great show of welcome.

"Blu-dog, we better boggie." Blu responded by continuing to sniff out the footprints. "I mean now! You want to be the next sacrifice? This is a great spot, but I'll pass on spending eternity here." Although the area really interested him it didn't take too much to coax him inside. The mosquitoes were horrendous.

When I turned on the ignition I had every intention of heading back up the firebreak. Temptation struck again. I couldn't leave without getting a picture of Blu and our Jeep sitting on a gravel bar in the middle of the river. There wasn't much time. The light would be gone soon.

We found a very narrow section of bank that was not quite perpendicular. Over we went making almost a nose dive into the river six feet below. Our front tires hit bottom only inches before the front bumper. The reverse would have been disastrous. The water was two to two and a half feet deep. I drove about forty feet across its rock bottom emerging onto the picturesque gravel bar.

Daylight was fading fast. I really had to move. I unpacked my camera and stepped out onto the bar and into a swarm of mosquitoes the size of hummingbirds. (You can believe that if you want to.) I tried to get Blu to come out to sit beside the Jeep, but he had more sense than his master, refusing emphatically. I would opt for a picture of the Jeep with Blu in it.

I got half way back across the river when the mosquitoes became too much for me. I could think of no picture that was worth that torture. Turning to head back to the Jeep I fought off the attack.

By the time I reached the bar the mosquitoes had called up reinforcements. I swear that, if I had not just acquired the added weight of wet pants and boots filled with river water, they would have carried me away to their nest where they would have systematically bled me to death.

The light was nearly gone. We still needed to winch back up the bank. I knew that we would be poking our way up through the marshy tussocks of the firebreak in the blackness of night.

Stretching and wrapping winch cable was no easy matter when forced to defend one's hide from the merciless mosquitoes. It was not until a half an hour later that we were back up on the bank with the cable wrapped snuggly on its spool and heading up the firebreak.

There had been a slight breeze on the river but in the thick woods there was only moist, still air. Memories of our encounter a couple of nights before haunted me sending a chill up my spine. But the labor required to winch off of the first tussock we high-centered on erased all recollection of that earlier night.

Three high-centers later I wearily drove our vehicle up the road bank and onto the highway to Alaska. I stopped for a moment to stagger out and unlock the front wheel hubs. Then we were on our way, again searching for a suitable place to lay our heads.

Blu's head was already at rest. In fact, except for the dirty looks he had given me each time we would get stuck and I'd inadvertently awaken him while operating the winch, he had been sleeping since we had left the river. Well, excuuuuuse me!

His attitude at least had kept me going with thoughts of how I would make him pay for his lack of encouragement. All the while, while I would be pulling out cable or guiding it back in, I would be rebuking him under my breath with strings of mumbled frustration. My jealousy of his life of leisure had gotten the better of me.

We arrived at Ft. Nelson for coffee and a burger. The rest and strong coffee gave me a new lease on life. We continued driving in rain that had begun to fall until we reached Kledo Creek campground. Other travelers there had long since drifted off to sleep.

The rain had ceased and the sky was clearing so I simply laid my sleeping bag on my ground cloth, crawled in, and was instantly asleep.

What seemed to be only moments later, we were awakened by shouts from across the campground. When I opened my eyes the sky was confusingly bright. A confirming look at my watch shocked me to the realization that it was already 8:00 A.M.

The shouts were still coming loud and strong. "What the heck is goin' on, Blu-dog?" He was standing next to me, legs set, teeth bared and growling low. The night had not been cold so my sleeping bag was already unzipped. I sat up quickly to see what Blu was so upset about.

At fifty yards distance the caretaker of the grounds was shooing away a black bear that had been busying itself in the camp's garbage. The bear was retreating under a shower of rocks as the caretaker pursued it at a fast pace.

My first thought was that that was certainly a cruel way to treat a native of the forest, but on closer examination my heart went out to the poor man who was responsible for cleaning up the mess. The mischievous bruin had made no attempt at an orderly sorting of the trash. Garbage was strewn everywhere. From where I sat I saw at least a couple of hours of work cleaning up.

I arose and ushered Blu, who seemed to be aching for a morning brawl, into the Jeep. Then I went over for a closer look. I didn't get too close however. The keeper of the grounds had a job to do and I don't think he would have appreciated some idiot tourist's interference. Besides, he had a handful of rocks...and was a pretty darn good shot.

The bear beat a hesitant withdrawal as he tried to decide how much punishment that delicious trash was worth. Finally, though, he must have come to the realization that there were other campgrounds and there would be other days to raid them. Hesitant withdrawal turned to hasty retreat and the last we saw of him was his black rump bounding over deadfalls as he made for deeper cover.

I cooked, ate breakfast and we were on our way by 9:00. Our priority that day was to find somewhere to wash clothes and bodies. Blu looked like a white lab rather than a black one and if the balding of my head wasn't enough, it was turning white as well. I looked like an old man who was taking what would probably be his last vacation.

A few hours later, crossing a bridge over the Laird River, we noticed a little pull-off that led behind some thick brush. It seemed the perfect place for getting naked and getting clean. I had only brought along one change of clothes. Everything else I had shipped. What I had to do was wash the already dirty clothes first. After I had done that and hung them to dry in the warm sunlight and soft breeze, I fixed and ate lunch and took a short nap.

Upon awakening I had a clean, dry change of clothes. I stripped off, or rather peeled off, the filthy rags I was wearing and took a bath. My body went numb in the cold water. After I'd scrubbed down thoroughly it was time to clean the caked white mop on my head.

Cupping my hands I scooped water onto my head to wet it down. Then I lathered up. I worked the soap into my scalp for a full five minutes before I was confident that each and every hair had been cleansed. Then came the shock of my life.

Scooping water to my head had not been too bad. It was cold, but easily bearable. In order to rinse, however, a more abundant water source was required.

I plunged my head deep into the swift waters of the Laird River. Instantly I experienced a headache that almost rendered me unconscious. The unrelenting throbbing caused me to clutch and dig at my head with my fingertips. Fortunately the pain remained only as long as it took the sun to reheat my remarkably feeble brain. I continued to rinse with the "a little here a little there" technique.

Being bathed and dressed in clean, dry clothes was a welcome treat. All that was left to do was to pound my dirty change on the rocks until they were clean.

Doing the laundry had gone well. I had finished and hung to dry shirt, underwear, socks, and was in the final rinse of my jeans when disaster struck.

I had had what I thought was a firm hold on the waist band of my trousers. I was wrong. The powerful waters suddenly jerked them from my grasp and my only spare pair of pants was on its way to the Pacific.

I followed them along the bank while they were swept under, around and over rocks and tree limbs. I had hoped that I would have an opportunity to reach them if they came close to the bank. Blu trailed along beside me staying out of the way.

"Wait a minute! You're the perfect tool for this job! Why should I have to get these dry duds wet? Hut!"

Just before he plunged into the swift waters Blu looked at me as if to say, "That's all you had to say. I've been waitin'."

For nearly three thousand miles I had been doing all the work. Blu finally had his opportunity to contribute to our adventure. The mighty current seemed to kidnap Blu as it forged toward the ocean.

I was proud of him as he bulled forward. The sea-worthy jeans were inching their way toward the opposite bank. Blu had quite a distance to travel but he was focused on the wayward jeans and he surmounted all obstacles in his quest.

Fighting those rapids was no easy task but he finally reached out and clamped the jeans between his teeth. He turned sharply and started back toward me. He was fifty yards downstream of me. I closed the distance as I climbed over boulders.

Though he fought valiantly in my direction, the current continued pulling him downstream. By the time he emerged on my side of the bank we were about three hundred yards below our starting point. He shook himself and displayed before me my limp, wet blue jeans. He was duly praised and we started back up the bank.

An hour later, after another nap, the clothes were dry and we were again heading north toward Yukon Territory. That would be the last Canadian plot of real estate before reaching

Alaska.

We made only a dent in the Yukon before heavy eyes brought us to rest at Watson Lake campground. It was a wonderfully calm and cool night and I was ready early the next morning. The closer we got to Alaska the more anxious I became. Even the most beautiful of scenery couldn't slow me. I did notice, however, the definite change in my surroundings.

We had left the large-girthed and stories tall trees of British Columbia behind. In the Yukon the trees became dwarfed and spindly. They stood mute testimony to the harsh climate.

The countryside was no less beautiful for it. On the contrary, it possessed a beauty all its own. Rather than gawking at it in amazement as I did in lower parts of Canada, I stared with admiration and respect. The road to survival was not an easy one for the living things in this territory yet they thrived and retained their magnificence.

Yukon was not the picturesque scene from postcards. Rather it was a wild, foreboding, mean, yet beckoning land that seemed to dare me to try it on for size. It was a land that sent shivers of fear and excitement down my spine.

We stopped in the town of Watson Lake to gas up. After filling the tank, checking the oil and scrubbing the white clay off of the windshield, I paid our bill. Then I climbed into the Jeep and called for Blu to follow. He was out of sight.

I started the engine and slowly rolled the Jeep away from the pumps toward the west side of the station where I was going to park while I searched for Blu. My search was over. There he stood rigidly squaring off with another dog.

The other dog was only half Blu's size. Blu was obviously in its territory so it felt obliged to do something about it. Just as obviously it seemed regretful that its primitive laws forced it into such a situation. He circled Blu with teeth bared and hackles raised. Blu followed its progress by moving only his head.

I knew it was only a matter of moments before the mangy-looking mutt felt that to save face he would have to attack. Blu knew it too and waited patiently looking forward to a little diversion.

"Sorry for the trespass," I said as I grabbed Blu's collar and moved toward the Jeep. No need for the smaller dog to be humiliated in front of his friends and neighbors by a transient. The smaller dog appeared thankful and relieved though he continued to strut his stuff.

"Blu, you don't really need this do you? You that bored?" Blu never released his gaze on his adversary who trailed behind us all the way to the Jeep.

Looking north there had been nothing but tens of thousands of square miles of wilderness. Some had probably never been trod upon by human feet. There lay months of daydream material.

The overwhelming splendor of the savage land was so exhilarating that it spurred me to a five hundred eighty mile gain that day. We lay to rest in a gravel pit that night. Nothing fancy. But we were in Alaska.

12. Our New Home

    The next morning we began the last leg of our journey. That day we would be in Eagle River where my cousin Bill lived.

    Low hanging clouds prevented us from seeing the surrounding mountains. Sightseeing was unnecessary though. We would make a point of seeing it all as soon as we were settled in.

    It was mid-afternoon when we pulled into Bill's place on Meadow Creek Drive. After customary greetings we were made a part of Bill's landscaping crew. Bill, his lady friend, and me. Blu supervised. Bill had only recently bought the house, so with summer approaching it was time for planting.

His neighbors had opted to incorporate the usual "lower 48" (as Alaskans liked to call the other states of the Union) ideas in their landscaping plans. Lots of grass. I suppose they didn't want to leave everything behind. My cousin, on the other hand, preferred the natural look. He used rocks and trees collected locally and sea shells he'd harvested and brought all the way from Ketchican. Ketchican, in southeastern Alaska, had been his home for a few years before he was transferred to Anchorage.

After a couple of hours of hard labor Bill showed me the inside of the house and what was to be my room. Then he and I unloaded my gear.

Blu evidently approved of our new home. He tinkled on everything outside that stood at least two inches above the ground. Where he came up with all the water I'll never know. The amount of urine he voided would have shriveled a two hundred pound man into a dehydrated shell of a human being. Without a doubt he was the one to have along in case of fire.

Blu then strutted into the house. He sauntered over to a cozy spot in front of the fireplace, tiptoed a half dozen ceremonial circles on the thick shag carpet and nestled down into his imaginary nest. It was time for his afternoon sack out, without even so much as a "Cousin Bill, may I".

Later that same evening, while Bill and I sat in front of the fireplace consuming a drink or two, Bill's neighbor Fred came over. Fred was relatively new to Alaska too. Between the two of us we kept Bill buried in questions.

The questions got increasingly harder as the night grew longer and the bottle emptier. Like me, Fred had all kinds of ideas as to what he wanted to see and do. We needed knowledge as to how to go about it. Bill was helpful in that respect but, like anything else, experience would be the best teacher.

The next day would be the longest day of the year. Blu's

and my first real taste of the Alaskan outdoors would come then. Bill and I had decided to climb one of the mountains on the right bank of Eagle River Valley. We would spend the longest day's midnight on top.

Late afternoon the next day, after some more landscaping, we drove a couple of miles closer to Anchorage in order to cross Eagle River. We turned left off of the highway and took a gravel road till we chose a suitable mountain. We drove up the mountain till we found a small level spot just large enough to turn the Jeep around. Parking there, Bill, Blu and I began our climb. There was no technical climbing involved…just a steep hike.

Not used to such steep walking and, quite honestly, in pretty poor shape, I had to stop frequently to catch my breath. At the same time I would smoke a cigarette in order to clear my lungs of the fresh air. I knew then that something would have to be done about that habit. And it would have to be soon.

We reached the summit at about 11:00 P.M. I felt as though I had just climbed Mt. Everest. Bill and Blu acted like they had just walked to the corner store.

The sky was cloudy. In fact, we were in one. The eerie mist snaked along the ground enveloping our feet and making everything feel clammy. There was no breeze. In Alaska that means quiet. We stayed hoping that by midnight the clouds would dissipate, but without a wind we knew it was unlikely. When midnight arrived we were still in soup and unable to see the rays of the midnight sun.

There was more than sufficient light, however, to make our descent safely. I'd had that first feel of spongy tundra under my feet. That first taste and smell of the Alaska wilderness. A wilderness that could be found within walking distance of Anchorage. A new, fresh, unspoiled country. Blu had been in seventh heaven. It was as though Bill and I didn't even exist. There were so many new smells and so much new land to explore. He had been in a world of his own, barely able to contain himself.

The next couple of weeks were spent getting acquainted with the country around our new home. We familiarized ourselves with the towns of Eagle River and Anchorage and hiked up Eagle River and Meadow Creek valleys. We toured up Peterson Valley and explored the Eklutna and Portage Glacier areas.

On the evening of the fifth of July, Bill, Blu and I were again sitting before a cozy fire after spending that afternoon planning a back porch and deck. We were shootin' bull and throwing out some jokes when my roving eyes noticed a particular book in Bill's library. It was a book about the Brooks Range.

I pulled it from the shelf. Its text and photographs fascinated me. The color, the broad valleys, the majestic mountains, the rushing rivers. That place was surely the closest thing to Eden left on earth.

Actually it was time to look for a job because funds were running mighty low. Before I did though, we had to go to that place. "Hey, Bill, where's the Brooks Range?" I asked thinking that it was a park of a few hundred thousand acres. Bill pulled out a large map of Alaska and swept his hand across the whole northern third of the state. A couple hundred million acres was more like it. It was larger than most states. I needed to narrow down my objective.

The furthest we could drive north was Circle City. That was the end of all connecting highways. From there we would have to charter an airplane. We would spend tomorrow, Tuesday, in Anchorage getting supplies and Wednesday packing. Bill and Fred suggested that I spend more time planning but as far as I was concerned the trip was already planned. We planned to leave Thursday.

I knew that trip would completely deplete the money I'd

saved. It would be imperative that I look for work when we returned. Even more so that I find some.

With one restless night under our belts Blu and I headed for Anchorage to buy what odds and ends we would need for our adventure. At the first store I bought some spinners for what I hoped would be some excellent grayling fishing. At the same time I got a non-resident hunt/fish license. There wasn't much else I needed at that store but the owners were kind enough to direct me to businesses that could supply our other needs. They even called around to find a retailer who had dog packs.

We got freeze dried food, mosquito repellent, a vinyl tarp (I couldn't afford a tent), plenty of film and a nylon doggie pack.

That evening, back in front of Bill's fireplace, I sat mesmerized while rereading the book about the Brooks Range. Butterflies started their fluttering in the pit of my stomach. They would be frequent companions for the next fourteen days.

The next morning I started by sorting my belongings. I would take only bare essentials. The final tally was what fit into a medium size pack that Bill loaned me, an over-the-shoulder bag, and the doggie pack that carried all Blu's food. In addition were a sleeping bag, camera, rifle and handgun.

We were ready. In fact it was all I could do to keep from packing the Jeep and leaving that afternoon. I kept telling myself that a good night's rest would be necessary to start the trip properly.

I still wasn't convinced and probably would have left if Bill hadn't come home with fresh king crab as a going away celebration. Crab legs with white wine, and a cold beer for dessert can keep a man from almost anything.

13. Above the Arctic Circle

Even after the big, rich meal of crab dipped in butter, the night didn't last long. My eyes opened at 3:30 A.M. and would not shut again. We packed, breakfasted and were on our way by 4:30 into a clean, crisp, fresh morning.

It was made crisper by having put the top down. I didn't want anything getting in the way of all we were about to see. Blu was eager with anticipation. He took his place seated on the passenger's seat. His back was straight, his head was high and his ears flapped in the breeze.

Mt. McKinley quickly came into view on that hazeless day even though we were still a hundred miles from her. Its majesty increased as the miles separating us decreased. It didn't seem to belong in a land that generally sported mountains of under ten thousand feet. But then nothing is ordinary about Alaska.

We stopped for lunch at a scenic point just past a place called McKinley View. There we soaked in the awesome ice-covered mountain that soared before us in the brilliantly blue sky. I rested in the knowledge that even such a monument fell short of heaven.

Finally we reached the boom town of Fairbanks. We took a relatively fast tour of the city then gassed up in preparation for the last leg of the journey. Looking at our map I estimated we had a hundred miles to go. Two, maybe two and a half hours.

One hundred and sixty-eight miles and five and a half of the most grueling hours I had ever spent, on the worst road I had ever encountered that was still called a highway later, we hobbled into Circle City. Our thirty mile an hour average could have been construed as reckless driving. A totally safe speed would have clocked in an average much less impressive.

We had made two stops along the way. Both were necessary to rest my abused body and repair my wounded vehicle. The ruggedness of the road actually caused the welds holding on the spare tire to break. The second-teamer made the trip atop my gear in the back of the Jeep.

When I finally stepped out at Circle I felt as though I had been mugged or had played a full sixty minutes of puppy-dog football.

We were five hundred miles and fourteen hours from Eagle River. On the banks of the Yukon River. In the thriving metropolis of Circle City, where all of North America's connecting roads ended. From there north only aircraft could get us where we needed to go.

Circle, for the most part, is made up of an air field, some old log cabins, an old log hotel, a campground, and a building serving as general store, gas station, cafe, air terminal, and tourist information center. Genuine wolf skins spread-eagle on the wall of that building went for $395.00.

While Blu slept off the beating he received on what someone with a sick sense of humor had classified as a highway, I inquired as to the availability of a flight into the Brooks Range. A pilot told me that to get to the Brooks Range by helicopter would cost me somewhere in the neighborhood of $1500.00. After I regained my composure he said that another possibility would be to take the regular sightseeing flight over to Ft. Yukon. There I might try to have a float plane take me the rest of the way up at a much more reasonable rate.

I didn't like the idea of spending $50.00 for me and $50.00 for Blu to take the flight to Ft. Yukon on a "maybe". "You think you could ask for me when you make your next flight tomorrow?" I inquired. "If a plane and pilot's available, and if I can afford 'em, I'll fly back up with you day after tomorrow." The pilot didn't seem pleased with my request.

Actually, that unusual delay in my plans was due to cold feet. It had nothing to do with frugality. Frugality had not even been a part of my vocabulary till I reached for a word that would cover up my cowardice.

We had just driven through some mighty forbidding country. It was rugged, treacherous and unconcerned with the courtesies and cordiality of civilization. But at least man had been there long enough to build a road through it. North of where I stood the land lay virtually undisturbed. Man did not reign supreme there. Like everything else, he stayed alive as best he could or not at all. There was no one to bail him out.

I had never done anything even remotely similar to what I had in mind. Sure I'd done my share of weekend camping and spent some weeks at Boy Scout camps but if emergencies arose I was always within ear-shot or walking distance of someone who could help. On the Brooks Range, the time it took to fly to safety could be more time than I had. And I was thinking of having someone drop us off…and take the plane back with them.

From the coziness of Bill's living room it had seemed adventurous and fun but things had started to get serious. It was, put up or shut up time. It was, if I don't like the heat get out of the kitchen time. It was, put my money where my mouth was time. It was, out of the pan and into the fire time. How about, don't and say I did time?

The country we had just passed through was mean enough to suit me. It was at least sparsely populated. Where I was thinking of going was umpteen miles from the nearest corner store. It was in an area where human presence was rarely, if ever, felt. The fun-loving adventurer had transformed into a cold-blooded, chicken-livered, gut-crawlin', yellow-bellied poltroon. The man who had considered finding a nice spot in the wilderness and living out the rest of his life on it as a hermit was looking for a congested subway to get comfortable in.

Time for bed. Safe from the mosquitoes I slept between the seats of the Jeep. My feet were on either side of the gear shifter and four-wheel drive shift sticks, my back was against Blu's, and snagged against my stomach, chest and face was my stuff. My mind raced with every conceivable evil thought but when I shut my eyes I slept like a baby.

A gorgeous morning arrived and I hastily cooked breakfast. After that good night's sleep I was able to see things in a different light. Rather than simply admitting to myself that I was scared stiff, with a little rest I was able to develop reasons and make excuses.

Things like, I wasn't a kid anymore, and as an adult I had to be a little more cautious. It would be safer to just go back down the road apiece, find a nice spot and camp for a week or two. Bill was my older cousin, so if anything happened to me the whole family would hold him responsible. I even had the audacity to think that it wouldn't be fair to Blu since he wasn't used to that sort of camping.

I was laying it on pretty thick. I almost fell for it but I caught myself in time. After all, I wasn't born yesterday. I heard all sorts of similar excuses before from someone or other and I was not going to get suckered in. No siree, I was not going to stand for those excuses. The fact was I was scared gutless and nobody was going to try and convince me differently. By golly, I would stand firm on that. I would fight the first man who tried to convince me that I wasn't a coward!

What would make that trip different was the fact that in case of trouble there was nowhere to go. We'd be entirely on our own. But that's why I chose the trip back there in front of Bill's cozy fireplace. That's what was going to make the trip so different from all the others.

"Well, what do ya say, Blu?" The wet tongue traveling up the side of my face wasn't a "yes" or a "no." Like always it was a "Whatever you decide will be OK with me" lick. His great love and faith put his neck on the line many times. His urge to please me was so strong that he did it over and over. Men should have such faith.

The fact was that I'd been wrong. We were not going somewhere where there was no one to help if things turned bad. Blu would be there to help me and I to help him. How could we go wrong? We would leave that morning...if we weren't already too late.

I rushed to the general store and checked with the pilot. He had two seats left. "I've got the room," he said. "But I'm leaving on schedule in fifteen minutes. If you're not ready I *will* leave without you."

I bought fare for both of us, hurried back to the Jeep, strapped Blu's pack on him, mine on me, put the shoulder bag and camera around my neck, and with rifle in hand and six-gun on hip headed briskly to the runway. We got there just in time to board. With Blu seated next to me we took off for Ft. Yukon, across the Arctic Circle.

Blu handled his first plane ride with bravado. He slept. The land we flew over was nothing near what I had expected. Ninety-nine percent of it was marshy bog. Thereby, for all practical purposes it was impassable on foot until winter would freeze it. I had finally discovered the source of all the mosquitoes.

The way I got the story was that the Brooks Range, along with its southern and northern slopes, was actually classified as a desert due to its low average annual rainfall. But even though the rain and snow that falls on this lonely land is minute, when it does fall it has nowhere to go. The frost line that remains all year, permafrost, is measured beneath the surface in inches. The water can't soak in. It sits on top waiting for the shallow-rooted plant life and evaporation to use it up.

Remove the brush and there'd be no way of telling where rivers ended and land began. It was not exactly the kind of place the average civilized human being would care to build a summer retreat.

The moose liked it though. On a number of occasions the pilot left his flight path and descended. He would circle the contented animals as they grazed knee deep in bog to the ooooos and aaaaahs of the short-sleeved, flower-shirted, bermuda-legged, multi-camera-toting, storybook touristy-looking passengers.

The flight took about forty-five minutes. Before we realized it we were circling in over the largest village north of the Arctic Circle, Fort Yukon. The largest could not have been too much larger than the smallest.

It was mostly made up of log cabins. A fancy two-story building was identified as the village hotel and restaurant.

Once landed, the rest of the passengers boarded a waiting van for a tour of the town and lunch at the hotel. Then they would be hustled back to the plane for the return flight to Circle. I instead made for the desk in the air terminal to inquire as to the possibility of hiring a plane and pilot for a flight farther north.

I was informed that the only available man for such a flight was not scheduled back for another five hours. That gave us time to see the town and grab a bite to eat. Blu and I headed out of the terminal, found a road and followed it into town.

On our way we were passed repeatedly by young native children on small motorbikes. Everyone, it seemed, had some kind of vehicle, or two kinds, or three kinds. It was amazing. The roads in Fort Yukon went absolutely nowhere. That was one of two forms of recreation that I noticed. The other was drinking.

I steamed as I thought of what my government was doing to demoralize yet another American native race. It's a broad generalization because I did see and meet some constructive, sober, friendly individuals. But my admittedly limited observations found them to be in the minority. Many of the people I saw were depressed, drunk, or both and stared at me hatefully.

Normally looks like that made me fighting mad, but in that case I couldn't blame them. To them I represented those who had taken from them their will, their proud and hardworking ethic. I represented those who had converted them to hopeless derelicts. They had for centuries struggled every waking hour to survive and had been victorious. No easy task in that land.

Now, because of big government bucks, they had free time coming out their ears and nothing to fill it with but alcohol. Bogus good-hearted legislation enacted for vote-grabbing by bleeding heart beaurocrats had given a proud, industrious, life-loving people nothing to live for. They should be punished for the lives they've destroyed. I hung my head in shame and disgust.

There was one particularly inhospitable log house that looms strongest in my mind. Blu and I were touring the streets of town when we passed the structure. In residence, sitting on the front porch, was a large family laughing and talking and drinking. That is until they observed us coming down the street. Then all activity ceased. The only thing that moved on that porch were a dozen pairs of eyes.

As we got closer I smiled and nodded a hello. The only response were those assaulting eyes. As we passed I would turn my head on occasion till we were out of sight, only to lock gazes with those bitter, bitter eyes.

What hurt most was that even the small children took part. They exhibited a hatred every bit as deep and full as their elders.

After lunch at the hotel (Blu sat outside) we went back to the airport. We were in for a pleasant and welcome surprise.

Just when I was beginning to think that every native in town was in total disgust over my being there, Blu and I made the acquaintance of one of the happiest, friendliest, most optimistic individuals I have ever in my life encountered.

He was as native an Alaskan as a brown bear. I took him to be a man in his late fifties or early sixties who had seen many traplines and caribou hunts. Yet he stood only five feet two inches tall and weighted in at no more than one hundred ten pounds. As a young man I envisioned him a real tiger. And he could spin a yarn bigger than Alaska herself.

He rocked and swayed a little, due to a constant friendship with a bottle of hooch, but unlike many of the other inhabitants, the booze had no apparent affect on his jovial personality.

Not knowing whether anyone would have objected to Blu being inside the terminal I had told him to sit and stay outside next to the door. I had first sprayed him liberally with Cutters Insect Repellent to ward off mosquitoes. Then I'd found a bench inside that gave me a good view of Blu whenever someone entered or left. That way I could keep an eye on my belongings inside.

When my Indian friend had approached me for the first time, I had been a bit leery and standoffish. That was the conditioned response I had acquired while touring the village. But the smile in his eyes even more than the one on his lips was unquestionably a display of honest friendship.

After he saw that he had broken through my defensive attitude his lips parted in the fullest grin imaginable showing some of the dirtiest, rottenest teeth in creation. Teeth like that must have hurt. Even with one hundred proof anesthetic. If he could keep a sincere smile on his face while enduring that pain he had to be a genuine good Joe.

I resisted but it was impossible for me not to smile back. I offered him the seat next to me even as he asked if he could have it. He plopped himself down, twisted over my way with an uncertain jerk, grabbed my right hand with both of his and shook it vigorously. "Very please to make your acquaintance," he expounded. He spoke with delight and the foulest breath I had smelled since Blu had gotten into horse manure. As he spoke he sprayed me with unintentional spit.

No matter. Anybody capable of preserving his joy in a place so filled with hatred was somebody worth knowing. Foul breath, body odor, unsightly teeth and spit in the face were only minor flaws in an otherwise perfect personality. After all, if I could stand these and worse faults in Blu, who I loved dearly but was in fact just a dog, how much more should I be able to endure from another man like myself?

I was smoking a cigarette at the time of our meeting. "Care for a smoke?" I offered.

"You bet!" he responded gratefully.

"I'll roll you a tight one." In his state of intoxication I figured I'd do him the favor. I rolled it, lit it and placed it between his smiling and beckoning scabbed lips. He closed his eyes, tilted his head back and took a long, pleasant drag to show his appreciation.

Being a hand-made smoke, his neglect at continued puffing caused me to have to relight it three or four times. I took care not to ignite his long gray hair that fell in disarray over his face.

We sat and talked for a long time that afternoon. Or rather he talked and I listened. He told stories of sailing around the world. He told of many exotic ports. Of great hunts all over the United States and Africa. And of many dangerous flights as a bush pilot.

Somehow it was understood that in actuality he had probably never been south of Fairbanks. He never insisted that I believe his stories. He seemed more to just want someone to listen to the adventures he had wished he had had when he was a young man. He wasn't bitter at not having had the opportunity to live his fantasies. Rather, he seemed thankful that he had them when so many others had nothing but sad memories and evil schemes for the future.

Every now and then we would rise to stretch our legs with a turn outside to visit Blu. On our first stretch, the meeting of my new friend and my dog was heartwarming. Blu took to the old storyteller right away. And he to Blu. Neither bad breath nor profuse slobber had any effect on their immediate liking for each other. The old man had no more difficulty telling Blu his stories than he had had telling me. I think Blu believed every word though. I have to admit I was a tad bored hearing the tales twice.

We would smoke ourselves out while inside so when we would make our pilgrimages to the out-of-doors it was time for a chew. I've since eliminated both addictions and my new found freedom has made me feel guilty that I contributed so greatly to his.

He would accept my offered tobacco plug and take a big juicy bite out of it with those yellow, green and black teeth that were caked with plaque to twice their size. Then he would hand it back to me for my turn. The first time, I took a long gagging look at the extras he had left behind on the half-circled edge that marked where he had left off and where I was to begin.

Friendship won out in the end. I would take my bite. After all he had lived with it to old age. It was probably more repulsive than it was hazardous and that tobacco juice would most likely have killed anything harmful anyway. I would have rather had my lips fall off than insult that wonderful old man. The taste of his saliva was soon lost in the sweet tobacco flavor and our relationship progressed as openly as before.

The afternoon waned into evening. My friend excused himself with regrets and headed home. I missed his company. He had tenderized me to a state that had me unprepared for what was to happen next.

I was sitting on the bench in the terminal. Blu was asleep just outside the door. A family of mother, father, two children, aunt and uncle entered to buy fare for a flight to Fairbanks. The father was blind, staggering drunk. He was also rude and obnoxious.

The wife would openly scold him and on occasion strike out violently with her hands. He would rebuff in a drunken and arrogant yet submissive manner. The rest of the family remained quiet but would grin cynically. This infuriated the man's wife to even a greater frenzy. They shouted in their native tongue, interjecting an occasional English swear word.

It was impossible for me to determine the exact cause of the domestic disturbance but it was definitely a doozy. A few more minutes of abuse by the wife and she became so intense that she shooed her husband out of the terminal with an extremely violent physical and verbal onslaught.

Staggering indignantly toward the door he looked over his shoulder and mumbled something, most likely obscene, under his breath. He had reached the closed door a broken man. Knowing that the door would not hit him back he clumsily punched and kicked it open.

In the instant that the door remained open I saw Blu raise his head groggily from a sound sleep. At the same instant I witnessed him receive a hard kick to the shoulder by that ignorant, drunken coward. Before the door slammed shut I saw only Blu's rump. He made tracks in bewilderment away from that cruel man who was reaching down and picking up rocks while he swore profanely.

My first reaction was complete disorientation. I gazed at the two dozen or so people in the terminal with disbelief. They were all looking at me because they knew that Blu and I were together. All had seen what I had seen.

Almost in unison everyone looked away from me giving the impression that they would turn their backs on whatever retribution I saw fit to deal upon this bully. My shock and disbelief turned to raving anger as I reached for the .44 magnum at my feet. I hesitated deciding that I would much rather wring his neck. I stormed from the terminal hoping that he was not too drunk to fight.

As I stepped outside he had just followed through with a rock that chased after Blu. It missed miserably.

"Hey, ___ ___!" I bellowed as he reached for another.

He stopped, pulling his shoulders up around his ears and turned sheepishly. He peered at me from under a lowered head.

When he saw that I was standing still rather than beating a trail for his throat, his head came out of his makeshift shell. He straightened up a bit and a frightened smile appeared on his face.

"Hello, my frien'. Is da your dog? He's all righ'. We were

jus' havin' a liddle fun, das all." He squirmed as he apologized, all the while coming closer to me with his right hand extended. I trusted that man as far as I could drop-kick Mt. McKinley so I stood with my eyes riveted on his.

When he was within reach I glared at him, then down at his extended hand and back up into his eyes. I made no attempt to shake it and it slowly sank to his side as his smile began to quiver.

"You want to shake hands?" I questioned.

"Ya man le's shak' han's an be frien'."

"All right. I'll shake your hand. After you apologize."

"I did apologi'," he said a little befuddled. "I'm sorry, ol' buddy. I din mean nottin'. Everythin' be OK now. OK?"

"No," I answered. "You have to apologize to the dog."

I knew that would get a reaction. I hoped enough of one for him to throw a punch but all he said was, "Wha' you mean da dog man? I don' apologi' to no dog."

"Oh, yes, you do," I said sternly, and advanced on him. "Or I'll wring your scrawny neck!"

His hands went up submissively to protect his throat. "OK, OK, man. Bu' I don' thin' we be able to fin' him now. Maybe lader."

"Nah," I returned. "We'll find him now. And there better not be a mark on him for your sake."

I stayed behind him menacingly while we walked around the back of the terminal. He never attempted to bolt. I guess he figured I'd catch him and doomsday would begin. I smiled as I thought that he could leave at any time, at even a slow jog, and I'd never be able to catch him on my gimp leg.

We looked behind the terminal. There was no sign of Blu. But as we passed the open overhead doors at the rear of the building I heard a growl coming from inside. Blu was backed into a corner staring viciously at the coward. Shock and bewilderment had left him. His first reaction of "Oh, my gosh, what have I done now?" had been replaced with the realization that he had done nothing wrong. Punishment without cause made Blu mad.

"There he is," I said. "Apologize."

"Tha' dog crazy man. He wan' gi' me!"

"Then you'd better apologize fast, because this is between you and him. I'm stayin' out of it."

"Sorry, dog!" the sloppy drunkard said angrily as he stormed off back around the building. He didn't leave though without giving me a dirty look. I simply stood with a smile on my face and my hand out.

Until he was out of sight he would occasionally make a quick glance over his shoulder like a frightened animal. I guessed he had visions of a big black dog lunging for the back of his neck.

Blu trotted out to me and looked up seriously. His unspoken words were, "That guy's one miserable slob." I agreed and we went back around to the front entrance.

Someone must have been watching the whole episode through the door between the waiting area and the back shop. When I went back inside everyone had taunting smiles on their faces directed at the man who had just apologized to a dog. His face was bowed in a combination of anger and embarrassment. I felt gratified at this. Somehow though I also felt sorry for the man. Though he would pierce me intermittently with hateful stares I kept straight faced. A man like that tortures himself twenty-four hours a day. He had enough hurt.

A short while later, the man who was to be our pilot arrived from Fairbanks in a small single engine aircraft. We were introduced to Kent by the gentleman at the ticket counter who also related my desire. We shook hands and retired to his quarters in another section of the terminal. There he unrolled a large map of the Brooks Range and asked, "Where do you want to go?"

"Well," I responded, "I saw a book that had some mighty pretty pictures of this northeast corner. But what I've got is $400.00. You tell me how far I can go on $400.00."

"I'm afraid I can't get you all the way there. Here," he said as he penciled in a large circle, "This is where we can go for 400 bucks."

I looked for a moment at the area within the circle then said, "I'll tell ya, all I know about this place is what I saw in that book. You got any suggestions?"

"The Chandalar Lake area's pretty scenic." The map showed in blue a large lake.

"What are all the little black squares?" I queried.

"Cabins. A lot of people have cabins on the lake." he said. "There's great fishin', it's accessible and, like I said, it's mighty pretty."

"Well, I'll tell ya, I'd really like to find somewhere as far from any signs of people as I can get. Is there any place in that circle that you know of where nobody's been?"

"Honestly, it's possible that someone may have been everywhere at one time or another, but this area here," he laid his fist on the map just outside the circle, "I've never taken anybody there and I don't personally know of anyone else who has. It's a little outside the circle, but if you want to try it I'll take you up there for the four hundred. I want'a see it too."

The area under his fist was in Wind River country on the south slope of the Range. After only a moment's thought I said, "That'll do fine. Where do we land?"

He looked up at me from the map, smiled, and said, "We'll find that out when we get there."

We left his room and went to the restaurant for dinner. There he introduced me to a couple of guys who flew for the Bureau of Land Management looking for fires in remote areas. I was also introduced to a weatherman for the Geological Survey. We exchanged greetings and then I managed to ask one of the dumbest questions of my life.

Thinking that I'd take the initiative and break the ice between new acquaintances I turned to the weatherman and asked, "Say, Burt, what's the weather forecast for up on the Brooks Range in the Wind River region?"

The four of them slowly exchanged glances, then smiles and the weatherman turned to me and said, "Right now we couldn't even tell you for sure that there is weather on the Brooks Range." With that my four new friends enjoyed a good laugh at my expense. The stupidity of my inquiry hit me between the eyes.

Just fifteen minutes before I had been looking at a map that showed 99.9 percent of the Brooks as being uninhabited. I was asking for a weather report as though I had dialed a time and temperature number on the telephone.

I lowered my head smiling, admitting my ignorance and accepting their ridicule as being well deserved. Keeping it fun without becoming insulting Burt volunteered, "Tedd, what I can tell you is this. For the most part there's very little rainfall. And this time of year highs can be in the eighties and lows in the thirties. I'm afraid that's about as specific as I can get." I nodded in gratitude.

It was the place I had dreamed of for much of my life. A place no one knew very much about.

Blu lay with his head on the door step. He watched us through the open door as we drank beer and talked of life above the Arctic Circle. He wasn't about to fall asleep again with all these strangers traipsing in and out. I could hardly blame him.

A couple of hours passed. Finally I felt that Blu and I should be getting some sleep for our big adventure that would begin the next morning. I excused myself and Blu and I made our way back to the terminal where Kent had offered me the spare bunk in his room.

We found the terminal door locked so we climbed up into a plane to be out of the wind and out of sight of the locals, one in particular I thought might be interested in causing some trouble. There we curled up together waiting for Kent to get home. He arrived in about an hour.

"I don't believe they locked the door. They never lock the door. Sorry, Tedd."

"No big deal, Kent. It was kind of nice listening to the wind whistle over the wings."

We three spent the rest of the night comfortably in Kent's quarters.

14. The Brooks Range

In the morning something was not sitting well with me from the night before. My head ached and my stomach was a bundle of cramps. A fabulous way to fly.

By 7:00 we had driven to the float plane, gassed it, loaded it, unhitched it from its moorings and were airborne. The usual bumping and dipping contributed greatly to my aching stomach and head.

For an hour we flew over uninhabited land. The landscape was the same as that which we had seen on our flight the day before…flat and wet. I began to wonder if ten days would be enough for me to evolve into an amphibian. Eventually, though we reached the foothills of the Brooks Range and there, although the valleys were still wet, the higher elevations displayed some dirt.

I knew Kent thought he was doing me a favor by suddenly leaving his course once in a while and dipping sharply to show me a critter or some unusual real estate, but he came mighty close to getting his cock-pit filled.

Finally we arrived at the area we had agreed on. We circled a group of lakes while Kent tried to determine which might be suitable for a landing. He chose one, settled into the wind, and began a somewhat fast descent. "Gotta clear these trees and touch down quick so we'll have time to stop." he explained.

"We won't be using near as much lake to land as I'll need to take off." he added. "Sure hope the lake's deep enough."

If I had felt secure at all, that passing remark nixed it.

The landing was successful. Blu and I disembarked on a lake a long way from the nearest convenience store.

"There's a storm movin' in. You'll have to unload quick so I can get out of here."

Kent was right. It was already starting to drizzle. The shoreline was too shallow to allow for the plane to beach. Blu jumped out, swam and waded the forty feet to shore, and waited. I waded to a bank that wasn't too much more solid than the lake. I piled gear hurriedly on shore and waved good-by as Kent taxied his plane to the north end, turned and took off into the wind.

To add to my stomach cramps, headache and hunger pangs from having had no breakfast, a sinking, desperate feeling came over me as I watched our last link to civilization become a small dot and then disappear in the southern sky. Blu was not feeling too chipper either. He was listless, his head and tail dragged noticeably.

We had to force ourselves to turn our attentions from our illnesses. What looked to be a heavy rainstorm was nearly upon us and a camp was far from being erected. In fact, from where I stood I couldn't even see a good spot to put one. The danger of hypothermia became more apparent than it ever had before.

I knew what hypothermia was, what it's symptoms were, what it could do. Till that time I had always been in situations where, if the shakes began from a loss of body heat, I would either hop into the car and turn on the heater or start up the Coleman stove inside a cozy tent. Our circumstances found us many miles from the nearest warm bed.

I quickly reconnoitered the surrounding area looking for a suitable campsite and found none. The entire east bank seemed to be nothing but dense brush and standing water. We had no choice but to pack up what gear I could carry and head south, even though rain had begun to fall heavily. I was too weak to carry everything at once and Blu would have been unable to heft his pack. I'd have to make another trip. That morning was a depressing time. Hungry, sick, wet and cold and nowhere to lie down.

Our journey took us about a mile through water and mud, some places knee deep, and one hip deep stream crossing at the south end of the lake. After crossing the effluent, that drained into a series of other lakes, we turned north along the west bank until we found a site for camp.

The spot I chose was muddy but at least we couldn't drink it. We had traversed halfway around the lake to a spot almost directly opposite from where we had been dropped. As I unloaded gear and covered it with the ground cloth a small shore bird skirted out from the bank followed by her minute young. She scolded me all the while. That was all I needed…to be hollered at by a bird.

Across the lake, on a small peninsula near where we had landed, a cow moose and twin calves grazed. Moose were still a rarity to me but right then I couldn't care less. I thought of covering us both, along with the gear, to wait out the storm.

Had we not been so remote I would have. I realized though that when alone and that far from the nearest helping hand, comfort comes only after all necessities have been assured. Otherwise we might find ourselves "gone beaver," as the old mountain men used to say. Besides, we were already soaked and cold and could only get colder and no drier sitting still under the ground cloth. In order to keep our blood moving we left, carrying only the handgun, on our return trip for what was left of our belongings.

An hour and a half later we were back, exhausted. Everything was wet. I had no choice but to pull the gear together in a heap, brush the beaded water off Blu, lay down with him on the bags, and pull the ground cloth over everything. We were instantly asleep.

In a couple of hours we awoke shivering. Blu was in an especially bad way. He could not even stand or at least he felt so poorly that he preferred not to. I knew it was imperative I get a fire going.

I pulled myself out from under the ground cloth. I grabbed the ax and, with legs quivering from hunger and the rest of my body shivering from loss of body heat, I headed across a bog toward three standing dead trees a hundred yards distant. At least the rain had stopped falling. Some arid climate!

I downed all three trees, they being only fifteen feet tall and no more than six inches in diameter, and dragged them back to the campsite. The mosquitoes were murderous. Blu had crawled out from under the plastic cloth and was listlessly fighting off the hordes of bloodsuckers. Before I did anything else I covered all my bare skin with Cutters Insect Repellent and sprayed Blu as well.

Trying to stay one step ahead of nature who, in all her beauty could just as easily make an ugly, bloated, decaying lump on the ground of any human who underestimated her, I commenced to tunnel out some deep dry holes in the steep bank behind us. In them I would stow our gear and, after cutting and splitting it, our firewood.

Blu, wanting to help, even though he found it even difficult to stand, dragged himself up alongside of me. We two desperate, sick, fatigued compadres dug side by side into the virgin earth of the Wind River Valley.

"Sorry, ol' boy," was all I had strength to say. We kept digging.

When we had finished three holes, one for wood and two for gear, I turned to reach for the equipment that needed to be stuffed into them. When I turned back, there were only two empty holes left. Blu had crawled into one in order to have a dry spot out of the wind and away from some of the mosquitoes. I didn't have the heart to evict him. There was room for another hole.

Before digging it though I was more inclined to build a fire. Maybe dry out a little too. I cut the tree trunks into fourteen inch lengths and split them uncovering the dry inner wood. With my knife I carved off some shavings. Before long my quivering body was perched over warm, welcome, dancing flames.

When I'd absorbed a little warmth I reached into my pack for a couple of handfuls of raisins, my first meal in about twenty hours. I opened the doggy pack and scooped out a couple of handfuls of Blu's food. He ate none of it. Before leaving Anchorage I'd packed his dry food in plastic bags before zipping it into the doggy pack. My reason for doing so was to keep the new pack from being soiled by the greasy food but after our welcoming shower, if the food hadn't been in plastic it would have been nothing but soggy mush…ruined. I probably would have had to shoot that cow moose to feed him, or at least one of her calves.

The clouds were breaking and sun was shining through. I grabbed my bags and climbed the bank. There I unpacked all my wet things and spread them out over the scrub brush to dry. Then I removed the cloths I had on and did the same with them.

While my things dried I finished cutting and splitting the rest of the wood, dug another hole, and stashed it. Blu was still feeling peaked but I tried to get him to eat. It was still no use. I figure if his instincts told him he needed rest more than food then that was what he was going to have without any interference from me.

I retired to the fire with a packet of freeze dried food, noodles Romanoff if I remember correctly. Water was obtained from the lake in a small pot and my coffee pot and set to boil. A feast was in the making.

Minutes later my stomach almost applauded as the warm food and drink hit bottom. When I had finished I had the strength to set up camp. Finding a spot for the vinyl tarp was not difficult. There was only one spot large enough with the ground solid enough for the purpose.

Two sticks were driven into the ground ten feet apart and left sticking up three and a half feet. A cord was staked into the ground at one end, pulled over both poles and staked at the other end as well. That cord ran parallel to a mound of earth about four feet high and two and a half feet away. One edge of the seven by nine tarp (a nine foot side) was staked into the top of the mound through its small brass grommets. The tarp was then pulled over the cord and staked into the ground at the lake's edge. And do I ever mean the lake's edge. When winds would get the lake agitated, waves would lap up under the tarp missing my sleeping bag by inches, if indeed they missed.

Not the best of campsites. But it was either there or lug everything up on top of the mountains west of us. There there would have been even less shelter from wind and we would have had a two hour round trip for water.

Though fed and feeling a little more energetic, my head

and stomach still ached. That, and the fact that Blu's condition had not improved, the mosquitoes were as thick as smoke, and no one would be back for us for ten days, bolstered my depression to a point where I could have given up Alaska and all wilderness contact forever. But I couldn't get out!

One thing was for certain. The more I slept, the faster the time would pass. Before I crawled into my half-dry sleeping bag I rolled out the aerial map Kent had given me to take one more look. A closer one.

I knew there were no villages close to our position but to illustrate just how desperate I was, I hoped that when I unrolled the map one would appear that hadn't been there before. Nope, there were no new dots.

I followed the river systems back to Fort Yukon with my finger. The Wind River to the North Fork of the Chandalar, the North Fork of the Chandalar to the Chandalar, and the Chandalar to the Yukon. Then up the Yukon to the village of Fort Yukon. It would have been a four hundred mile trip. Guess we would stay.

The fact that there was no way out depressed me even more. Despondently I wedged my way down into my sleeping bag. I called to Blu to join me, which he did gratefully. What the heck, it was 6:30 P.M. That meant it was 10:30 in Nebraska. Time for bed.

Morning came and I was glad to see a clear blue sky, but I was weak from hunger. The one meal from the day before did not stay with me long. We were both still wet, the skeeters were unbelievable and Blu was still sick. That same cow moose was back with her calves but this time at the north end of the lake. Like the day before I was in no mood for sightseeing or picture taking. I had no desire to do anything that would in the future remind me of that which I considered the biggest blunder of my life.

I crawled out of the sack, reapplied Cutters, got a small

cooking fire going, and prepared breakfast and coffee. I had barely the strength to lift the fork from the plastic pouch to my mouth but it did raise my spirits when Blu was able to swallow some down.

After breakfast I decided to go back to sleep and kill some more time. I knew that soon I would be slept out and wondered what I would do then. I was still naked from the day before, but I just didn't have the ambition to do anything about it.

Two hours later I reentered the real world. The breakfast I had eaten had had time to get to where it needed to go. My renewed strength improved my temperament one hundred percent. Five hundred percent, however, would have only improved it to that of a prisoner on death row. At least I came to the conclusion that I had been wet and naked long enough. I started another fire to warm me and finish drying my clothing. I also opened my sleeping bag and spread it over the scrub to finish drying. Then I discharged my .50 caliber rifle and seated a fresh charge.

I proceeded to pull the ground cloth from under the tarp and take the tarp down to give the soggy ground under it a chance to dry. It would probably never dry completely, but I had hopes that it might reach a state where it didn't feel like a waterbed.

After that was accomplished I even had the ambition to investigate our surroundings. Our site was nothing more than a small mud beach twenty-five to thirty feet long. The distance from the bank to the lake at its deepest point was fifteen feet. The bank rose steeply to approximately eight feet and leveled off into the scrub and tussocks that were drenched with standing water. Our beach had some washed out hills of mud on it that rose here and there to a height of up to four feet.

The day was becoming quite warm. Actually, hot. But despite the high temperature and the hooded sweatshirt I had covering Blu, he was still shivering and could barely open his eyes.

Later that day I repitched camp, cooked and ate supper, sharing some with Blu, and with his head in my lap, dozed off in the shade under the tarp.

Waking with the chill of the night hours upon us, I crawled into the sleeping bag pulling Blu in with me. It was a bit crowded, but I could keep him warm that way.

By the next morning Blu's fever had left him. He was weak, but otherwise running true to form. That removed a heavy weight from me, but I was still in a down hearted state, so our third day on the Brooks Range was much the same as the first two. Even the profusion of wildlife which I had expected to witness was lacking. The only animals of any note had been the shore bird and her young and the cow moose and her calves and since the second sighting even they had failed to return.

On our trek around the lake we had followed and crossed some extremely wide and deep game trails, but other than that there had been no sign of life accept for the chirp of a bird now and then. That harsh and rugged wilderness seemed to be too bitter for even the wildest of creatures. What were we doing there?!

Most of the third day I spent reading a book. It was a book that, as a young boy, I had begun many times. I had become bored with its unusual and hard to comprehend style and had never finished it. I thought that our stay on the Brooks would afford me plenty of time to have at it again so I had bought a pocket publication of it before leaving Anchorage.

Had I known what was in store for me in those first chapters I never would have brought it along. As it turned out, it was quite violent and frightening and was similar to what was in store for me in that lonely land. There were soon to be times when I wished I'd never opened the pages of the Bible.

As I read, the sky grew darker and darker but I didn't notice the impending storm until, suddenly, everything grew quiet. I looked up from my reading and nothing was moving. I mean nothing at all. The surrounding country appeared as a still photograph. Not the hint of a breeze. Not the peep of a shore bird. Not even the buzz of a mosquito.

It was as though I were in a vacuum. Or standing outside looking in. I know I wished I were.

I had just finished reading of a devastating flood, an all consuming fire, people being turned into pillars of salt, and I, one of the humdingerest of sinners I had ever known, was witnessing the gathering of the cruelest looking storm I had ever seen. In a land that wasn't even supposed to get much rain.

I was in the wilderness, alone, with only a dog and a gun to defend against all that God could bring down upon me from the heavens, from out of the earth, and from off of the land itself. Sure made me feel insignificant.

Reading of the wrath of God, the bloody stories of whole civilizations being destroyed for going against his commandments, was not exactly what I would have preferred to learn of at that time. I mean, some of those who were lost had done no worse things than I had at one time or another.

After all the countless millions who have come and gone throughout the centuries, after all the great ones who have fallen, who was I to stand in defense against the Mighty One? Seemed like a good time for me to surrender. I just hoped that He recognized a white flag.

There was no cellar to run into. I had only a paper thin vinyl tarp separating me from the impending holocaust. It was over! That was it! God had deceived me into going to that place, then suckered me into reading that book just to give me a taste of how I was going to go. He wanted to see me squirm. No swift felled stroke for me. It was going to be torture!

Movement on the north shore caught my eye. The trees. It was as though some great force had them by their roots and was shaking mercilessly. The wind had hit them with the force of a hurricane, had passed through their defenses, and was making its way across the water toward my little shelter. White capped waves showed its tracks as my invisible enemy approached.

In panic I made for my shelter. A shelter that would afford me as much protection as a clump of grass would a rabbit against the blast of a shotgun. I settled in as the wind struck. Without effort it tore my tarp loose from its stakes and sent it sailing across the campsite.

Blinding rains accompanied the wind and beat down on me ferociously. In the time it took to lay my rifle on my sleeping bag to hold it down, I was, once again, soaked to the bone. As I rose to retrieve my tarp, which had hung up in thick brush at the end of the beach, the wind nearly pitched me face down into the mud. I fought to regain my balance and remembered Blu. I looked around desperately only to find that he had found safety in his hole in the bank.

When I reached the tarp I found that the grommets had been ripped out. There seemed no way to retie it to the stakes.

The storm was relentless. All I could do was get under the tarp, curl the two bottom corners under my feet and hold the two upper corners to the bank behind me with my outstretched hands. In that sitting position I could barely hold on against the gale. In fact on two occasions I couldn't hold it and was forced to chase after my shelter when I lost my grip.

Large pieces of brush, bark and twigs flew through the air as though they had been shot from catapults. All the while I shivered from cold and fear thinking that that was my final hour. Prayers were on my lips in profusion. Let me rephrase that. I was not praying. I was begging.

After nearly an hour the wind died to no more than a

steady breeze but the rain continued to fall heavily. I was exhausted but before I could rest I needed to somehow erect my tarp. The torn corners were just ragged vinyl. No chance of tying them to anything. My only recourse was to lay the bottom end flat on the ground and bury it under rocks and mud. Then I pulled the other end up and over the cord, flattened it out on the mound, and likewise buried it. That would have to do.

I removed my garments. Wrung them out. Put them back on. Wrung out my sleeping bag. Squirmed into it. And fell asleep. I was alive.

I'm not sure how long I had been asleep when I was abruptly awakened from my sound slumber by a very loud and sharp slapping sound. "Lord! Now what?!" Just when I was beginning to think that I would live through this insanity, some monster of the north woods was going to eat me alive.

Blu was in the bag with me. I don't remember when he crawled in, but I was glad he had. He was warm, and he was an ally.

"Slap!" It happened again! Whatever it was could not have been more than twenty, maybe twenty-five feet from my house of straw.

Again there was silence. The wind and rain had ceased entirely. It was too late at night for birds or mosquitoes, and there were no such things as crickets. In the dictionary, next to the word "quiet," there should be a picture of the Brooks Range. There is no quiet on earth to match the one found there.

Again the stillness was broken by the loud *slap!* I could feel my body stiffen from tension, and fear.

Blu's head had come out of the sleeping bag. His eyes glared, his teeth were bared, and a muffled growl that could not have been heard five feet away emitted through his clenched jaws. Oh, Lord, that indicated something big and mean. What now?

Slap! There it was again!

No nearer. But no further either. It was not going to leave. Sooner or later its curiosity or maliciousness was going to bring it right inside with us. I had to do something. I had to do something, quickly.

But I didn't want to do anything. I just wanted to pull the covers over my head and wish the monsters away.

Fear and necessity forced me to slowly unzip my sleeping bag. I kept a good hold on Blu so he would not rush out and start something that only our deaths would end. I freed my legs. I pointed at Blu and commanded him to stay with a very quiet, "Ssssssss." I rolled over onto my hands and knees and grabbed hold of the .44 magnum. I started poking my head slowly toward the opening of the shelter.

Another *Slap!* unnervingly jerked me to an upright kneeling position pushing my head up into the tarp. That pulled it loose from the mud and rock holding it down and the tarp, the mud, and the rocks fell in on us making a racket that would have awakened the dead, had anybody other than me ever been foolish enough to come there and stay long enough to die there.

The suddenness and noise spooked Blu. In scurrying out he knocked my legs out from under me and I fell hard bringing the whole mess down on me. I struggled desperately, the adrenaline removing all stiffness. All I wanted to do was get out and get ready. I knew that Blu was going to need help. Or worse, he would be taking off for the hills, and the intruder was at that very moment headed straight for the panicked movement under the tarp—me!

It seemed a lifetime before I was free of the vinyl and mud that had obviously taken up sides against me. But finally I was out with arms outstretched, .44 in hand. I turned my head from side to side straining for a glimpse of a target.

There was nothing. Nothing of a threat anyway. The cause of the destruction of our sleeping quarters and the near heart failure of man and dog was nothing more than an inquisitive beaver bent on making our acquaintance.

As my eyes locked on his he ducked his head under the surface of the lake and, with a *Slap!* of his tail, he submerged. As it turned out, he was slapping his tail on the water to awaken us. He wanted to meet the new kids on the block.

Blu sat at the water's edge calmly watching our neighbor. A few seconds after his dive he reappeared treading water and gazing at us.

My first urge was to blow his brains out. But all at once I was aware of splendor surrounding us. I dropped my hands to my sides and looked up in awe.

The storm had departed. It had left behind an exact duplicate of what Shangri-La must surely have been like. Black thunderheads were still visible moving to the south but where I stood was the most peacefully serene environment I had ever experienced, framed by a bright and full double rainbow.

God is a Mighty One. First He had given me a taste of what He was capable of if crossed. Then, merely the wave of His hand over a foolish man who had finally discovered his own insignificance changed what had been a private hell into a vision of heaven. Sheer ugliness into unsurpassed beauty; terror and fear into peace and tranquillity; pain and misery into comfort and ecstasy! And I never had to pay one red cent. Simply admitting His existence was payment in full.

My whole outlook made a complete about-face. I was finally feeling the way I had dreamed I would be feeling when I was back in front of Bill's fireplace. I was enjoying myself. Even though cold and soaking wet.

After three days of being alone, the animal population had decided that we posed no threat and had resumed their affairs.

Blu danced up and down the bank. The lake was busy with activity. Beavers, muskrats, ducks and shore birds covered the mirror lake and left wistful "V" wakes in all directions. Boy, did I welcome their company. "Helloooo!" I shouted. Some friends looked up in acknowledgment but most went on with their business. There was no fear in them. No longer were we alone in the wilderness. It was as busy as downtown Chicago at rush-hour.

Slap! Whoops, I had been completely ignoring the welcome wagon. The beaver, reminding me of his presence, almost at my feet, laid another one on the lake.

"Sorry, Bucky. Forgive my rudeness," I said bowing. "Where have you guys been for three days? I was beginning to think that Blu and me were the only living things for a million miles."

Neither my speech nor my movement fazed the beaver. He never answered me either, but that didn't matter. I told him our whole story anyway. It was a one-sided conversation to be sure, but a bona fide conversation nevertheless.

Speech seemed to intrigue him. He floated quietly in the water or aimlessly swam back and forth, his eyes almost never leaving me. I believe I was the first human being the animals of the lake had ever laid eyes on. There was little fear in them. There was extreme caution. But isn't that to be expected from creatures that live every day only one small wrong move from death?

The calm remained. It was remarkable. What contrasting change. The sky, the earth and the waters had been torn by a calamitous tempest. Moments later it seemed that we were indoors, out of the elements, surrounded by lifeless props. The semi-aquatic animals on the surface of the lake were like wind-up toys. Blu and I seemed the only animate things around and, at times, I even questioned that.

The slightest breeze was unfelt. No crickets clicking,

mosquitoes buzzing, frogs croaking. There was virtually nothing to convince me that we were not a part of an exquisite masterpiece over someone's sofa.

I had meditated on the quiet for quite a while. Then, when preparing to leave my mental fixation, the silence was broken by an ethereal sound coming to me through the still, dusk-lit air from far to the north. The mournful cry of a single Arctic wolf. It brought goose bumps and sent my head reeling in an ecstatic natural high.

The wolf seemed to feel the same way I did about our flawless environment. But he, irrefutably, was far better at expressing it. Tears flowed as I watched to the north and listened to the final, lower pitched portion of the song. I wished, as the final echo left me, that I could disclose absolute appreciation in such a way.

The rain had cleansed the air. What I smelled whetted my ravenous appetite more than a prime rib could have. I drooled not only for food for my stomach, but for my eyes and ears and mind and spirit of adventure. Tomorrow we would strike out and explore the untouched wilderness.

Bucky had been like an angel sent from heaven. He had given me the will to savor the beauty around me and to crave the land from whence had come that glorious and noble call of the wild. Only minutes before, exploration had been the furthest thing from my mind. Well, not entirely so. I had thought about it, but I had also been making every effort to keep from accommodating it.

That night, right then, I made a proper camp with the materials at my disposal and then, by golly, I went fishin'!

15. Untouched Wilderness

Out came my ultra-light rod and reel. On it went a gold spooned and feathered spinner. The trout in the lake were mine.

My first and second casts yielded bumps against the lure that were most promising. On the third cast I let my spinner settle slowly into the cold waters hopefully inviting the curiosity of an unsuspecting fish. With a sudden jerk, that I hoped would jolt the observant fish to action, I began to reel in the line at a fast pace.

The attack on the spinner was one that nearly pulled me off of the mound upon which I stood and into the lake. Line was tearing off my reel at a rate that made me think I had hooked a nuclear submarine.

"What the heck is it, Bluper?" He saw the pole bobbing and knew a fish was on the other end. He started to turn on. I kept up the chatter with him until we were both beside ourselves.

"I've either got a world record grayling or I've snagged the monster of the lake. Yeh, that's it. I've latched hold of some prehistoric monster, supposed to be extinct. He's been trapped, living in this lake for eons just waitin' for some dumbo to reel him in. When I get him to shore he's gonna eat us both!"

I joked with Blu, but was perplexed at what sort of fish could be putting up such a fight. I thought there were only grayling there.

"Keep watchin' the line, Bluper. Nessie's cousin's gonna rise any second, frothin' at the mouth. I hear he especially likes the taste of dog. Partial to black ones. Ones with long pink tongues. Bow-legged's his favorite." Blu was just about at his peak, trying to jump through his skin. I loved it when he got that way.

There couldn't possibly be any grayling large enough to do what that fish was doing. I became obsessed. I had to get a look at that fish. I hoped that the abrupt halt in the action did not mean that the creature had escaped.

Ever so slowly my left hand began to turn the handle that rewrapped the line onto the spool. Five or six revolutions later there was still no struggle and only slight resistance. I increased the retrieval to a moderate pace. A dozen revolutions later and there was still no counter-reaction.

I'd lost him. "Dang, Blu! He's gone!" I said as I reeled faster. "All he's left me is some brush. Maybe an old tree branch. Doggone, I wanted to see what that thing was! You know, if we weren't where we are I'd think he snagged me into a tractor tire. This thing's heavy."

Suddenly my tire came to life. "Yo! The tire's got fins!"

Line peeled off the spool at a staggering rate. "Man, Blu, he's gonna use it all up. Here goes nothin'." I began to wade out into the lake to save what I could.

Before all the line was expended the animal turned to the right and raced toward where the lake emptied. After going about twenty yards it abruptly reversed direction swimming toward the lake's influent.

While it ran parallel to the bank I reeled in as much slack line as I had time for, reducing the distance between us somewhat.

I was up to my knees in the cold northern lake. Blu ran and jumped up and down the bank, cheerleading. On occasion he'd splash into the lake and dance around in a circle.

The fight continued for twenty more minutes. Finally my catch began to tire. I was up to my waist in the lake when I got my first glimpse of it. It was a very long, very broad northern pike.

He was a pleasant surprise; I had expected only small grayling. But I was not prepared for fish in his category. My lightweight rod and reel and six pound test line was insubstantial.

"How'm I gonna beach this thing? This line's barely holdin' him in the water."

Wading deeper into the lake I managed to put the fish between me and the bank. With some gentle coaxing and, sometimes, not so gentle coaxing I was able to chase, push and kick the large fish onto the bank. All the while Blu kept cheering me on waiting anxiously to help, which he did in pawing the northern farther up onto the bank.

Even though there had been a lot of commotion with all the splashing, shouting, running and jumping, life had gone on as usual for the animals of the lake. After dressing, or rather undressing, our fish I changed into dry cloths and Blu and I resumed our vigil of our industrious neighbors.

Bucky had remained just off-shore as we made camp and through the entire fishing escapade. He appeared quite interested. I wished he could speak for I felt that there was far more that he could teach me than I him.

Suddenly I smelled something unusual. It was faint, but definitely distinguishable from the other, familiar, odors. I wondered about it for a moment, then wondered why I wondered.

Why had the scent bothered to alert me? So what? In my world my nose had been used to distinguish between something to eat and garbage or something pleasing and something repulsive. Why had it then, all of a sudden, triggered an instinct to identify this odor for other reasons?

It didn't activate my taste buds. It didn't smell exceptionally good, nor especially bad. It simply alerted me to the presence of something different and insisted on identification.

The feeling puzzled me just long enough for the moose to step out from behind the bank. She caught sight of me, came to a halt and stared, poised for attack, flight or the resumption of her intended business. I supposed it mattered only which would seem the most prudent to her.

Had it been a stalking or mischievous bear, my ignorance of its particular aroma could have cost me my life. As it turned out, a surprised cow moose is nothing to sneeze at, but her intentions were purely honorable.

After concluding that I intended no threat she waded out into the lake. She seemed nearly as curious as Bucky. She stayed a little beyond where Bucky was treading water, standing shoulder deep and watching us in amazement.

Following extended observation she made her way across the lake to the peninsula on the east shore. She'd probably grown tired of my blabbering. There she remained, fearless of us, for the next hour.

While fishing I continued to observe with wonder the

industriousness of the animals of the lake. The urgency with which they collected food and repaired their homes was evident. Summer there lasted only two, maybe three months. But how did they know? Instinct, sure. Instinct might tell them to hurry because they felt winter coming. What tells them how much food to collect to sustain them through the long winter or how well to repair homes and dams so that they last till the summer thaw? He who created all that loveliness must also be concerned about maintaining it.

The vast majority of the beavers and muskrats lived at the south end of the lake. Supplies and building materials were more abundant at the north end. All night long the procession from south to north and back again could be witnessed in the light of a never-dark sky. Dusk is probably a good term to describe the darkest the sky became that time of year.

There seemed to be lines drawn that only the diligent swimmers could see delineating the lanes of travel. The users of the liquid highway appeared to keep to the right and the lanes were always the same distance offshore.

As is the case with any major thoroughfare, the inevitable fender bender occurred. A muskrat returning south with a mouthful of grasses and one tuft of Alaska cotton crashed head-on with a beaver heading north.

Like commuters on a freeway, a verbal battle broke out as the muskrat, who was knocked loose of his burden, and the beaver, who had apparently fallen asleep at the rudder, collided. Words led to physical violence as the two rolled and splashed up a storm for a few moments. But, as quickly as it had begun, it ended.

Without another utterance from either, the beaver continued on his way north and the muskrat, after collecting his floating grasses and one tuft of Alaska cotton, continued south. Why the one tuft of cotton, I wondered. Perhaps a bouquet for his mate.

About the time that Bucky decided he had better get to work, the cow moose headed back in our direction. On her return trip she stopped about thirty feet from shore and watched me fish. I told her of the finer points of pike angling. At the conclusion of my lesson she strode out of the lake and up and around the bank and left the way she had come.

At about 11:30 P.M., as the sun dipped into the north northeast, disappearing temporarily behind a mountain peak, a wistful cloud formation, on fire with the red of the sun, blended into a pink sky and reflected off of the mirror surface of the lake. The sight consumed me, capturing my attention, making it impossible to be mindful of anything else.

Then at midnight the sun reappeared on the other side of that mountain and rested in a chasm between two peaks. It seemed to need that moment to appreciate the beauty of the river valley. Showing its approval it sank slightly lower into the vale of the mountains and sent out a single ray to the heavens in homage to He who had made it, and another, a reflection of the first, out across the lake terminating at my feet where land touched water.

That had been a glorious day. I felt privileged to have been allowed to see so much in so short a time. In only a few hours I had experienced a lifetime. It was difficult to close my eyes to it.

Although we had spent a late night, morning came early. I was anxious to start exploring. Blu bird-dogged through the scrub above our campsite while I busied about breakfast. While I worked I sang every cheery song in my repertoire.

Bending over the fire, I was removing freshly perked coffee and thinking of nothing but the adventure that lay before us as we would go up and over the mountain that lay to the west. In that position, any activity to the west was obscured by the steep bank. Likewise our camp was hidden from view from anything in that direction.

Suddenly, only a few feet overhead, and from my blind spot to the west, came a loud, nearly deafening *Shhhhhhhhoooooooooo*. Convulsing in fear, I threw the coffee pot to the ground while I involuntarily screamed at the top of my lungs.

I turned reaching desperately for my rifle, sensing that whatever was coming down on me would need a bullet to stop. I lost my balance falling into the mud but continued scrambling on knees and elbows. I reached the rifle and clutched it to me pulling back the hammer. Rolling onto my back I forced myself as deeply into the mud as possible, in the ostrich maneuver, while I pointed the barrel of the rifle at sky.

Above me, at about one hundred feet and rising rapidly, almost vertically, was a bald eagle. Apparently he had been as surprised as I at our sudden meeting. He wasted no time in putting me behind him.

I thought that if those birds were in the habit of such meteoric materialization I had a good theory as to the reason for their perceived baldness. In fact, his rude intrusion had not done a whole lot for the conservation of my hairline.

Before I was over my humiliation, my personal representative of our national bird was already across the river flying along the south slope of the bare mountain to the east. The five second encounter had added fifteen minutes of work to our morning agenda. I needed to perk another pot of coffee and scrape a few pounds of mud from my clothing.

Clean-up completed and breakfast gobbled down as fast as Blu could eat beefsteak, I packed some Pilot crackers and raisins for lunch, shouldered my rifle and started off while the day was still young and refreshingly cool. I had even packed my gold pan. I intended to pan in the stream that most likely flowed in the valley on the other side of the mountain. Quite possibly, it was one that may have never been panned before.

It was a quarter of a mile to the base of the mountain. The whole distance was a bog that took nearly an hour to traverse. It consisted of five- to six-inch diameter tussocks that stood from only inches to nearly a foot and a half above the ground and were surrounded by standing water. The little mounds were spaced from two to eight inches apart.

If I opted to walk on them, and they were too tall or too small in diameter, my weight would break them sending me up to a foot and a half lower than I had intended. If, on the other hand, I decided to try and walk between them, my feet on occasion would get stuck between them. Stumbling on an unseen submerged one was common as well. If that obstacle wasn't enough, the stagnant water was also home to millions of mosquitoes.

Each step into their lair would bring a cloud of the vampires to torment us. By the time we had reached the base of the mountain we must have looked like no more than two balls of moving insects. It became necessary to wave my hand frantically in front of my face creating a tunnel through the insects through which I could see where I needed to go. I had covered us both with Cutters so we weren't being punctured, but the annoyance was nearly unbearable.

Hordes of blood suckers or not, when I reached the foot of the mountain I stopped to rest. Blu was frantic to be rid of them, however, so he continued up the mountain in hopes of rising above them.

I sat for ten minutes, engulfed by them, wondering where my second wind was and trying to retain my sanity by attempting to name as many of the critters as I could. Or did that merely confirm my insanity?

I proceeded upward to where Blu had found a rock overhang a couple of hundred yards ahead. It was above where the mosquitoes cared to rise. The spongy tundra was a pleasant change. It was comfortable on my feet and it was dry, but its resilience made it necessary to rest frequently. There was joy in being able to take a breath without acquiring a mouthful of bugs.

Each step nearer the summit revealed more of the fabulous valley below. I reasoned that God's intention in creating such beauty was not to show off his talent to a greatly inferior mankind. This land lay in the middle of nowhere, far from admiring eyes. He had made this, not necessarily for our enjoyment, nor selfishly for His own pleasure, but rather because He is simply incapable of making anything that is less than perfect. Even with the harshness of climate, the misery of bloodthirsty insects and the difficulty of travel, it is the beauty that prevails.

Game trails laced back and forth across the face of the mountain. Being impatient, I disregarded these well-worn paths preferring to make a straight one to the top. In the wilderness man is clearly the subordinate, at least for as long as it takes him to learn how to exist and be comfortable at the same time. It took a dozen breathless rest stops before I had sense enough to try the native trails. I discovered that those who knew the country far better than I also knew the easiest way to travel through it.

From the mountain top we saw mile upon mile, at every point of the compass, of unspoiled grandeur of the highest order. There we sat to eat before proceeding down the other side. It was a pleasant revelation to know that we didn't have to get back before dark. That restriction, this far north, gave us at least to the end of the month.

Another restriction, however, was becoming apparent in the northwestern sky. Large black clouds were taking shape over the far mountains. The urge to see the valley below overrode caution. We started across the tundra covered rolling top of the mountain headed for a descent on the other side.

My eyes were on the ground in front of me wondering at the delicacies of the tiny flowers rising only fractions of an inch above the ground. In that posture, had it not been for Blu's low growl, I would probably have walked into something that I do not believe would have accepted an "excuse me".

At his sound, my eyes casually shifted to him as we reached the brink on the far side. I looked at him with disgust for having disturbed my contemplation of the fine thread that connects delicacy with hardiness. But when I saw the urgency and resolve in his expression, a cold shiver made its way down my spine.

Blu's legs were braced, his shoulder hairs were erect, his lips were curled back and his eyes were glued straight ahead of us. Something worthy of that reaction was not something to arouse by any sudden movement. Ever-so-slowly I began to lift my head.

As the gradually rising curtain unveiled the massive form of a barren-ground grizzly boar, my lungs inflated to well beyond what I had thought their capacity. Every joint froze. Every muscle tightened. Even my heart, if I remember correctly, ceased beating. The cold shiver turned into a yellow streak. My lungs refused to release their reservoir of air, afraid that it might be their last.

The grizzly stood no more than fifty feet from us. He watched me as though he were wondering whether or not it needed to do something to protect himself or, at the very least, to be sure that we knew who was boss.

I was perfectly content in the knowledge that he *was* boss. I made no attempt to assert myself. In fact, if he needed copies made, a cup of coffee, claws buffed, anything at all, he just needed to ask.

Just in case he was the type that took pleasure in molesting his subordinates, however, I slowly pulled back the hammer on my rifle. Blu was still at peak readiness showing submission only in the fact that he hadn't attacked.

"Lighten up, will ya?" I whispered without taking my eyes off of the bear. I didn't want Blu provoking anything. I guess, though, that Bluper had done pretty well, considering. Actually the bear didn't pay much attention to Blu. The grizzly flat-out ignored him. Come to think of it, maybe that's what made Blu so mad.

I'm reasonably certain that we three didn't stand there staring at each other for as long as it seemed, but it wasn't any twinkling of an eye either. Finally the bear, not feeling threatened and not being hungry, I assumed, nonchalantly turned and ambled down the mountain. Now and then he would look over his shoulder. His glances seemed to question what I was, rather than to show concern about me back-shootin' him.

The bear had detained us sufficiently. The thunderheads had moved in close enough for caution to override my urge to gold pan in the river below. Besides, that grizzly was down there. I had no intention of giving him a reason to believe that we were following him. Though he had chosen to let the intruders go the first time, I don't think that creatures of his stature are inclined to be charitable often.

Going back down the mountain took one quarter of the time that going up had. Crossing the muskeg swamp, however, was even more difficult on tired legs. It was a drudgery I could have done without.

The last few hundred yards were in a drizzle. The fury of the storm could be seen in the tree tops at the north end of the lake as we crawled under our shelter. Only the tracks of the invisible wind could be seen as it came down the lake. I took up my position with my hands holding the upper corners of the tarp and my feet firmly planted on the lower corners as the gale struck.

It hit us with a fierceness equal to what we had endured

earlier. My change in attitude, though, made it more easily bearable. Actually, it was rather enjoyable. I was able to appreciate the savage intensity as the splendid display that it truly was. Besides, I had refined my technique for holding our shelter so that it was never lost again. The only wet we got was from slight spray blowing in the open sides, and from the waves of the lake lapping up at the seat of my pants.

The storm passed in twenty or thirty minutes leaving in its wake another grandiose aftermath. While starting a fire for my evening meal I watched the storm continue on its way south. It reminded me of loud and boisterous politicians on the campaign trail. They hit you with the same stuff over and over again, never tiring of listening to themselves speak, and trying to shake up the whole world. But, after they're gone, and the hollow words are ignored, business goes on as usual.

After dinner, some more good reading and a little more fishing. Even Bucky came back for another visit. With his arrival fishing, this time, became useless. Every time I would cast he would swim toward the splash curiously, scaring off the fish.

Being a part of the life of a thoroughly wild creature could only be experienced in a place like the Brooks Range. Blu and I cherished Bucky's company and were disappointed when he would leave to get back to business, but we wanted no part of the possibility of him not being prepared for winter.

It was time for sleep. The next day we would travel east to the other side of the lake. We would reach the banks of the Wind River and cross it to explore the bare mountain that stood as the sentinel over our park. We might even be able to find the nesting place of the bald eagle that had scared us that morning. How perfectly fitting it would be for a bald man to find a bald eagle on a bald mountain.

The next day was a disappointment in that we were unable to ford the river. It was frustrating to watch the eagle soaring across the face of that barren pinnacle, beckoning with an occasional screech.

Twice I disrobed. Bundling my cloths into my pack and onto a log I tried swimming the fifty yards of water. Both times I was defeated and had to turn back. The river was too deep and too swift. The other side remained just out of reach. I had to leave that place, the place where eagles cry, unexplored.

I had to resign myself to the fact that we had to be satisfied with only the millions of acres on our side of the river. We covered as much ground as we could that day, and all the days remaining until the time we had scheduled for our departure.

We ran into a problem. Everything had moved along swiftly since those first miserable days. The sun had never set. I wasn't sure what day it was. I only hoped I wasn't wasting my time sitting on the beach waiting for a plane that was not to arrive till the next day.

I took one precaution. Though everything else was packed and ready, I would not tear down my masterpiece of primitive architecture, pieced together with vinyl, mud, and rocks until I saw the plane touch down on the lake.

I had obliterated all signs of our habitation there. There was not even a boot print left to mar that which had been loaned to us.

As the plane buzzed the lake then circled, landing into the wind, I hurriedly tore down our home, stuffed it into the pack, finished clean-up of the area, and had enough time to give thanks to those who had unselfishly tolerated our presence. I promised to return one day to say hello. Then I gave a very special thank you to the One who had made everything I had just saluted.

16. Bummin's Over

The flight back was not the happy time that I had perceived it would be during those first three days. I felt as though I were leaving lifelong friends. I did not have much to say flying back to Ft. Yukon, and even less flying to Circle.

Actually no one was very friendly to me. After two weeks without a decent bath I must have been a tad ripe. The half-dried trophy northern pike head, I had wrapped in my pack, probably didn't help much. And Blu wasn't what you would call a carnation. I saw one elderly lady even retch once or twice.

In Circle I packed our gear into the Jeep and we headed south, anxious to relate our adventure to Bill, Fred and whoever else would listen. But even with my adrenaline pumping, Mt. McKinley was as far as we got that day. We pulled in to rest about midnight.

It wound up that the anxiety I had for relating our adventures got shot in the shorts when, after arriving home, Bill was away on business and Fred was off fishing. I quelled my depression with a glass of wine and fresh king crab legs and practiced telling the story to Blu.

Blu was at peace. Snug in front of Bill's fireplace where there were no big, hairy, brown creatures that smelled atrociously and had ugly humps on their backs and no bloodthirsty parasites. I must admit that I was a lot more appreciative of the comforts as well, though in a sentimental way I missed our pieced together shelter and our old friends.

Fun time was over. Our cash was gone. It was time to find a job. Out came the newspaper want ads and resumes. I wanted to do something different than I did in Nebraska but I did not know just what. I wanted something with a little more opportunity. Something a little more exciting.

"Wait a minute, mister." I said to myself. "You better take what you can get. Just get a job you lazy bum."

With that bit of wisdom, my finger made a blind stab at the want ads' page. I looked to see where my first call would be made. My finger had fallen on an ad for a place called Yukon Office Supply in Anchorage. Well, if I got the job it would certainly be different, selling pencils and paper clips behind a cash register.

I made the phone call and set an appointment for an interview. The next day at 10:00 A.M. I would see about getting back to earning a living.

What I had expected to be a small store turned out to be one of the largest and most modern buildings in Anchorage. Was I glad that I had decided to wear a coat and tie instead of blue jeans and flannel shirt.

I was hired as an office furniture salesman. I had never sold anything in my life since my days at the nickel-a-glass lemonade stand in front of my families apartment in South Chicago. Heck, that had been a disaster. On those hot, humid summer days I wound up drinking so much of the stuff there was little left to sell.

I was assigned the task of selling desks, chairs, file cabinets and other related paraphernalia worth thousands of dollars. Had I been able to comprehend the broad responsibilities and the enormous dollar figures I would have rejected the position out of shear fear. Only my ignorance saved me. It seemed I was making a habit of jumping into unknown situations. I rushed home to tell Blu I would be able to keep him in doggie biscuits.

Bill and Fred had long since returned home. Fred's wife Jane had also arrived with their two daughters Eve and Janelle from a visit to the lower forty-eight. Blu had been getting more attention than a cover girl on Devil's Island. His personality and temperament were suited perfectly to young children. He'd become more domestic than a grandmother. In nightmares I saw him wearing a housecoat and slippers with curlers and a babushka on his head.

For the last three months Blu and I had not been separated for more than a few minutes. When I had prepared a place for him to stay while I was at work, he'd howled when I'd hooked him to his chain. He actually had a pretty nice place, able to reach his dog house, the back of Bill's house and even Meadow Creek, but he didn't like being alone.

On my way home, regret and fear were fluttering through my stomach and filling my mind with all sorts of negatives. But I had my best friend waiting for me.

Desperately needing his reassurance I didn't even bother to go into the house to change clothes. Instead I rushed around the side and to the back of the house to free my shoulder-to-lean-on. What I saw when I got around back stopped me dead in my tracks. There was Blu sitting on the back porch consuming what was left of the back door frame.

When he saw me he stood up abruptly and joyously, forgetting for a moment the damage he had just caused. Seeing that I didn't instantly return his happiness but rather stood with my mouth ajar, he remembered what he had just done. His head dropped, ears drooped and his tail disappeared between his legs.

I took deep breaths calming myself. On top of the already monumental day's events, that had been a devastating blow. It was disappointing. It hurt.

In deep depression and disappointment I walked toward Blu. Though there was anger inside me I justified Blu's action by telling myself that he had done it out of panic, despair and loneliness and not for pure joy of vandalism. When I reached Blu's side I squatted down and released the timid, withdrawn creature from his chain. I petted him and reassured him with comforting words.

He revitalized immediately, dancing and loping around the backyard. His display accomplished its intention as I smiled and chuckled. He became even more frantic as he narrowed down his territory dancing all around me. I lifted my eyes from him to go in the back door. What I saw made my blood run cold.

Not only had he chewed the door frame to pieces, but also the door. Two full panels of siding were scratched to ribbons all the way up to the bathroom window whose sill was virtually nonexistent.

Blu must have felt the heat radiating from my body. He had assumed his previous submissive position as I stood steaming. The tension within me coiled tighter and tighter.

That was it! Lonely or not that was too much! Sternly I turned, refastening his chain to his collar reeking punishment with my words. The more I shouted, the angrier I became. The back of my hand came in hard contact with Blu's hind quarters as he retreated into his dog house. The force of the blow caused him to stagger a step to the left but he still escaped to the sanctitiy of his house.

The fact that my boy was retreating rather than taking his well-deserved punishment steamed me even more. I crawled into the house to reach the scruff of his neck and dragged him out into the open. The more he resisted the angrier I got. Finally I lost all control and dove onto him pushing, shoving, slapping and squeezing.

That's when Blu figured enough was enough. He was right of course. In my berserk state, his snarl and snap at my arm only infuriated me more. It had become a no holds barred, free-for-all. An all out brawl, and may the best man win. At least may everyone take the opportunity to quell their frustrations.

He bit, I punched. But because he pushed more than bit, it was difficult to stay balanced well enough to land a really good one. Throwing caution to the wind we rolled and kicked and bit each other...Blu growling and barking and me growling and shouting.

A few minutes of that sort of intense fracas was enough for both of us. Each still on the defensive, we backed away making clear that there was more where that had come from if the other wanted it.

I was scratched, punctured, bruised and dirty. Though not as readily visable through his thick hair, I was certain that Blu carried some battle scars as well.

Boy, I felt better. From the looks of Blu, he seemed more at ease too. But, man, was I a mess. Oh God! I still had on my sport coat and tie!

I stood slowly and began brushing myself off, occasionally rubbing an especially sore spot while Blu sat licking his wounds. As we preened I complimented Blu on a good fight but at the same time got the unmistakable feeling of being watched.

I turned to see Fred's visiting mother standing with her hands at her sides and her mouth wide open. She'd seen the whole ruckus.

I had thought that Blu and I had had a private argument. I felt as though a deep secret had been uncovered. As though, finally, we had been found out. Two primitive aliens trying to make it in a civilized society had been revealed.

I stopped brushing wanting only to escape. Sheepishly, smiling and nodding a good afternoon, I backed clumsily toward Blu, released him, and we two disappeared through the dilapidated back door. Fred's mom never moved a muscle.

Drat! And I hadn't even met the lady yet. I only knew that she had been due in that day from the lower forty-eight for a two week visit. I could imagine the impression that poor lady was getting of Alaska and its inhabitants. And we were supposed to be the civilized ones. If Fred had still been a boy I'm sure that his mother would have grabbed him by the ear and marched him all the way back to Illinois.

Bill took the destruction of his house better than I did. For the next few nights, and that weekend, I spent my leisure time repairing as best I could. Bill seemed to accept the job as adequate, but you never know about that guy. He's the quiet type. I'm still waiting for him to tear off my back door to get even.

17. Kodiak

That's how it had been. Through the good and not so good we had stuck together. Blu got used to us being apart weekdays and we both looked forward to the weekend adventures. We'd made it, and it looked as though we were going to make it through our winter ordeal up Eagle River.

Walking was stiff and painful at first but, with that first mile or so under our belts, muscles and joints loosened and the trek to Jack and Irma's Garden of Eden Lodge became bareable. Soon, however, after breaking through the crusted ice and sinking to my knees or even my thighs on occasion, I began to feel the weariness of a long hard day.

Seeing that Blu was again strong and vibrant, following his

near drowning, I wished that I had just walked him in circles around the fire for awhile and then slept out the rest of the night in our camp. I suppose, though, that if I'd really wanted to I could have stopped anywhere along the way and rolled out my bed. It was the thought of that toddy by the fire at the Garden of Eden Lodge that kept me going. With each labored step the thought became an infatuation.

We reached Jack and Irma's non-stop some time after midnight. Seeing fatigue written all over my face, and not having expected us back till much later in the day, they both knew that we had just been through some sort of an ordeal. Without a word they kindly served up my drink and poured a dish of water for Blu. After a little time to rest Jack asked what had happened.

I don't believe I did a very good job of relating our experience, but they got the idea. Where adventure and danger is to be found behind nearly every tree, much is understood that goes unsaid.

Many more weekends were spent at road's end up Eagle River Valley. It was hard to pass up the hospitality, good food, good entertainment and good company at Jack and Irma's. And even though our latest excursion had nearly killed us, I couldn't resist its wonders.

That stretch of Eagle River had been the original route of the dog sleds carrying mail from Seward to Nome. At each bend in the river I could look up its course and visualize those hardy men of old racing at me while mushing their yapping sled dogs on the perilous journey to boom-town Nome.

Other than the weekend trips our next extended adventure came when I took my first vacation from work the following September.

For years I had heard or read tales of the gigantic brown bears found on Kodiak Island. Finally had come my opportunity to hunt and spend time with the magnificent animals.

I had done a bit of research before making the trip. A few new articles accompanied us that were not along on the journey to the Wind River country.

For one thing, more substantial shelters were purchased. A tent for sleeping, and a lean-to for cooking and storing gear. Kodiak Island's climate was considered near-rainforest. I did not want us spending all our time hanging onto a piece of vinyl. I guess I had grown older and softer. I also upgraded our armament from a .50 to a .58 caliber muzzel loader and even went so far as to buy a short double barrelled twelve-guage shotgun as back up.

We drove to Homer, Alaska, and there boarded a twin engine plane for the hop over to the island.

At the airport in Kodiak I discovered that my ammunition had not made the trip with us. I was furious. I took a cab to my bush pilot's home and place of business and his daughter was kind enough to drive me to town where I bought extra powder and balls for the .58, and slugs and 00 buck for the shotgun.

Before leaving home I had moulded a heavy bullet for my .58, especially for the hunt. On the island I had to settle for a lighter round ball. The granulation of powder I preferred was not available either. They would have to do though, because even if I had to throw rocks I intended flying in that afternoon. I only had two weeks.

After making the purchases, the young lady drove us to the docks where we awaited the floatplane that would fly Blu and me to our destination in the heart of the island. Sitting on the docks waiting, I was about to take off my boots and dangle my feet in the cold ocean waters when I noticed a myriad of jelly fish hugging the pier. I left my boots on, my feet on the dock.

The plane was not long in coming. After quickly stowing our gear, we boarded and were off to the island's interior.

Landscape below was thick and lush, something I would have expected to see in the tropics. Soon we landed on a beautiful lake surrounded by mountains.

"Salmon run's just about over." The pilot said as we touched down and taxied toward the beach. "The bears are sick of the stuff by now. You'll be safe making camp in the lowlands. The bears are high in the mountains. That's where you'll want to do your huntin'." Then the pilot did something that startled me.

From my last experience I realized that those planes were restricted to water deep enough to float their pontoons. We were only able to get within fifteen yards of shore. For that reason hip waders are a common form of apparel in Alaska. I knew that, I even owned a pair. They just didn't make it to my final list of necessities. I chose to wade without them.

I had climbed down through the door of the plane and was standing on one of the pontoons reaching back in for some of the gear when I heard from behind me, "Okay, hop on."

Questioningly I turned to see the pilot standing in the waters of the lake with his back to me. He was slightly hunkered down with his knees bent and arms bowed out from his sides looking like a teapot.

"What are you doin'?!" I asked in surprise.

"Let's go. Come on, hop on. I'll ferry you to the bank."

"What are you talkin' about? I've gotta get all this gear over there." I retorted. Still in disbelief.

"No prob. I'll get you to dry ground, then I'll bring your stuff."

"I don't believe this." I said. "You don't need to be cartin' me around this island on your back. I knew what I was gettin' into."

"I don't care. I'm gettin' you started dry. Now get on!"

I could tell from his resoluteness that he wasn't going to let me set foot in that lake so, feeling extremely foolish, I hopped aboard my temporary beast of burden and was carried to dry ground. Blu was already there. He'd dove in as soon as the first door had been opened and was already nosing through the thick grass and brush above the beach. Good thing too. It would have been a bit much to have had the pilot piggyback him ashore.

While I stood in amazement, with a thumb in each ear, the pilot neatly stacked all of my gear on the beach. Then with a parting comment of, "Remember now, don't be too concerned about bears around here. They're all in the high country by now," he climbed into his puddlejumper and was on his way back to the town of Kodiak.

The setting was perfect. A clear lake teaming with rainbows and silvers, a gravel beach, and all around us lush, dense and wild country. The day was hot and calm.

As I left the beach, pushing my way through the tall grass in search of a campsite, I became aware of a problem that surpassed even the mosquitoes of the Arctic. Exceptionally tiny black flies were everywhere.

If I left my mouth open they were in there. Otherwise they were only to be found in nose, ears and eyes. The scary thing was that they seemed immune to the repellent properties of my bug dope.

While taxying toward shore I had covered all bare skin with the stuff and I'd sparyed it on Blu in readiness. I knew that our coverage was less than a half hour old and the mosquitoes were at bay, but the black flys were oblivious to it. Heck, they seemed to thrive on it.

Unlike the Brooks Range camp, our Kodiak camp was made only one hundred yards north of where we were dropped off. And we were on firm, high and dry ground. We were only twenty feet from a four-foot bank that eased down to a twelve-foot gravel beach.

The tents were pitched in grasses that were from two to five feet in height. In short order, normal camp tasks sufficiently matted down the growth around us.

Remembering tales of the rain that is supposed to almost constantly fall on Kodiak Island, Blu and I braved the flies long enough to put in a week's supply of wood under the lean-to, even though the skies were clear that afternoon. Then we dove into the sanctity of our mosquito-netted tent where we hoped to breath without coating our lungs with black flies.

Having read the Old Testament we began the New. We read until cool evening breezes sent the hordes of microscopic annoyances scurrying home. I imagined home was a nearby dung heep. Then we crawled forth to survey our neighborhood.

Our lake was surrounded on all sides by mountains. Its valley was thick with tall grasses, fireweed and alder thickets. At the south end, where fresh mountain water feeds the lake, was a large beaver dam. In the center of the pond that it formed was an immense beaver hutch. At the north end, where our lake emptied, a rocky stream poured through thick alders on its way to the ocean about a mile distant.

The night overtook us a hundred yards from camp, but a bright moon guided our path home. I built a fire, cooked and ate dinner and turned in for the night.

Waking early in the morning it was already shirt sleeve weather. We expected and got another hellaciously hot day and, you guessed it, the ever-so-lovely black flies. If you can believe it, I wished for more mosquitoes.

Something curious was transpiring at the south end of the lake that caught our attention and sent me into the tent to retrieve my binoculars. Magnified examination revealed a group of eight bald eagles in the tall bushes.

We watched for half an hour while they flapped from the bushes to the beach, to the bushes, and back to the beach over and over again. Finally, one by one, they took off in a flight pattern that led them almost right over our camp to the summit of the mountain that stood east of us. We watched a while longer as they flew circles around the peak until the plague of black flies drove us to the confines of the tent.

The eagles performed the same ritual many times in the next two weeks. That morning I decided that some time during our stay, we would make a point of climbing that mountain in order to view them more closely. We'd missed the one on the Brooks Range.

The day was far too hot and the air much too full of flies for us to venture out of the tent for anything but food and that other haunting natural urge. It didn't matter. We still had the better part of two weeks ahead of us. The usual rains would come soon, putting to rest the flies and the heat. Then we would be off exploring and hunting. Until that time I had the best in books and Blu could catch up on his favorite sport other than hunting: snoozing.

Following another hot, uneventful but nevertheless luxurious day, we were to bed early after the darkest night I had ever experienced came over us. Just before sunset a total and thick overcast had moved in. It completely blotted out star and moon light. Being far from any city lights the last possible form of indirect illumination was eliminated.

The darkness was so complete that a mere three or four feet kept even the brightest of colors from being perceived. The night was also calm and quiet unto death. A feeling of complete solitude crept over me.

I don't remember when I finally dozed off. I most certainly will never forget what awakened me.

Some time in the middle of that blackest of nights I was blasted awake by a loud explosion that seemed to shake the ground. It brought Blu to a rigid but quivering stand at the zipped-shut front flap of the tent.

Fully awakened only instants after the eruption, I could not imagine what it was that could have blown up. First I thought of my gas lantern, but I was certain I'd turned it off before retiring. Besides, there was no light dancing through the sheer fabric of my sleeping tent in the direction of the kitchen tent and no dirt or sticks or pieces of equipment were hitting on the rainfly.

With my mind still pondering other possibilities I began crawling out of my bed. It was only moments before all my questions would be answered.

I wasn't yet completely clear of my sleeping bag when I was shocked into almost the same position Blu had assumed. The explosion again shattered the tomb-like night. Unfortunately, it was not an explosion at all.

What I had thought was a blast was the angry roar of a brown bear. It seemed to be somewhere between our camp and the beaver pond two hundred and fifty yards away.

For a moment my mind blanked as fear raced through it. With its leader immobilized the remainder of my body was without direction, unsteady.

The third roar was what was needed to bring me back from my semi-comatose state. Hurriedly but spasmodically, I finished shedding my sleeping cocoon. I grabbed my .44 magnum from its holster with one hand, my slug-loaded shotgun with the other and crawled quickly on hands and knees toward the closed entrance of my home. Reaching the zipper of the door I began sliding it upward but stopped abruptly.

It had been only a short while since the last bellow of madness but, nevertheless, certainly enough time for the animal to cover the distance necessary to reach our camp. I had no desire to rush out into the darkness only to rise up into the waiting grasp of nearly a ton of bad. My tent, I knew, would not keep him out. But at least I would not be a locked in target for a paw swipe that could break the neck of a horse. The way I saw it, getting my neck broken once was enough.

I waited with my thumb and forefinger on the zipper

listening for anything that would be a clue as to the bear's whereabouts. I remember being furious with myself because I could not stop shaking. The racket I was making against the nylon fabric of the tent made it difficult to hear clearly.

Except for the step to the side Blu had been forced to make while I crawled past him, he had not faltered from his gargoylian posture.

A few moments later another resounding, drawn out roar erupted from the direction of the beaver pond. Closer, but not yet an immediate threat. The flap was back on the tent and I was out standing and looking back over the top of it in the direction of our challenger.

I laid the .44 on the front roof of our shelter. Gripping the shotgun tightly with both hands I peered into darkness waiting for something to unload it on.

Blu was two feet to my left in the same position he had been in inside the tent. It was as if two men, one holding his snout the other his tail, had lifted him, carried him out of the tent, turned him one hundred eighty degrees and set him down.

The situation was not what I had expected. Nor was I accustomed to it. Never before had I had my prey come to me. Nor had they ever had the gall to wake me in the middle of the night. The audacity!

A man was supposed to be allowed a good night's sleep. Then an enjoyable, unthreatened morning of game bagging while his quarry ran before him. After which, a leisurely afternoon rest before more game bagging in the evening.

That bear's display was uncalled for. How dare he break the rules and get my bowels to rumbling to near uncontrolled release. Had I been deer hunting it would have been too easy, being able to shoot my quarry from in front of my tent. Somehow, though, instead of making the hunt effortless, the turn of events had made me feel that maybe I was not necessarily the hunter. I would have felt comfortable only had

I had a flame-thrower to replace my shotgun and a full case of hand grenades substituted for the .44.

The roar came again. It seemed further away and was accompanied by the sound of wood being violently ripped and splintered. Splashing sounds told me that the bear was in the beaver pond. The only wood was in the beaver dam and hut.

The bear was not hunting beaver. He was destroying in a fit of rage and I believed that it was my presence that drove him to it. The destruction continued for a few minutes. All the while I never knew if the bear's fit of frustration would turn on us and he would decide to reek havoc where havoc was due.

Presently, the commotion ceased. Again silence prevailed. Curiously, Blu still would not budge. In the silence I heard his low, deep growl. It meant threat, warning. It bore undeniable assurance that any aggressive action would be met by him. No matter who the perpetrator. No matter what the consequence.

I bent down and stroked his head, neck and shoulders. "It's all right, boy. Let's go back to bed."

His growl never stopped. His vigilance never averted. I surmised that he knew something I didn't. I resumed my previous attitude with shotgun at the ready.

We watched and waited for twenty more minutes. I knew what I was waiting for but watching seemed useless. The darkness had not brightened one iota. As hard as I strained, my eyes could not penetrate the inky night. I could barely make out the back of my tent seven feet away.

Had the bear decided to attack, my first shot would have had to be only at the sound of his charge. I would save the second for that fraction of a second it would take him to cover the seven feet of visibility. At that moment seven-foot basketball players seemed awfully short.

During the silence, for what good it would have done, I worked on a plan B if the worst happened. I thought I would save most of the .44 magnum rounds for close quarters firing. The first shot from the .44 would be fired in the air when I became certain that the massive beast was on a collision course.

Then, if he persisted, I would let loose no more than one at the sound of his approach. Throwing the .44 to the ground to my right I would next use the shotgun and blindly fire the chamber I had reloaded with 00 buckshot in the direction of his approach. I'd then stand ready for that instant of visual contact letting go the other barrel with the slug in it. At the same time I would dive to my right averting his headlong rush and grabbing the .44.

Spinning on my back I would fire the remaining four shots placing them perfectly at the upper neck of the animal who, I was sure by then, would be being diverted by trusty old Blu.

The animal would drop to the ground paralyzed. Within seconds thereafter I would reload and administer the finishing shots with the twelve-gauge putting an end to my adversary. Triumphantly Blu and I would sit on his corpse and celebrate with a short pull of hooch and a few loud yells of victory. All I had to do was somehow contact the bear and give him a copy of the script.

Needless to say my valiant plan was no more than a way to pass the time. Only the end of the encounter would show who had won and who had lost.

My daring idea could only have been carried through if I were cool, calm and unflinching. Even then there would have been no guarantees. As tense as I was, I would have been lucky if my fear-frozen finger could have jerked off one round. And that one probably wouldn't have done any more than blow out the back of my tent. No, our only hope lay with the bear's present emotional stability.

Blu stopped growling. Then, gradually he relaxed. Still, though, he stayed where he was for a few more minutes. His head turned slowly from side to side. His nose was raised high in the air sniffing cautiously and thoroughly.

His senses giving him the all clear, he slowly moved back into the tent without giving me so much as a glance. I got his message. "Way to go, Dumb-bo, so much for another of your great ideas!" He was serious.

If Blu said so, it was safe. I retired after him to our sleeping quarters and eased back off to sleep.

Awakening shortly before sunrise the first thing that caught my eye was Blu. He was lying with his head up, on his elbows, eyes staring intently at the front flap of the tent. "Did you sleep at all last night, Bluper?" I got no answer but I just knew that he'd spent the night on guard. For that matter, I don't believe he slept at night for the remainder of that two weeks. Had he not been such a vigilant sentinel, I have often wondered if I would have lived through the remainder of our days on the island.

At any rate, by our second morning on Kodiak Island, I had had enough brown bear hunting to last me a lifetime. It is certainly more exciting but not nearly as much fun when you are not sure which role you're actually playing in the age old hunter/hunted conflict.

Before breakfast Blu and I went to investigate the site of last night's hell-bent madness. Our pilot had been so sure that there were no longer any browns in the area. After that last night, for some odd reason, I had my doubts. I carried with me the shotgun and a pocket full of slugs. In fact, from that morning on, I never ventured even from one tent to the other without it. I had liked calling it our "equalizer." But I lengthened the name a bit to "provided-we're-exceptionally-lucky-almost-equalizer."

The beaver dam and hut were in an unbelievable state of devastation. Water poured through a gaping hole in the dam and the hut, that had stood nearly seven feet above the water, had been reduced to a low crater of broken sticks and oozing mud.

There was no sign of dead beaver so I hoped that they had had time to escape through their underwater passage. A feeling of guilt and compassion overcame me. I had been the indirect cause of that carnage. The unfortunate family of beavers had many days of hard work ahead of them if they were to repair the damage before winter set in.

Closer inspection revealed tracks in the mud that were enormous. We returned to camp in awe. We had breakfast. I reconsidered my idea of hunting those giants with a muzzle loader.

Back home, dreaming of the adventure, it had seemed like an exciting change of pace. While visiting the captive brown bear at the Anchorage Zoo I had been fascinated. But, being in the cage with one (one heck, there were thousands of them on that ocean encircled pile of dirt and foliage), the idea did not seem quite so noble. In fact, instead of spending our time hunting, it seemed that we might be wiser to spend it trying to stay off the menu.

That day, like the others, was full of flies. But not wanting to be cooped up for the rest of our stay, flies or no flies, we went fishing. Fishing proved excellent in both the lake and the stream which fed it. The beaver pond wasn't bad either. The lake generously coughed up silver salmon and rainbow trout while the stream and pond abounded with dolly varden. If we could keep from being eaten, we sure would eat well.

Blu wasn't enjoying himself much. Wherever we went he seemed to go on his tiptoes, alert to every sound and movement. He couldn't understand why we didn't pack up and get the heck out of there since the natives were so unfriendly and so overwhelmingly huge. "So tell me again," he would have said, "What's so boring about rabbits and pheasants that brings us to this God-forsaken land of the not-so-jolly brown giant?"

After a dinner of silver salmon, night again began to overtake our lake. The uneasiness that had left me during the daylight hours began again to creep up my spine in proportion to the creeping darkness.

Uneasily I dozed off only to be rudely awakened a short time later by the same commotion of the previous night. Actually, I had expected it. Having once come through the experience without a scratch, the second encounter was somewhat less frightening but still respected enough to bring us both flying out of the tent armed. We assumed the same battle stations as the night before.

I knew the bear's intent. He was clearing up a few things. That was his territory. His domain. He wanted us out and was giving us a chance to make an exit. "Get out peacefully," he said, "or you'll force me to do the job in my efficient, yet messy way."

Lord, how I wished we could oblige. If there had been a way out we would have taken it. But there wasn't. If only there had been some way of relating to him our dilemma. But then again, even if we could the bear seemed in no mood for compromise.

Somehow I believed he would keep his distance so I reveled in his magnificence. Blu, on the other hand, had assumed a no less rigid stance than on the previous night. He seemed not as willing to believe that our tormentor would be able to control his hateful temper.

That night's ostentation ended without mishap. When Blu was certain that the beast had retreated into the surrounding hills we slept the rest of the night…at least I did.

Next morning an overcast had brought a slight drizzle reducing the fly contingent substantially. Blu and I had an important decision to make. The question we needed to answer was a straightforward one: What the heck were we going to do?

Had we some form of communication with the outside world the question would have posed no difficulty whatever. I would have simply notified our flying service that we wanted out and if they were there in five minutes they would have been late.

As I fixed breakfast I said, "We can't get out'a here. You know that, don't ya? He's comin' back. And ya know that."

There was only one answer. I desperately tried to come up with another but, "Bluper, there's only one thing we can do. We've gotta go after him." Having finally said it a chill swept over me.

If the beast persisted, we would have to discard our defensive position and take the offensive before it was too late. We would have to leave the false security of our camp and attack.

I was not an experienced brown bear hunter. All I had to go on while preparing our plan of attack was plain common sense and what I had heard and read on the subject. No, we need to eliminate common sense. If I'd had any we wouldn't have been there.

Stories of what it would take to kill one of those monsters ranged from one round in the ear from a small caliber rifle, to thirteen rounds from large calibers finally putting one under after it had killed one man and severely mauled another. Some of the large bullets were said to have ricocheted off its scull. There was one story about a bear that ran half a mile after a bullet had obliterated its heart.

These stories told me a great deal. I would have to shoot it from one to thirteen times. The shots had to be vital. But by all means, never shoot it in the head or the heart. And, however it turned out, probably expect to wrestle a little bit with a guy that outweighed me by a thousand pounds or more, carried eight knives permanently affixed to the ends of his fingers, stood in the neighborhood of nine feet tall and, with one punch, could knock a moose off its feet.

Well, my mind certainly was at ease since I knew exactly how I would handle things. All that was left was to start packing, and write a will.

We were going extremely light, but it still took the rest of the day to pack. I knew what needed to be done. I just wasn't overly anxious to do it. I figured if I really moved slowly it would be too late to leave that day. The bear had tried for two nights. Who was to say that he wouldn't give up and go up into the hills where the pilot said he was supposed to be? We'd give him one last chance.

Blu and I sat awake that night. We waited for what we knew was going to happen but prayed wouldn't. Sure enough, not long after dark, it began again.

First I watched Blu gradually become a rigid, growling mannequin. That signaled the unheard approach of our nightmare. Five minutes later the maniacal roaring and breaking of wood began again. Blu and I were in our usual positions in front of the tent peering in the direction of the unseen holocaust. Then something that froze my blood occurred.

I had grown accustomed to the nightly charade. The fear of it had left me. The only reason I came out of the tent at all was because I could listen better. What I thought might happen at any time, but never really believed would, transpired so quickly that I found myself back in the same state of shock that I had been in on the first night.

The rapidly nearing sound of foliage being trampled and the increasing volume of snorting and bellowing meant that the beast had finally lost patience with our intrusion and was charging our stronghold.

I looked down at Blu for help but his fighting instinct had made him so intense that his only concern was channeled in the direction of the fast approaching one bear army. He was waiting only for an instant's glimpse of his adversary. He'd then turn on his fighting machine and enter into combat that he must have known he could not win.

I, on the other hand, was not so anxious to die bravely. I had to do something, and right away, before the crazed animal appeared out of the darkness. I shifted the shotgun to my right hand, lifted the .44 magnum in my left and fired two successive rounds into the night sky.

I stuffed the handgun between my pants and belly and aimed the shotgun in the direction of the bear's advance, just in case my feeble attempt at quelling the uprising had failed and Blu had been right after all.

The sound of the shots still echoing was the only sound I heard. The advance had stopped. But where was our enemy? In front? Behind? How far out? I don't know which was worse, expecting him in our camp at any moment, or wondering if he already was?

Our only hope was Blu's senses. Kind of like flying by instruments. Rather than peering hopelessly out into the blackness, I glued my eyes to Blu. As he shifted direction so did I. And so did the barrel of the shotgun.

The ice had been broken. Fear was gone from me, and so too from Blu. We were relying on senses that were performing objectively. The battle had begun.

We were horrendously disadvantaged, undergunned and outnumbered. There was one of him and only two of us.

From Blu's actions and the confirming sound of rustling and breaking plant growth, I could tell that the bear had begun to move once again. He was making a slow circle around camp. He was no more than one hundred feet out. But I didn't think closer than fifty.

After making the circuit from south to east to north he splashed noisily into the lake to the west. At a run he proceeded down the shoreline and out of hearing, at least my hearing, and was gone.

First thing, come light of day, we had no choice but to begin our offensive.

18. The Hunt

We ate breakfast in the dark. Blu and I were in pursuit of our opponent as the sky grew red from the awakening sun.

With us we had packed the lean-to, sleeping bag, rain jacket, enough food for three days and enough firepower to assault and besiege the town of Kodiak.

It was not what I was accustomed to taking along on a hunt. But then it was more a contest to see who might live and who might die. Though heavily armed, I still felt that the brown was far better equipped than we. I only hoped that he didn't know it.

Before leaving camp I remembered stuffing my brown bear harvest ticket into my pack. I couldn't help laughing at having spent hard earned money for the opportunity of going out and getting myself killed. If I had to buy one of those, how come the bear didn't?! And it was called, of all things, a harvest ticket. As though all I had to do was go out and pick one. The bear that we were going out to meet was not a vegetable.

We easily picked up his trail at the head of the beaver pond. One of Jimmy Tebs's favorite sayings was, "It was easy as trackin' an elephant in ten foot of snow." That was the case on our counter offensive. In the low scrub and marsh we trudged through the trail could have been likened to the path of a bulldozer.

Not only was his trail visually evident, but it was olfactory evident as well. Every branch, every leaf, every rock that he brushed against carried the stench of rotting fish and filth. Alder thickets reeked of him. Wherever he excreted, and it seemed often, the flies were maddening though the sky dripped precipitation. We were hot, wet, covered with flies and subjected to that nauseating aroma all day.

The trail led east between mountains and then swung south hugging the east side of the valley. Later in the day it abruptly went across the valley floor and up the side of the mountains before continuing south. The walking was made easier then it had been in the swampy bottom land.

It seemed as if the bear wanted to lead us away from the region of the lake. That was okay. But if he started to edge back down the mountain and back the way we had come, we were in deep trouble. If he got back to camp before we did he would destroy it in a matter of minutes.

The growth on the side of the mountain was thick with brush and alders up to eight feet high, where as in the valley we had been mostly in grass. Our visibility was dangerously limited. We were forced to slow our pace to a slow stalk for safety's sake.

If he'd had a mind to, the bear could have doubled back

anywhere in that area and waited for us only feet off of our path. If I were lucky I would have had time for one unaimed shot. Blu's nose was what I was depending on. I watched him as much as I watched the trail.

Now and then Blu would freeze, the hair on his neck would rise and his nostrils would flare and quiver as his eyes tried to penetrate the choking undergrowth. At times like those condors would be flapping their wings in my stomach. My breath would come in short gasps and cold shivers would race the well-worn track down my spine. The hammers would be eased back on the shotgun then, too. Our time of do or die would come if Blu ever added his low growl to the other signals.

I would stare at Blu and only Blu at those times. I would wait for his lips to part and that eerie threatening sound to roll out from between his clenched teeth. When it didn't come and he calmed, we would push on.

Blu did no wandering that day. If nothing else came of that hunt, Blu learned to stay within gun range. Actually, he never exceeded spittin' distance.

That first evening of the hunt found us physically and mentally exhausted. We found a small level area close to a trickle coming down from the mountain and made camp. It had drizzled all day and I was soaked. I removed my clothes and hung them by the fire under the lean-to.

The night was colder than we had become used to but with the fire reflecting back onto us from the back of the shelter we stayed as comfortable as was to be expected. Our enemy, for some unknown reason, did not harass us. I was permitted a good night's sleep. Blu remained uneasy and vigilant.

Hard on the trail by sunrise, it led further and further up the mountains. In the thickets, where no breeze could penetrate, the day became sultry, even up high. How I wished the bear would venture only a few yards higher where the alders thinned and a cool breeze blew. But he knew better than to leave cover and risk a bullet.

It had been so long since we had been subjected to any menacing encounters that my guard had worked way down. My gun just swung in my left hand as I walked head down and stooped, clearing low hanging growth. I was noisy and nonchalant.

Suddenly startled, I heard the ominous growl coming from Blu. I froze with the feeling that I was lost. My lackadaisical attitude had left me unprotected. I deserved to die. Stupid! Dumb! Ignorant! Nonsensical! I was never more mad at myself than I was then. Momentarily I had resigned myself to the reality that the bear had earned himself a victory. Had the bear made his move then he would have had me. Without a fight.

He didn't take advantage of my vulnerability, however, and I was able to regroup. I spun to look at Blu. Through lack of concern I had let him get behind me. He was facing the way we had come, growling and braced to fight. There was no doubt that the bear was there, very close, intent on attack.

I cocked both hammers, the stock of the shotgun was at my shoulder and the muzzle was pointed in the same direction as Blu's hideously contorted snout.

Blu would show fear only when confronted with unknowns. Then, his enemy was unmistakable. He was ready. No matter what the odds. We stood still and awaited the bear's next move.

He had circled behind us. I'm ashamed to say the tactic had nearly worked, and would have, had it not been for Blu. The bear's hesitation, though, told me that he was unsure of his superiority. That was fine with me.

Minutes later my senses picked up on the bear's whereabouts. Brush began breaking as he swung down the mountain to the east and then back up in front of us to intersect the trail we had been following south. It amazed me that so little noise was made by a half-ton creature.

"Bluper, you could be in Kodiak by now. What are you doin' here with this crippled up idiot wonderin' where your next breath is comin' from?" Without a sound, without a look, Blu took the point.

That night we were again drained from the day's events. Unable to find a campsite along the trail we climbed a short distance to a spot above tree line next to a pocket of snow. A cold wind blew as we sat by our fire boiling water for a freeze dried dinner and coffee.

I was glad I'd stretched our three-day ration of food. Since we had been so close, we would dog his trail again the next day.

I didn't want to sleep as soundly as I did, but I couldn't help myself. I had grown dependent on Blu. Morning inspection uncovered evidence that our bear had been only a few short yards from us during the night. Blu was a wreck. I felt for him. I appreciated him. I loved him. I wished I could have flown him home there and then, but we were committed to our isolation for eight more days. We had to be certain that our host was of a mind not to return to our base camp, or dead.

The bear could have easily outdistanced us in the last two days. He had obviously felt no pressure from us. He was testing us to see how badly we wanted him or at least wanted him to leave us alone. If we turned and went back I was sure he was still of a mind to follow. That day we would press hard. We would drive him. Caution would be discarded. I would depend on Blu's senses even more. We had to convince our adversary that we meant business.

By early evening he had led us back down into a valley where flies were swarming. After the day's fast pace I hardly noticed. He had stayed just ahead of us all day. We had accomplished nothing. All the pressure I could muster had not put him to flight as I had hoped. That night I went to bed feeling that I had failed. We would have to head back on the morrow, and I was afraid that the bear would then be trailing us.

My dilemma did not afford me the luxury of sleeping as soundly as the night before. Suddenly I was awakened to Blu's alarm. He was braced and growling deep and low, peering into the dark brush to the south.

It was impossible to see anything and the noises I heard could only be guessed at. The frustration was unbearable. We had really pressed him that day, but here he was again, undaunted, threatening our existence. We hadn't even winded him.

I was so perplexed, exhausted and frustrated that I was on the verge of a charge into the thick brush to once and for all force a confrontation. I said perplexed, exhausted and frustrated. Note I did not mention delirious or suicidal, so the charge was not initiated. I knew I had to do something though. Something that would show our tormentor that we were no longer going to be intimidated.

I pulled myself out of the sleeping bag, left the shelter of the lean-to and backed against a tree. Breaking the double-barrel shotgun I replaced the slugs with three-inch magnum buckshot but kept the two slugs in my left hand. Nervously I pulled back the two hammers and raised the gun to my shoulder. I would either force him to show himself or, preferably, run him off for good.

Intending to spray the area, I aimed slightly to the right of Blu's gaze, took a deep breath, and pulled the first trigger. The sound of the blast was still ringing in my ears as I swung slightly left and touched it off again. I quickly broke the gun, removed the spent shells and replaced them with the two slugs. The gun was again at my shoulder as I waited expectantly. My eyes stared intently into the brush where the few dozen lead balls had gone searching for the hide of the bear.

It was then that I realized that I had forgotten my .44 next to my sleeping bag. No matter, at this range I would only have time for two shots anyway.

The noise of the blasts was dying away when another sound found me. It was the unmistakable sound of brush rustling and branches snapping. Thank God, it was fading up the valley.

The brown was making his retreat. And it wasn't just a saunter. He was going full bore. The feeling of relief that swept over me buckled my knees and sent me to the ground.

Lying there with my forehead on my forearms a smile crossed my face as I recalled what Blu had done when I'd fired. He had temporarily forgotten what we were about. At the sound of the shotgun blast his conditioning had sent him at full speed toward the brush curtain that hid the bear. But before disappearing into the thicket the gravity of the situation had hit him like a sledge hammer. He had slammed on the brakes and backed and side-stepped back to where I stood remembering that that wasn't a quacker out there.

At daybreak Blu and I scoured the area which the bear had occupied and a couple hundred yards down the bulldozed path of his retreat. We looked for blood that would have been evidence that some of the buckshot had found him. There was none.

At that discovery I felt an odd combination of disappointment and relief. Part of me wanted to trail after him. Evidence that he had been wounded would have made that wish an obligation. But there was also that part of me that was hungry, tired and unwilling to put an end to such a noble beast…or, have such a noble beast put an end to me.

We were into our fourth day and our stretched three-day food supply was nearly gone. I still thought it best that we continue on his trail for at least a couple of hours to be absolutely certain that he was leaving.

The trail was fresh but it was comforting to know that it wasn't steaming. We walked slowly, conserving energy, till mid-morning. The bear was well ahead of us and heading in a southerly direction, away from base camp. It was over.

We turned and made for the less confining though wetter land in the valley below. The flies were worse, but conserving energy and shortening our return trip took precedent over livable annoyance.

Blu sensed our destination. His prance urged me to go faster. I was anxious. The thought of fresh baked trout and salmon wandered through my thoughts. But I was weak. Blu would just have to wait a little longer.

The bear had led us on a meandering south-southeasterly course. I felt that if we kept to the valleys, staying on a straighter passage, we could be to base camp in twenty-four hours; maybe a little more. The prevailing wind would be in our faces most of the way. Once again I would rely on Blu's nose to keep us out of trouble. I was confident that the bear would leave us be. I knew though that I would still be making occasional glances over my shoulder.

We had been walking a couple of hours and were in a narrow section of valley about a hundred and fifty yards wide. The western mountains were only thirty yards to our left when a bunch of magpies broke cover like a covey of quail. We froze in our tracks. Straining our senses we tried to identify what had broken up the party. A couple of long minutes later the question was still unanswered. It was probably no more than a fox or other small critter, but we were a little paranoid. We backed to the other side of the valley, crossing a shallow creek, before continuing.

The rest of the day progressed smoothly enabling us to make good time. Preferring an early start over more of the late afternoon heat, camp was made early. We would get rested for the final push to base camp.

We went to bed hungry. I decided to save our remaining provisions for what I hoped would be our final breakfast on the trail. If I had figured wrong and had more than a day ahead of us, we'd have to stop and search for something to eat.

As I drifted off to sleep in our three-sided shelter, a strong wind rose from the north-northwest. On the morrow I sensed we would be walking into a storm.

After breakfast we left straight away without taking time to look for signs of an intruder. The wind and rain came on strong all day. Actually though, they were a welcome relief from the heat and flies.

We fought the storm with few rests realizing that if we didn't reach camp that night we would have to sleep on muddy ground. Around mid-afternoon I recognized, ahead and to our left, the barren-topped mountain that lay south east of our base camp. I knew then that we had only a few hours to go. Soon we would enter the head of the valley that led to the beaver pond.

Camp was found a little before sunset. We ate a hurried freeze-dried meal, Blu's was mixed with his dry food, and turned in to our enclosed tent. As a treat I lit my small backpacker's stove and set it on the dirt floor of the vestibule to take the chill and dampness out of the air. Toasty warm and dry I slept satisfied with where we were and how we had fared. Blu, on the other hand, would not be content till we were back in Anchorage.

Waking, I felt we had won a great victory. The night had gone without an attempt at camp-crashing. After checking the pond for fresh bear sign, the remainder of the day would be spent resting and feasting. Throwing the shotgun over my shoulder and grabbing my fishing pole, Blu and I headed for the pond.

A thorough search produced nothing new. Surprisingly, I noticed that the gaping hole in the dam had been completely repaired. The beaver hut was near total restoration as well. Remarkable.

Time for breakfast. The pool below the dam was teaming with dolly varden. Fifteen minutes of fishing was good for eight twelve-inchers. I cleaned them on the spot and we went back to camp.

Baked to perfection over hot coals they went down fast and easy. We two bloated gluttons crawled back into our, for the most part, fly-free tent and took a nap.

An hour later I awoke in a pool of sweat. The overcast of the last five days had moved off to the southeast and the sun beating on our tent had turned it into an oven. Panting heavily we crawled into fresh air where we found a light, cool breeze blowing that worked well with the bright sun to create a perfect day. So long as we stayed out of the tall grass, where the breeze could not penetrate, we were even free of flies.

Sleeping was not the way to spend such a day. Packing a lunch of Pilot crackers and raisins into the fanny pack and grabbing fishing tackle and shotgun, we made for the lake. As a treat I tucked in a bar of soap. A bath would do nicely.

At the northeast end of the lake, where the fresh water flowed out to meet salt a mile away, we stood on the bank and cast into deep water that produced excellent fishing. The problem was that we were in neck high grass. The sign of bear was strong there. Trails wound like mazes through the tall grass. We wanted only enjoyment that day and were not the least bit interested in surprises. We moved back south where we could fish comfortably.

At our new spot, closer to camp, fishing was best when I waded out twenty yards. There, in hip deep water, I was at the edge of where the bottom dropped off to a substantial depth. Silvers and rainbows were caught in profusion.

After my arms had become tired from battles with fish I decided to take a break and take a bath. I waded back to shore where I laid down pole and shotgun on the gravel beach. Then I waded back out into a foot of water and sat down to wash my cloths. I scrubbed them with the soap bar and then rolled in the shallows to rinse. Back on shore I disrobed laying my cloths out to dry and reentered the lake to wash my birthday suit. You really don't appreciate a good bath if you take one every day.

Bath time over, I went back to shore for shotgun and fishing pole and resumed fishing. I had cast out into the drop-off and had cranked the reel a half dozen times when, wham!— a big one struck. He hit so hard that he nearly wrenched the pole from my hands. Blu, back on the beach, saw me stumble at the strike and he perked up.

"Wooo, Bluper, this is a monster!" I screamed. "I'm gonna need your help! Hurry up I...I...I, can't hold on much longer!" That got him goin'. A couple of spins, a couple of high jumps like a bucking bronco and he dove into the lake with a clumsy splash and came swimming out to me. I fought the fish with desperation. Okay, so I exaggerated a little.

"Help, Bluper, Help! He's gittin' the best a' me!" I staggered and stumbled to the left ten or twelve paces then, holding the pole high over my head, spun around once or twice and then staggered and stumbled back to the right. Then I fell into the lake and rolled around a bit disturbing as much water as I could.

Blu was in a jubilant frenzy. With my face just under the surface, for effect, "Hellllpppp! Blulululuperperper!"

As the fish took the line from side to side Blu swam after it, even diving under trying to grab hold of the fish.

"Reel faster?! No! What the heck are you talkin' about?! I can't reel any faster! He'll snap the line!" I swayed forward, wavered back and fell in again. Rising, "Jerk the line?! What kind of fisherman are you anyway?! Everybody knows you don't jerk the line around like that!" I tottered, pirouetted and toppled backwards.

By then Blu was so overwhelmed with excitement he was choking. Time to get him back to shore for a rest. While reeling in line I walked back to the beach. Then dragged the giant silver out of the lake so Blu could do a victory dance around it. He felt as responsible for the catch as I.

I squatted down and removed the hook. Reaching under to cradle it I picked it up and set it in only inches of water, faced it in the direction of the deep and gave it a little shove. Blu looked up at me startled for an instant then dove headlong after it.

The fish was long gone, but Blu searched in desperation, diving well beneath the surface. I quickly floundered out after him, naked except for the shotgun slung over my shoulder. When he came up for air, I dove on him and we wrestled and splashed up a storm.

The cold waters were invigorating. We had both needed that diversion. Exhausted, we crawled joyfully onto the beach and lay there panting, soaking up the warm sunshine.

We fished and played till dark. We were beat when we dragged ourselves and the twelve-pound silver we had saved to camp. "Nothing smells quite like baking salmon, uh boy?" Blu sat by the hot coals staring at the sizzling fish, saliva pouring from the corners of his mouth. "Just a little while longer now and it'll be fallin' off the bone." I slurped in a little of my own.

Blu and I stayed up late that night talking, singing, playing the harmonica and staring into our campfire. We had an important matter to concern ourselves with. After all, we had come to the island to hunt brown bear. There we were ten days into our hunt and we'd spent only half of it hunting. True, they had been five grueling days on the trail of our camp marauder, but the fact remained that they had also been exciting ones. The chase had been grand, even though sometimes it was difficult to tell who was the chaser and who the chasee.

I argued for spending our last three days hunting. Blu, on the other hand, had a strong argument for fishing and swimming. We compromised. The next day would be spent fishing, playing, resting. The day after we would hunt down the effluent stream to the coast. The day after that we would play by ear. A fair and equitable accord.

There was something different about the next day. The difference was that the fishing was even better than the day before. How was it possible? After that second day of R&R we were ready to see the coast. Toward evening I dried and cleaned our armament and packed a lunch and incidentals in case of emergency. We were ready to leave come morning.

Early morning birds sang in a large tree by our camp. The sun was a long time coming over the mountains as the birds watched us disappear down the beach to the north.

We remained on the easy-going beach as long as it lasted. Finally we climbed the bank and were enveloped by the neck-high grass. Blu had known that that was not another fishing day. He didn't like it. He stayed very close to my side and was ever alert.

As we progressed further and further into the tall grass Blu became more uneasy. When Blu was uneasy there was trouble nearby. Not more than ten minutes from camp and I had already got what I had so foolishly craved, goose bumps.

"You just fidgety about the sign, boy, or's there a beasty out there?" With the possibility of the latter looming I wasn't about to walk deeper into foliage that kept my next step invisible until I took it. We moved to our left, back toward the lake that was only yards away yet unseen.

The thick grass grew all the way to the brink of the bank. I nearly stepped off of it blindly and into the lake five feet below. I sat on the edge and scooted myself over into the cold knee-deep water.

Blu joined me but found that where I could walk he had to swim. Twenty yards of that was enough. He opted for the dangers of walking the bank rather than the constant strain of swimming. His senses would tell him when it was time to hit the drink.

I was thigh deep, about ten feet from shore. Not much field of fire, but I would have time for a shot should a bear charge over the bank.

Where the lake ended at the stream that carried its waters to the ocean, I stepped out onto the shore once again. My legs were numb from cold. The grasses had given way to alder thickets. Walking was more strenuous than through the grass but visibility, although still limited, was improved. I would have liked to continue on in the stream, but it was strewn with deadfalls and large boulders.

As we continued along the stream, we watched large fish slithering their way among the boulders and snags. The fish seemed too large for such a small rivulet. I felt as though I were walking through a fisherman's dream.

Watching the fish I was almost in a trance when I heard splashing ahead of us. It was then that I noticed that Blu had already assumed the warning position. We stopped, trying to ascertain what was causing the commotion. Too far ahead for an accurate explanation, we inched forward taking care not to break any of the tangled mass before us.

As we drew closer the splashing was so loud that I decided it could only be a bear. There was nothing else on the island big enough to make such a racket.

The brush was too thick to see our quarry, let alone have a shot, so we went east up the slope to see if we could find a vantage point above our target.

The racket that the bear was making made it easier for us to move unheard. I was hoping for an ideal situation. We would get within range without spooking the animal. His adrenaline would not be pumping so one well-placed shot might drop him in his tracks. And, if my adrenaline theory didn't work, he might bleed to death in the time it took him to locate us. The best part was that we were less than a mile from camp and could float our take of the carcass nearly all the way back.

When we were high enough, and behind a small ridge, we edged north to a spot that put us directly over our prey and about fifty yards distant. Slowly pushing my head over the lip of the ridge I searched for our quarry. There it was.

To my dismay and joy (there were those two conflicting feelings again) our bear turned out to be two bears. A sow with a cub.

Not being legal to shoot either I simply watched the festivities for a while. When I remembered that we were not in a zoo and at any moment they might decide to stop playing and go home, we moved back into the depression of the ridge continuing north toward the coast. Home might have been right over us. A sow with a cub may have proven to be unstoppable. That cub wasn't any midget either.

Soon the stream burst from cover. It poured through a rock-strewn cove. The waiting ocean welcomed it into its noisy surf. We sat on a ledge overlooking the tranquil picture until the heavenly view was permanently etched into memory. Thank God a brown bear did not appear at that moment for I may have walked up to it and given it a big hug and kiss.

We climbed down the steep slope and walked onto the open beach. The rest of that morning and into late afternoon we hunted up and down the coast. There was much bear sign, but most was old. Not very promising.

As the sun got lower we went back to the stream, backtracking to camp. We were cautious as we neared the area that had sported the sow and cub but they were gone. Their tracks told us that they had gone up the mountains to the west, so passage the rest of the way to camp was safe, at least from them.

Just after sunset we were back in camp and had time to catch another large silver for dinner. Sleepy-eyed from full bellies and an exhilarating day, we retired to our sleep tent.

We had served the purpose of hunting. As far as we were concerned we would spend our last day fishing, wandering and resting. Then we would say good-by to a place that had provided us with some genuine thrills. I felt relaxed and mentally ready to take on the rigors of the big game my job would provide back in Anchorage. In three days I would be pounding the streets in coat and tie, making a living.

What we had thought was to be our last day was a drippy one. But we spent it catching more big ones and wandering around the valley. In the afternoon I shouldered the shotgun and Blu and I went up the mountain behind our camp to see if we could reach the nesting area of the eagles.

The going was difficult. The plant growth was very thick and, unlike our hunt, we didn't have a trail to follow. The mountain was steep, it was hot and muggy and the black flies were out in force. My curiosity to see the home of the eagles was strong however, and we pressed on. Now and again we would get a glimpse of a soaring eagle through the low canopy.

It became evident that we had begun a tad late in the afternoon. The sun was getting low in the west. It would be difficult to get back to camp before dark.

Frustration began to mount. "Darn it, Bluper, why didn't you tell me to leave earlier?" I was afraid that once again I'd be deprived of viewing our national bird up close. A surge of adrenaline facilitated a strong push up the mountain.

We were within twenty minutes of the peak. I would satisfy myself with a quarter of an hour of observation. That would leave us only an hour to get back down the mountain. No way. We would be hiking through bear country in the dark.

Finally we pushed through the jungle coming out at the base of a perpendicular rock formation. It stood from fifteen to twenty feet high. Through binoculars from camp the formation had not looked so formidable. Its face was shear. It had few foot holds and, after traversing its base for fifty yards in either direction, I found no safe passage to the top.

The frustration was nearly unbearable. I started to climb. At one point I was six feet from the ground, hanging on by the tips of my fingers and toes. The top was no more than a couple of feet from my outstretched hands but I could hang on no longer. I slid down the rock hitting hard at its base. I was skinned in a few places and gouged in a few others. No more climbing. We started back down the mountain after again being deprived of sharing the place where eagles cry.

Next morning, Blu and I awoke to a strong wind blowing across the lake from the northwest. The pilot had said that he would pick us up as early as he could so down came camp. Everything was carried to the beach to await the plane.

After securely stacking and covering our gear, we two and the shotgun made a last call. We said good-by to the beaver pond, the stream, and other favorite spots near camp.

The wind had risen steadily since our awakening. Enough even to make walking difficult. But it would have been bad manners not to personally thank all that had made our vacation a memorable one. We walked up the creek then crossed it. We went to the other small feeder stream and walked down it into the wind. The wind blew so strongly in our faces that we were unable to pick up the pungent aroma of rotten fish and decaying filth that persistently lingers on the big bears. It blew so strongly through the grasses and brush that the bear was unable to hear our approach.

My eyes were torn from the waters of the stream they had been glued on. The sound I heard could only have been made by a brontosaurus or a brown bear. Being the experienced backwoodsman that I am, my next move was quite predictable. I froze in utter horror!

Though my shocked mind kept repeating, "Defend! Defend! Defend!" my frozen muscles were unable to bring the shotgun to bare from where it lay casually on my shoulder, my hand gripping the barrel.

Apparently the bear had been lying down munching on long-dead salmon when we had startled him. He rose to the occasion. As he stood staring at us he seemed in the same state of shock that had Blu and me paralyzed. We stood facing each other for what seemed an eternity. Twenty yards separated us.

As suddenly as he had appeared, the bear turned and slammed to the ground in the same fluid motion. He was off like a horse at the starting gate. In only a few steps he was at full speed. A speed which stunned me.

How could an animal that large move so swiftly and effortlessly? Thick brush that stood in his way neither slowed nor altered his course. He went through tangles of alder as though they were spaghetti noodles. His power was awesome.

I thanked him for seeing fit to go south rather than east even though the going would have been much easier. East would have been through light grass and right over me.

At one hundred yards he stopped, stood and, facing us, strained his weak eyes but state-of-the-art nose trying to determine if we were threatening. Threatening, ha! I still hadn't moved. The bear returned to the ground continuing at a more leisurely rate. To my relief he kept to his previous direction of travel.

Control of my body returned to me. Frequent chills ran through my frame as I thought of what might have happened had the beast decided to attack rather than flee. He could have left pieces of us all over the island.

We returned to the beach. The wind had reached gale force. Blu and I retreated to a hole formed by the exposed roots of the large tree near our old base camp. We waited there and were lulled to sleep by the whistling of the wind. We stayed in hiding for many hours. The plane never arrived.

A couple of hours before dark we determined that even if the wind ceased it was too late for the plane. Crawling out of our cozy spot we fought the wind to the beach where we retrieved what we would need for one night.

Back at our old campsite we pitched the tent in a wind that had large trees leaning at precarious angles. Blu was inside long before I hammered in the last stake. As I crawled in out of breath, he greeted me with a wet tongue. I rolled onto my back breathing deeply. It was nice to be where the oxygen wasn't blown from me before I could inhale it. Blu rested his head on my shoulder. We lay that way till dark, once again hypnotized by the wind.

A startling quiet awakened us. The wind had blown away. Crawling out we witnessed another incredible calm. We were assimilating the tranquillity where nothing stirred and not a fly hummed when, from across the lake, a high pitched scream broke the solitude. The sound rang through the sentinel hills, bringing with it visions of some unspeakable horror. It persisted for many seconds concluding with a heartbreakingly mournful drawl as whatever it was succumbed to its fate. With the last echo of the morbid scream all was quiet again.

I wondered if I had actually heard what I thought I had. Looking at Blu told me I had imagined nothing. The sound was similar to the death scream of a rabbit but a rabbit could not have made a sound like that carry clear across the lake. Either some large, rare animal has a most unusual call, or something pitiful died there.

After dinner we sat up most of the night gazing into our fire reliving the events of the past two weeks. I wished our bear would return that night for one last symphony.

Next morning we were barely packed and down to the

beach before our chauffeur arrived. The pilot apologized for being a day late but explained that winds the day before had reached eighty miles an hour with gusts much higher.

Spending that night camped next to the airport in Kodiak, our flight left early the following morning. Landing in Homer I loaded the Jeep and made for Eagle River.

I had driven for about an hour and was in a section of straight road bordered by tall spruce. Ahead I saw three large dogs congregated in the middle of the road. They stayed together as I approached making no effort to move out of my way. I hugged the shoulder of the road as I began to slowly go around them. As I passed, from their huddle crawled a baby. A human baby. A baby with a diaper on.

I slammed on the brakes. Poor Blu slammed into the dash and onto the floor. Rudyard Kipling's *Jungle Book* flashed before me for a moment. No, the dogs could not have applied the diaper.

There had been a road house a mile or so back. Ahead all I saw was trees. Where had the infant come from?! Had someone abandoned it along this desolate road and had the wild dogs adopted her? No, that's what fairy tales are made of. She belonged somewhere. And it had to be somewhere close by. Literally, within crawling distance.

I pulled off the road. Leaving Blu inside, so there would not be trouble with the other dogs, I stepped out. The dogs circled the baby and stood braced ready to protect her. They growled with their teeth bared and stared devilishly at me.

If I had hesitated the dogs would have known that I could be intimidated. I would have lost the opportunity to take the baby without having to kill the dogs. I walked deliberately toward her, never even glancing at the animals. I did my best to give the impression that they didn't concern me. They parted reluctantly.

If I made a wrong move, they would react. Those dogs had

defied an oncoming vehicle. They would not hesitate to defend their charge if I showed any signs that could be interpreted as treachery. But they also seemed to know that the baby did not belong there and that they were not capable of taking her home.

I respected their position and knew that my well-being hinged on making the right moves. I tried getting her into the Jeep. The dogs didn't like that idea. Well, I would have to walk back to the road house. I turned in that direction and took a couple of steps. Nope, the dogs didn't like that either. Even though I kicked at them and scolded authoritatively they would not let me pass.

I faced north. I saw nothing that promised habitation. Great, I might be walking for hours. I struck out north, unopposed.

I had walked only thirty or forty yards when I came on an inconspicuous cut that ran into the woods.

"Is this it?!" The dogs growled and milled in response to my words. "Come on, you guys, lighten up!"

I took a few steps in that direction to test the guardians. They followed...in front of me. I could see where the two-track led down into the woods taking a bend to the left. The dogs escorted me as I proceeded. Following the bend I sighted a dilapidated shack canopied by the large trees.

I was amazed at the distance the baby had crawled. Appalled that she had crawled that far without being missed. I was sure her parents would be real doozies.

My arms were tired as I reached the ramshackle homestead. I had been carrying the babe out away from my body because not only was she dirty with native soil, but also with her own and the dogs' excrement. Her diaper bulged with oozing, squashy, brownish-yellow, doo-doo.

A woman nearly as dirty as the baby was hanging laundry behind the shack. The clothes looked as though she had forgotten to wash them first. No man was in sight.

Not wanting to venture any farther into the virtual pigpen that lay before me I called, "Hey, lady!"

I startled her. She turned abruptly stumbling and dropping a pair of trousers. Fear was in her eyes till she saw that I wasn't a bear or moose or human pointing a gun. Without any mention of the baby I held before me she let out, "Daaaaamn!" and bent to pick up the near rag that had fallen.

"Lady, is this your child?!"

"Yaaa. Why?" She showed no concern.

"Why?! Because I found her crawling out on the highway more than a hundred yards from here!"

"Daaamn," she said again. "That youngun's always a-crawlin' off'n somewhere."

"It took this kid at least an hour to get to…aw, never mind!" I was furious. I wanted to holler and scream up a storm at this woman who thought so little of her offspring. It would have gone unheard. I was of a mind to take the baby to some authorities somewhere. That wasn't my place. I handed the unfortunate child to her mother.

Without even a thank-you from the miserable excuse for motherhood, I turned and left. On my way I bent and, with great respect, petted each dog. "Keep up the good work, guys. Without you that kid's got nobody." If that child was to survive, it was surely God through those dogs that would see to it.

Down the road a piece my anger subsided. Thinking of the ill-fated child and its pitiful mother my eyes filled with water.

"Bluper, how the hell can I be angry at a woman who was probably brought up much the same herself? I can't think to keep her from havin' a kid. But man, I hurt for that baby. It's got nothin'. But them dogs."

Economies, budgets, deficits, foreign policies, social programs, taxes. Easy stuff. When someone comes along that can find answers to problems of the heart, there will be a wise man.

We were home late that night and to work early the next morning. Blu was happy to be back but he needed constant attention. The poor guy was a nervous wreck. The week of our return I took him everywhere with me. While I was in the office or calling on customers he sat out in the Jeep. At home he would tag behind an inch off my heels even when I went to the bathroom. When I sat he would lay at my feet, jumping at the slightest sound.

On our third day back I was returning to the Jeep from the office. Blu had fallen asleep on the passenger seat. When I popped the door open he jumped in fright. His front paws slipped off of the seat sending his snout smashing into the windshield. The windshield cracked and it gave Blu a bloody nose and mouth.

The poor guy definitely had a bad case of battle rattle. But with tender care he was back to his old easy-going self in a few weeks. I must admit, I have always slept a lot lighter since Kodiak.

19. Alcan in January

    Later that winter I flew to Nebraska for Jimmy Tebs's retirement party. There, my former boss offered me my old job back. It was not an easy decision, but having an opportunity to drive down the AlCan highway in mid-winter with a job waiting at the other end was too tempting a proposition. I could work a year or two down below and then go back to Alaska.

    Returned to Alaska after Jim's party I gave notice and, two weeks later, January 22, we started down. I left early in the morning, heading north to Nebraska.

    The morning was calm, overcast, dark and cold. My gas tank was full and so were two five-gallon cans. I had enough raisins and peanuts to last a lifetime.

Behind the front seats was everything we owned, including our new kitten, Painter. Blu had his usual spot on the passenger seat and on the floor in front of him was Painter's litter box. On the back over the spare tire hung chains for all four wheels in case conditions warranted their use and on top of them were strapped snow shoes in case the chains proved inadequate.

At Palmer the road turned northeasterly. Two hours out of Palmer there was still no hint of sun. We found ourselves gradually being engulfed in an ice fog. In fifteen minutes we were forced to stop, unable to see even well enough to pull off the road.

A white-out is a beautiful yet frightening phenomenon. Sitting in the Jeep I could not see the hood. I appreciated the feelings of a genie in his lamp. There was nothing to see that wasn't inside the Jeep. I felt an urgency to pull off of the road even though there was no way to determine where the edge of the road was. But if I couldn't see to drive, neither could anybody else.

Genuinely fascinated by the natural quirk I opened the door and stepped out into a calm, pure void. When my feet touched ground I began to loose equilibrium. Light from the rising sun reflected off of each and every minute ice crystal. The ambient light did not allow for shadows. There was not a hint of three dimensions.

The only way to keep my feet was to retain a constant hold on the door handle. With my arm outstretched the side of the vehicle was merely a vague, questionable form, only slightly darker than the stark white fantasy in which I stood. I became nauseous and closed my eyes.

I was certain that if I let go I would loose my balance, stumble and fall. I'd not know which way to get back up. Fighting against the nearly overpowering dizziness I stepped back into the Jeep laying my head on the steering wheel.

In half an hour the hazy yellow circle of the sun became the first distinguishable object. It signaled the death of the fog. Soon the landscape returned from whence it had disappeared. We resumed our journey south, going northeast.

The fog had not completely burnt away. Its remnants lay close to the ground like a thick white carpet. Moose and caribou, which were plentiful along the way, looked as though they stood to their knees in a cloud.

The roads had been heavily snow-packed all morning but there had been little ice. We traveled steadily though slowly. Late in the afternoon we reached the United States border checkpoint. There I was informed that the road ahead was in substantially worse condition. Snow had just stopped falling after nearly a full day of heavy accumulation. Plows had not yet opened the highway for normal traffic.

After their customary check of our belongings and a cordial, "Good-by and drive carefully," we were on our way again. I was unsure as to whether we would be able to continue or have to pitch camp.

Crossing into the Yukon Territory the path produced deeper and deeper drifts of freshly fallen snow. One vehicle had gone before us. It had made a welcome double track. Its wheel base was wider than ours but at least one side or the other could get traction when ascending hills. The vehicle had also removed the tops of two and three foot drifts that may have otherwise broken our momentum.

I would gain as much speed as possible before an ascent and fishtail to the top. Then we would merrily slide down the other side staying in the tracks as best we could. It had grown dark again. Daylight only lasted a few hours. The downhill slides reminded me fondly of late night sledding and tobogganing in Palos Park, Illinois, when I was a boy. For old times' sake I would holler and scream while we slid to the bottom. As alone as we were, I could do it if I wanted.

We continued that way for hours, deep into the Yukon. We had been driving for sixteen hours before I thought that I should be tired. The treacherous highway had given no time to think of sleep. Besides, at any moment, more blizzards could halt our progress, possibly for days. I decided to travel until sleep was necessary not customary. We forged ahead through towns with the names of Koidern, Aishihik, and Kluane. The names alone stirred my spirit.

Since leaving Tok Junction, more than three hundred miles back, we had passed no one and no one had passed us. The lane leading back to Alaska had only produced four large trucks. As they went by, the clouds of snow that they sucked up would obliterate our vision forcing us to stop and wait while it settled. Other than those trucks, whose headlights would speed toward us like the eyes of hungry trolls, we were alone.

A moonless and starless night, the only light was our own headlamps stretching before us like feelers testing the emptiness. As they revealed obstacles we would overcome them, one by one.

A little over half way between Haines Junction and Whitehorse the light from the lamps illuminated two large forms that ran left to right across the highway. At first glance I would have sworn they were elk. But elk didn't live in the Yukon. I pumped the brakes, slowly coming to a halt. Then I maneuvered the Jeep so that it sat sideways on the road. My high beams again caught sight of the antlered creatures.

They stood thirty-five yards out on the open snow staring back at us. Had I not seen them for myself I would never have believed that deer could grow so large. The bucks stood in a row, broadside. Both had racks measuring over thirty inches from tip to tip and their bodies were enormous.

We watched as they turned and continued on their way into the vastness of the Yukon. I wished I were a flea on their backs so I could see more of the wild, untouched wilderness that was their home.

One-inch diameter snow flakes began to fall lightly as we resumed our easterly course. Though Blu and Painter had long since nodded off to sleep, I drove through the deserted outskirts of Whitehorse and continued on feeling reasonably alert.

Painter had declared Blu his big brother and Blu had willingly adopted him. Painter followed Blu everywhere, ate out of a bowl right next to his and even slept with him as he did then, curled up against the back of Blu's neck.

Without those two to talk to all that was left for me was to concentrate on the road. It was like driving through a tunnel. The headlights made visible enough real estate to squeeze the Jeep through. Presently I began to feel the effects of nineteen hours behind the wheel.

At a gas stop outside Whitehorse the thermometer on the side of the station had read twenty-five below. The heater in the Jeep blasted full bore, bringing the inside temperature up to twenty above. I was dressed in woolen long underwear, jeans, wool shirt, down vest, insulated coveralls, heavy coat with hood, wool watch cap, down gloves, and two pairs of wool socks inside wool felt lined rubber boots. I was still shivering. I knew my body was tiring. It wouldn't be long before I would have to stop.

A short distance from Whitehorse the road made a near ninety degree turn right. As I neared the turn the lights of the Jeep left the road creeping along the snow straight ahead. A half dozen pairs of eyes flashed like neon from the edge of the woods. I stopped, staring at the elusive kings and queens of the wilderness. There stood the creatures that to me are the epitome of everything that is free, wild and uncorrupted. Wolves.

I watched as they watched, each of us waiting for the other

to make a move. On many still nights while camping in Alaska I had heard the mournful cry of those magnificent animals but that had been my first visual contact.

Finally the lead wolf began to move. The others followed trotting in the direction they had been going when my lights had first interrupted them. When they were beyond the range of the beams I stared into the empty blackness for a time and then resumed my journey. My shivers had left me, replaced by an inner warmth. Sighting the wolf pack had made me good for another few hours.

I drove on past Johnson's Crossing toward Teslin. We crossed the border into British Columbia but the road swung north again crossing back into Yukon. Before we swung south again leaving the Yukon for good I decided to make camp.

Pulling off of the highway we stepped out into a night, windy and cold. My breath froze in my beard. Blu relieved himself and Painter stretched but neither dallied too long. They jumped back in while I pulled out tent and other necessary paraphernalia. The wind grew stronger with every passing moment.

Blu and Painter lay snug on top of the gear and two wool blankets in the back of the Jeep. Over the roll bar I had draped another blanket to trap more of their body heat.

Pitching the tent was impossible. Stakes bent, unable to pierce the frozen ground. Following twenty-two hours of driving, the cold and exertion was quickly tiring me. Rolling the tent and stuffing it back into the duffel bag, I pulled out the nine by twelve canvas tarp we had used on our trip up the highway. It would at least break the wind.

I laid it out flat on top of the snow. While standing on the windward side I unzipped my sleeping bag and laid it on top of the tarp. I crawled in without even removing my boots. In my gloved hands was my Little Ben alarm clock. It was set to ring in one hour. I would check to see if I was freezing to death.

After zipping myself in I sat up and flipped one corner of the tarp over the foot end of the bag. Then, lying down, I grabbed the adjacent corner and started to roll. I rolled slowly, deliberately leaving loose air pockets in my canvas cocoon. As I flapped the top corner of the tarp over my head and squirmed as deeply into the bag as I could, the snow began to fall heavily blowing hard into the side of the tarp tube.

The next thing I remember was the Little Ben ringing and gyrating under my left armpit. I awoke long enough to wiggle my toes and fingers and squirm liberally to be assured that all parts contained warm blood. I reset the clock for another hour and drifted off to sleep.

The same procedure was repeated for the next few hours until I was more cold than tired. Though I shivered slightly, I remained in the primitive but adequate shelter dreading emerging into the rush of the cold wind and snow. Finally I summoned enough courage to face the elements and told my muscles to roll out.

Something was wrong. Nothing budged. I flexed and twitched all of my muscles. They all worked. What was the problem? Pulling my fingers from the gloves I unzipped the sleeping bag and reached out to the inside of the tarp tube. It was frozen.

My body heat had condensed on the canvas and had become ice. Good thing I had rolled the tarp loosely. Even then, it was difficult inching my way out of the bag and tude. Making matters worse was arising under a pile of snow that had drifted over me and my house. I imagine that the snow had contributed to keeping me warm while I slept.

The wind was blowing fiercely as I dug out my tarp and sleeping bag. How was I to get a seven-foot tube into my Jeep? That could wait. I needed to get warm.

Climbing into the Jeep I pulled the key from my coat with shaking hands and plunged it into the ignition. I wasn't optimistic. I tried a half dozen times but the engine would not turn over. Not wanting to murder the battery I ceased the futile attempts and put my iced brain to work on plan B.

I needed a heat source…fire. I was not enthusiastic about hunting wood in a blizzard under deep snow in fifty to sixty below wind-chill temperatures. Not to mention it was dark and I was unfamiliar with the territory.

The answer struck me. It was so rudimentary that I would have kicked myself in the backside if I could have bent my heavily clothed leg around that far. My backpacking stove. It certainly wasn't much, but in the confines of the Jeep it would do nicely.

I dug into the duffel bag pulling out the stove and spare flask of fuel. I went through the tedious process of getting it lit and then set it between the seats of the Jeep. I watched as the tiny blue flame struggled against the cold. I coveted its warmth.

My hands were cupped wide apart so that my face could also be bathed in heat. Not more than two feet separated my nose from the rejuvenating flame. Within minutes the interior of the Jeep was livable. It was time to get back to the business of starting the Jeep, getting packed and getting gone before the storm trapped us indefinitely.

I stepped back into the snow and wind. Blu and Painter jumped out at my command, probably more to the call of nature than to the call of Tedd. I began stuffing the frozen canvas tube through the passenger door. It was no easy task, but I was able to push, fold and buckle it into the back. We then reentered to get warm.

Soon I was ready for another go outside. This time the goal was to warm the radiator and engine. The tarp had thawed. I removed it and from the passenger side, which was also the windward side, I held one end and threw the rest to the wind that blew it over the hood. I lowered my end to the ground and packed it down with snow. I went around to the driver's side and packed that end of the tarp down in the same manner creating a makeshift canvas garage.

From between the spare tire and tailgate I untied my shovel and used it to pile more snow on the canvas. Then I sealed all around the undercarriage of the vehicle, leaving only a small space open in the middle of the front bumper. It was my camp stove's turn. I filled its small tank to capacity and pushed it deep into the opening I had left placing it under the engine. I sealed behind it with more snow.

Back in the driver's seat I could faintly hear the hiss of the stove through the fire-wall. When it had burned itself out I would give ignition another try. While I waited I munched on peanuts and raisins. I fed the boys too. I wished it was daylight so I could have explored the scenery with my eyes. No matter, the blowing snow would have obscured everything anyway.

Ten minutes of waiting and I was getting cold. I tried to keep warm by getting out and draping and hooking the rear tires with their snow chains. I knew they would be necessary...if the engine cooperated.

The rear chains in place I retreated to the confines of the Jeep. The hissing had ceased. Time to see if we were going to continue or stay there a few days.

I turned the key and received only a whining response. I tried again and got the same. The third time the whine was accompanied by a single cough. The fourth time only the whine. On the fifth attempt it coughed once and then twice more in rapid succession. Turn of the key number six produced a rapid round of coughs and a second or two of the sound made by an awakening engine. On the seventh turn she started, but after a few moments she gagged and quit. It was the eighth jolt that revived her.

I left the choke open for a full five minutes before disengaging it. While it purred smoothly I got out to retrieve my tarp and stove. I then shoveled away enough snow to attach the front chains. Climbing back in I discovered that the heat gauge was at a proper reading. Rolling the Jeep forward slightly, I went back out to tighten the chains and attach the rubber tension bands. That did it. We were once again on our way to the lower forty-eight.

Soon light began to blend into the southern sky. There was no sun though, nor would there be all day. The snow continued to fall heavily. Only two trucks passed that day heading to Alaska. We pushed on through deep powdery snow that parted easily when prodded by the nose of our Jeep.

The storm intensified. I was forced to reduce our speed to twenty-five miles an hour. It would be a long way to Nebraska at that rate. The sky remained dark and my eyes strained to make out the snow-swept highway. I didn't see the bull moose until he was in front of us.

Slamming on the brakes to avoid a collision we slid sideways till the deep snow brought us to a halt. He had emerged from the barren wastes on our left. The moose had been so close that even in those violent winds he must have heard the engine as he passed along our side dwarfing us. Never once did he give us so much as a glance. I guess he figured that if we caused any trouble he'd just pound us into the snow.

His majesty the bull trotted away with his head down. Antlers were poised, daring even the all-powerful wind to try and keep him from his appointed rendezvous somewhere out on the element battered tundra. The bull disappeared into the fierce wall of white on the side of the road opposite from where he had materialized.

We traveled at the same slow speed for the next two hundred and fifty miles. I was exhausted from an eighteen hour day when we pulled into a truck stop at Ft. Nelson. The engine temperature gauge was dangerously high. I had to see to it before resting.

"You don't need a mechanic," responded the station attendant as he spit a used up wad of chewing tobacco into his hand. "Your problem's simple. Happens all the time. Your radiator's froze." He threw the wad into the snow.

"How can that be? I've never turned the engine off, accept to get gas, since I warmed it up this morning."

The attendant stuffed his lip with a cigarette and lit it. "Hey guy, you've been drivin' into a thirty to fifty mile an hour wind. It's thirty below out there without it. There ain't no antifreeze made that can whoop that. Here, bust up this box and stuff the cardboard between the grill and the radiator." He handed me an empty carton that had contained a case of oil. "Go get yourself a burger and a cup of coffee. We'll just leave this in here runnin' till it thaws out."

I thanked him as I tore at the box. As directed I squeezed the pieces into place.

The burger and coffee sounded like one heck of a good idea. I left the boys in the Jeep sleeping and went in to feed. For the first time in two days I was able to take off my hat, gloves, coat, and vest.

A half an hour in the cozy cafe and my eyelids nearly slammed shut. Back at the garage I found the Jeep pulled outside, still running. The temperature gauge registered normally. That night I curled up with the boys in the Jeep right there at the truck stop.

I awakened stiffly five hours later. It was daylight and the truck stop was bustling. The skies were partly cloudy and there was little wind. I awoke the boys and we ate breakfast. We were off again.

We made excellent time that morning averaging forty-five miles an hour. I was saying good-by to mile after mile when I made a regular check of my gauges. The infernal temperature gauge was again in the dangerously hot range. I was feeling warm myself and wondered if I were coming down with something. Just before cresting a steep hill I pulled over at a wide spot to see if I could find the problem.

Stepping from the Jeep I was stunned. The temperature must have been near thirty above. I and my engine were cooking under our sub-zero clothing. Off came most of my outer garments and out came the cardboard. In less than two hundred miles the temperature had risen sixty degrees. We took a break.

The boys barreled out and began their exploration of the scenic pull-off. Sitting on the bumper I poured myself a cup of coffee from the thermos that I had filled at the Ft. Nelson truck stop. The pause was a welcome one. Blu and Painter had rarely been out of the Jeep for three days. They stretched, ran and rolled on the side of the road.

We languished for a quarter of an hour. I knew there would be many more stops that day. I had finished nearly the whole thermos of coffee.

Later we reached Dawson Creek where paved highway began. After fifteen hundred miles of unrestricted travel there was suddenly a strange light before us that stepped up from green to yellow to red. Suddenly I remembered what one of those was and came to a sliding halt. We were back in civilization.

The town of Hythe disappeared behind us as did Grand Prairie. But that was the best I could do. We pulled over to sleep before reaching the junction of Highway 34 with 43. It was not a cold night. I lay under the tarp and the boys, as usual, slept on wool in the Jeep.

We awakened early to a cold, humid wind, under a familiar overcast sky. After a quick pot of coffee we hit the road expecting more snow, or worse, at any moment.

A few miles after turning south onto Highway 43 we got the worse. Freezing rain began coating the road with ice. It poured relentlessly. It became cold; too cold, I thought, to be raining. Every few miles I needed to stop to scrape the windshield of a half inch thick coating of ice.

The defroster was of little help. After a scraping the windshield would gradually start re-icing. First a half circle of ice would form quickly outside the perimeter of the wipers. Slowly the radius would reduce under the wipers until all that was left open was a small hole right at the defroster port just above the dash. I would drive hunched over, peering through the steering wheel and the small hole until playing the part of a voyeur became uncomfortable. I would pull over again to scrape, or more accurately, to hack.

By 7:00 A.M. other vehicles had joined us inching along the glare ice. In another half an hour the ditches were becoming littered with victims. I had stopped to reattach the snow chains but the only advantage they gave us was that when we slid into the ditch, we were able to drive out again. On the ice of the road, however, we floundered like everyone else. Tow trucks were soon seen in abundance.

A few miles past Whitecourt the rains ceased. The roads were clear nearly all the way to Edmonton. Though an icy windshield was no longer a problem, large flakes of snow falling in abundance replaced the ice as visibility limiters. Snow was with us to Calgary where we spent the night.

The next day we crossed into the United States at the border station on the outskirts of Coutts. We avoided the mountain roads on the eastern slope of the Continental Divide.

Snow began to fall again at Oilmont, Montana. Conditions slowed us. At mile marker seven on Highway 87 near Roundup the snowfall had reached blizzard proportions. The light from our headlamps reflected off of each and every snowflake hypnotizing me. It was almost a better idea to drive in the dark rather than the glare.

The highway was made narrow by snow heaped onto the shoulders by the plows. I looked for somewhere to pull off but found none. My eyes and hands were weary. I held the steering wheel so tightly that I feared my fingers would remain curled for the rest of my life.

Around a bend in the road ahead, an eighteen-wheeler came barreling at me holding a course smack in the middle of the road. I pulled over as far as I could but kept driving. I was certain that the truck would soon pull to its side.

The distance between us shortened and still the driver made no attempt to ease his rig over. It couldn't be. No one on earth was so inconsiderate that they would run a fellow human being off of the road in a blizzard, in the middle of nowhere, in sub-zero temperatures. No, I was sure that he would pull over to let us by. I had faith in humanity.

Finally the distance was so small that I knew he could not maneuver a rig of that size, at that speed, on that snow-covered highway to go around us without sliding and jackknifing. So went my faith in humanity.

I tried to finesse the Jeep only slightly into the snowbank so that after the rude malcontent went by I would still have enough control to pull back onto the highway.

Contact with the snowbank was made. The right side of the Jeep raised slightly but maintained a straight course as the truck whizzed by only inches from our sideview mirror. It was past us in less time than it would have taken to take a breath, had I been breathing.

Attempting to get back on the road, I turned the steering wheel only a little not wanting to create too much trauma. With no warning the right front tire struck something under the snow creating enough resistance to start the left side sliding out in front. I lost it.

Tension and fear was replaced by relief when I knew that our lives were in the hands of Someone who was much more capable than myself of a happy landing. All I could do was hold on.

The left rear came around one hundred and eighty degrees slamming into the snowbank and plowing through it. We sailed upright out into the ditch spinning another two hundred sixty degrees before hitting bottom. On impact, when our left wheels came to an immediate halt in the deep snow, the unspent energy of our right wheels had to go somewhere. They did…straight up into the air, laying us on the driver's side.

If you will think back to my earlier description of how the Jeep was packed, you will remember that Painter's litter box was on the floor in front on the passenger's side. With this knowledge, it will not be hard for you to imagine where the litter box wound up.

At least we had stopped. Before the encounter with the truck Blu and Painter had been curled up on the passenger seat asleep. The spinning had awakened them. They had sat up watching in disbelief.

When we had come to our abrupt halt lying on our left side, the two of them and the ripe litter box had poured over onto me. Blu's legs moved a mile a minute in panic as he tried to regain an upright position. Painter, not being so exuberant but nevertheless in just as much distress, was dug in and holding to the right side of my face. The hood I wore eased the pain somewhat.

Blu finally relaxed so I could stop protecting myself from his left jabs and right hooks. Painter was then pried from my head. I took stock of our predicament. First I tested my limbs to see that none were broken. Then I concentrated on the rest of me to see if I could detect any unusual aches or pains. Other than a slight ache in my left upper arm where it had come in hard contact with the bar that supports the vinyl door, and a tingling on the right side of my face where Painter's claws had penetrated my hood, all was well.

The impact had been gentle considering our flight pattern. I concluded that we must have been in very deep snow. After having hit down on our left side we had bounced up slightly so that we had come to rest in a position similar to that of a stunt driver doing a "wheely" only we weren't moving.

Pushing Blu and Painter down between the seats I unzipped the Plexiglas window on my side. We were at a precarious angle but I determined that that was the best way for us to make our escape. Our side was buried deeply in snow and could tip no further. The right side tottered and seemed ready to fall with just the slightest shove.

The boys needed no coaxing. They were anxious to exchange the close quarters of the inside of the Jeep for the freedom of the out-of-doors. They fought their way over me vying to be first out.

I crawled out after them. Untying the shovel from behind the spare, I shoveled snow from the insides of the left front and left rear tires. Then, moving to the driver's side, I lifted and pushed until the Jeep came crashing down into the deep powdery snow.

Now that our vehicle was right side up I inspected under the hood. The battery had jumped out of its carrier and was laying between the wheel well and the engine and its ground wire had been torn free, but all else was in order. The damage was easily repaired and after a few tries I was able to restart the engine. I let the engine run with the heater on so that I would have a warm sanctuary to retreat to as I worked to extricate us.

The winch was on the front of the Jeep and we faced away from the road. A direct pull was not possible. We were high centered in many feet of snow. Digging out was futile.

That truck driver, whomever he might have been, would not have wanted to hear the many unpleasant things that I wished upon him. My feelings snowballed (no pun intended) until I believed that all truck drivers were just as rude and uncaring.

I paced off the distance to the closest pole on the other side of the highway. Forty-five yards, give or take a yard or two. My one hundred fifty foot winch cable would reach. That was encouraging, but how was I to get it there?

The snow would have produced too much resistance to stretch the cable around the side of the Jeep. That maneuver would have tipped us over. The only other alternative was something I had never tried. I would try tunneling under the Jeep from front to back and run the cable under. That might pull us out backwards. Then again it might just pull the nose deeper into the snow. Not the greatest of solutions, but it was all we had. If it didn't work, maybe the attempt would at least unveil another alternative.

Another problem was that I would have to stretch the cable across the highway. In all the time we had just spent in the ditch, nary a vehicle had gone by. I knew, though, that as soon as I laid that cable across the road I'd witness a parade.

I would have to keep the cable low on the post and stretched tight. Hopefully then vehicles could pass over it without entanglement. I began tunneling.

Blu and Painter had reentered the Jeep to keep warm and on many occasions, while constructing our escape tunnel, I joined them in order to thaw out. Two and a half hours after our misfortune had begun, the tunnel was completed, the cable passed through, and I was marching it up to the highway. A bulging inventory of curses and oaths rolling from my lips and directed at truck drivers, performed admirably at keeping me warm.

"If that no good ___-__-_____ would have stopped I'da made 'im choke on his own eyeballs. I'da stomped that dirty _____ _____ so deep in the snow that the _____-_____ wouldn'ta been found till spring. Truck driven ____ ___ __

_____ have no right bein' on roads with decent people. If I ever see another one of those _____ _____ _____ I'm gonna pull his tongue out and button it to his collar just before I rip off both his arms and feed 'em to polecats. Then I'm gonna watch while his...." Over the sound of my hollering and the raging wind the roar of a truck rang in my ears.

I stopped, thigh deep in snow with the winch cable over my shoulder. With the smile of a maniac spreading across my face and my eyes widening in a hungry glare I slowly raised my head to see a semi-trailer truck coming to a stop on the highway before me.

It was a dream come true. Before I winched myself out I would get to feast on a truck driver! All that would be found of him would be a pool of blood, entrails and bones. No, the entrails I'd save for later and the bones I'd hang on my wall as a trophy.

I dropped the cable and began my deliberate stalk to the truck as the driver climbed down from his cab. I was prepared to say every insulting thing I could muster to provoke him into a fight. Then he would belong to me!

When I was within speaking distance my mouth opened to begin my eloquent oration but I was interrupted by, "Boy, you're in pretty good."

"Yah, well, I got run off the road by a...."

"Well, we better see what we can do to get you out."

"Right, I was gonna do that when you..."

"Looks like you worked pretty hard gettin' that cable through. By golly I think it might'a worked too."

"I know, but first I'm gonna...."

"No need sweatin' anymore over it though. Let's just hitch you up. I'll pull you out'a there in a jiffy."

I was speechless, frustrated! How could I say what I wanted to say. The man wouldn't shut up! And he didn't say anything that wasn't nice!

While I stood there he took charge. With almost no help from me he rewrapped the winch cable and joined us with his chain. All the while he praised me for my ingenuity and reassured me that my theory would have worked. I wanted to ask him to leave before I lost my dislike for truck drivers but I couldn't get a word in edgewise! I felt cheated! Things were moving too fast!

He had the Jeep hitched to the back of his truck, pulled onto the road, unhitched and said good-by. He was on his way before I could even explain what had happened. And I didn't even get to bite off one ear! But then I didn't feel like doing that anymore. After many years I had finally come to realize how those townsfolk felt at the end of all those *Lone Ranger* TV shows. "Who was that masked man?!"

In a few hours we found ourselves in Crow Agency, Montana. I was tired. We spent the rest of that night there.

It was a short drive the next morning to the Montana–Wyoming border. By late in the afternoon we had traversed Wyoming and entered Colorado. That evening was spent in Colorado Springs.

An early start the next day got the three of us to Nebraska and Blu's most favorite spot in the whole world, Helen and Jimmy's. Blu hadn't laid eyes on their place for going on two years but the instant we pulled into their drive, he wouldn't settle down till I let him out. He ran straight to the back door and planted himself.

20. Canoeing the Big Blue

Jimmy and Helen had offered to let me stay in their second home. It stood on the Big Blue River. Jimmy called it "the old place." His parents had lived there and run a power plant that was generated by the dam they had built there.

The dam was no longer viable. It had been blasted open to let the river run free. But the ruins of it still stood as did the old buildings and the quaint cottage that his parents had abided in.

My plans were to stay long enough to find a place in the country. I soon discovered, though, that attitudes had changed in the short time I had been gone. No longer were old vacant farm houses looked upon as low rent commodities that no one but bums like me wanted. They had become "the thing". Living in the country and fixing up an old farm house was the new fad. Rents had risen beyond that which I could pay and still have money left over with which to play.

While Blu and I got back into the swing of things traveling our assigned river basins, and Blu catching up on his goal to water off of every bridge in Nebraska, Painter got accustomed to the territory around the cottage. All the while I kept my eyes open for a suitable country home.

It was good being with old friends and frequenting old haunts. Blu thrived on it. But the excitement had left our lives since we had left Alaska. Nebraska overflowed with easily accessible fishing and hunting areas but it was devoid of wilderness.

It did, however, possess a feature that I thought just might fill my need for excitement. That feature also made it possible to travel more than a quarter of a mile without encountering a fence. Nebraska had almost as many rivers flowing through it as it had roads. And they were navigable.

River banks were typically the last places to succumb to the plow and bulldozer. We would be able to paddle within throwing distance of a city and not even know it was there.

I located a second hand canoe and bought it. It had obviously been through the battles of Verdon, Iwo Jima, Pork Chop Hill and the Tet Offensive. I'm hesitant in mentioning its role in the Spanish/American War since its action in that conflict was minimal. Nevertheless, it only had one leak that required bailing so it was adequate.

There were still some weeks remaining before ice would be off the Big Blue. Unseasonably warm weather had however caused some rapid snow melt. The water on top of the ice in the river had kept the old mill pond on "the old place" flooded. That gave me an opportunity to bone up on my paddling skills. It also eased the frustration of having a boat and not being able to use it. At night after I'd get home from work, I would paddle around the pond under a bright moon listening to the coons wail.

As nature would have it, by the weekend the river had thawed drastically leaving a clear channel out of the pond and into the river. As far downstream as I could see the river contained only floating ice. Hot dog! With Blu sitting in the bow I slowly edged into the current.

It was great. All that was required of us was to keep ahead of the ice floating down behind us, and to dodge the flows we encountered in front of us. Once in a while I'd use the paddle to push off of bank ice. It was easy.

I had decided that we would remain a guest of the current until we had bypassed the western edge of town and a little of the country to the south of it. We would put out at the bridge a mile below town and walk back for the Jeep. At our rate of speed I estimated about three quarters of an hour. Plenty of time for our first taste of Nebraska river boating.

Rounding a bend on a bridge approach we beheld a sight that dashed our hopes of reaching the destination. The ice spanned the full width of the Blue. What was worse was that all the floating ice was pushing up and over or down and under the immovable barricade. To the river we were just another piece of ice. The pile on top and the jagged edges jutting out from below looked formidable.

In a few moments the wall of ice would be reckoning with us. I didn't much like that idea. Especially if it reckoned we go under. I scanned the banks right and left for a place to put in.

That stretch of the river flaunted eight to fifteen foot banks that rose perpendicular to the water. We had nowhere to go and not much time to get there. I searched for a solution up until the instant of impact.

Traveling in the neighborhood of two or three miles an hour, the collision was not violent. But on a river, unlike a road, the sudden stop is in no way the end of the complication. It's only the beginning. Millions of gallons of water were intent on getting to the ocean. Mindlessly they pushed at us ignoring my urgent plea.

Due to our buoyancy, the waters were resolute in pushing us up onto the stationary ice, the far more preferable alternative. But in pushing up the starboard, downstream side, the port sank. We were taking on water, in danger of capsizing.

If we were forcibly beached on the ice, rather than sunk, we would be stranded. The ice seemed strong enough to support the distributed weight of the canoe, but I doubted it was sturdy enough to support me if I were to make an effort to reach the bank across it.

I hastily stepped over the thwart in front of me to the middle of the canoe and leaned far over the starboard side. At the same time I dug into the ice with my fingers inching us toward the left bank. What I would do when I got there didn't matter.

The bank I headed for was the inside curve where the current was weakest. Water continued splashing over the port side. Soon the witless river would give up the notion of lifting us onto the ice and opt for pushing us under instead.

I was concerned for our welfare. Blu, on the other hand, still seemed to be enjoying the ride. "Bluper, I don't believe you realize the gravity of our situation. You keep leaning to the port like that and we're gonna die!"

He looked at me with an unconcerned glance and then, as if to say, "What do ya mean we?" he hopped out onto the ice and pranced to and up the bank. Wonderful! In my time of need he decided that it was every man for himself.

Pulling desperately for solid earth I heard from above, "Yo!"

I closed my eyes tightly thinking it was the Lord calling to me from Heaven. But then I thought, no, He would have used a better choice of words. Looking up I beheld a welcome sight.

On the bridge above stood two buddies I had gone to school with and their wives. "Hi, guys. Could I ask you to come over to the bank so I can throw you a line?"

The boys hustled off the bridge to a spot parallel with my line of travel and I heaved them the bow line. As they pulled one asked, "You crazy? What are you doin' on the river this early?"

In reply I merely said, "You just answered your own question."

The next few days were limited to paddling the mill pond.

That soon became boring again, but we were the recipients of a stroke of luck. Heavy rains and continued unseasonably warm temperatures brought the Big Blue out of its banks. The high water broke up and moved out most of the rest of the ice. What was normally a slow moving waterway was a turbulent, frothing torrent. Perfect!

With Blu in front of the middle thwart I launched our craft into the calm but rapidly rising mill pond. I paddled toward the rushing river. When the nose of the boat poked out to test the current, the force of the river grabbed hold and jerked us out of the safe waters of the pond. The ride was on.

Blu had become accustomed to a gentle ride. He enjoyed that. He would sit on the bottom with his paws on the front seat watching objects floating by or gazing at the landscape. That's the posture he was in when the current slammed into our starboard nearly sending both of us into the drink. He had quickly assumed his usual position when four-wheeling—spread-eagled on the bottom of the boat seeking maximum stability and wondering what had been so wrong with staying in the mill pond.

The waters were rocking us violently from side to side and splashing up at all angles. This was my first encounter with anything but a snails' paced stream. The differences in required paddling techniques became immediately apparent.

No time for laying the paddle across the gunwales and restfully drifting past the stolid banks. No occasion to paddle aimlessly from bank to bank dipping the paddle lazily ten times a minute. The flood waters also carried large trees and chunks of ice that needed avoiding.

"Bluper, I guess I've done it to you again. Sorry, boy," was all I could say for myself.

Predictably, there was no answer, but I knew what he was thinking. I had gone and turned another enjoyable form of recreation into a frightening, nerve-racking chore. He was disgusted, appalled.

At any rate it was too late to wish that we had stayed home. The paddle was in the water sixty or more times a minute. There were times I wished I could have stroked it two or three times faster.

The Big Blue winds almost continually. Many of its bends are ninety degrees, some even greater. For a short stretch adjacent to the city park it straightens and flows under that bridge mentioned in our earlier episode. Rounding the bend that brought the bridge into view I took a deep breath, in shock. The structure that usually spans the river at a height of twelve feet seemed only inches above the seething water.

Up until then I had been successful in avoiding the banks and floating debris. How was I to avoid an obstacle that stretched across the entire width of the river? Glances at the banks verified that there was nowhere to beach and there was no way around. Heck, it was too late to do either anyway!

I pulled in the paddle and lay backwards against the seat. Blu was already flat on the bottom…had it been possible he would have been lower. We passed under. The steel girders were only inches from my nose.

Regaining my kneeling position, the canoe had already turned broadside to the current. It floated parallel to a log that had attached itself to us. One of its branches had bobbed and twisted its way over the port gunwale, under the center thwart, and back up again. I had seen the tree rolling ahead of us just before I had had to duck the bridge. I'd disregarded it, thinking it easily avoidable.

Its normal rolling had been somewhat abated by its entanglement with our craft but its desire to continue rolling was evident from the way it precariously lifted our port side. It threatened to swamp us. Too much more water sloshing over the side, accompanied by our persistent leak, would precipitate a frantic swim in the frigid, churning, brown waters.

Leaning as far toward the log as I dared, keeping weight off the starboard side, I held onto the gunwales for support and stepped over the thwart in front of me. Getting to the spot where the thwart and branch were having their wrestling match I thought a double team against the branch appropriate.

Trying to push the branch back under the thwart proved futile. The whole weight of the tree trunk trying to roll over held the branch in place. Somehow I had to break the branch, which was four inches in diameter, or tear the thwart loose from the gunwale which was held in place by two rivets. Before I could decide how to do either, the roots of the tree caught onto a snag along the bank. Our progress was halted; our problem compounded.

Forces were brought to bear that our craft could not long endure. The merciless current slammed us broadside as we were trapped immobile. We slowly filled with murky water. It would not be long before the boat rolled into the current and sank beneath the snag.

I stepped over the center thwart to get to Blu, "Get out'a here, Blu! Come on, let's go! Get up on these branches!" He cautiously climbed onto the snag. There he tightroped it to the bank.

Suddenly a loud crack, not unlike a rifle shot, rang out and at the same instant I was nearly thrown from the canoe. Under the tremendous pressures that had been exerted upon it, the branch had snapped and the sudden release had rolled the canoe hard against the snag.

I was free of the tree at last. But the force of the current still pinned the boat to the snag. My better judgment told me to follow Blu to the bank and say good-by to our canoe. Following good judgment, however, was not one of my better traits. All I could think of was I had only recently paid $50 for that boat. I wasn't about to lose it. We still had other excursions to take. I was free of the tree. There was a chance.

I began pulling the craft along the snag in hopes of reaching open water. If loss of the craft became imminent I could always dive for the snag. But if I could reach open water I would again have freedom to navigate.

I felt in control so long as I kept the craft free to bob and rock with the current. Again and again, though, the boat would get caught on protruding branches or roots that would prevent it from riding on the current freely. At those times special care and added strength was required to keep from going under. I was ever prepared to jump for the snag.

Gradually the canoe worked to the end of the snag where the stern was hit by the current. I was pulled free. The wrestling match was over and I was again running for my life.

Blu followed along the bank harboring great concern. Even when it necessitated swimming across flooded areas, never once did he hesitate. Going under a series of bridges I was forced to hug the left bank. Blu ran across the first bridge to be on the same side.

I could not find a suitable place to beach the boat. Or rather, I was swept past those few suitable places that I did spy before I was able to react. I was at the southern edge of town in no time at all. At any moment I knew that the rubble of a second old dam would appear. I had never seen the remnants of that dam in high water. Would there be a rapid, or worse, a fall?

Sure enough there it was. The river funneled down to a shoot between the remains of the old concrete structure. It blasted out the other side as though it were pouring out a very large horizontal faucet.

The dam's remains were still enough of an obstacle, at flood stage, to back up some water. A flooded grove of willows stood off the left bank. My present course would take me within a few yards of that relatively calm water. An attempt at the sanctuary was feasible. Rather it was my only hope.

If I couldn't reach it it would be too late to get ready for the funnel. I would smash into the concrete, crumpling my canoe like you do the aluminum foil you take off of your baked potato…only I'd be in it.

Aim for the willows, or aim for the shoot? I aimed for the willows.

I back paddled a hard stroke on the port side to abruptly turn the bow toward the inviting willow slough. Then I dug in deep on the starboard side and paddled like all hell was chasing me. The muscles of my hands, arms and back were numb by then so I just willed them to do it.

By the time the prow of the canoe reached calm water the stern was headed downstream, still in the grip of the river's current. I couldn't lose being so close! Somehow I found the strength to paddle just a little faster and just a little deeper and the canoe inched forward until the front seat was over into calm water. Then the first thwart, but I was weakening. The canoe started drifting back into the river. I poured it on a little more and I started forward again. The middle thwart passed into safe harbor. Twelve dips of the paddle later the rear thwart inched to safety. Another dozen and I felt the fingers of the river's current let go and the boat gently lurched into the backwater. I slammed the paddle down, gunwale to gunwale, and dropped my forehead on it.

When I raised my head the boat was drifting up unto the muddy bank where Blu awaited, dancing with delight. Together we walked to the road to hitch a ride home for the Jeep. The Big Blue was well back to its normal, easy going self before we again paddled its waters.

21. You're Missed

    Still I had not been able to latch onto a suitable farm house. I did the next best thing. I bought a small, used trailer in Lincoln and pulled it near a lake a few miles out of Crete.
    It was April, the rainy season, when we made the move. With the help of the winch I dragged the trailer across a muddy field to the shelter of trees south of the lake's dam. There Blu, Painter and I set up house keeping.
    Our site was bordered west, north and east by forest, south by a tree-encircled milo field (in season). On the other side of the dam that lay a hundred yards north was a bass-filled lake whose banks were in natural grass prairie and trees.
    Our trailer was fifteen feet long. Inside were kitchen table

and benches, ice box, sink, stove and oven, heater and a sofa that turned down to a bed. With the bed down the empty floor space was thirty by sixty…inches. The trailer was used for little else but sleep. Most of the cooking was even done outside and for a bathroom we had one of the largest imaginable; one hundred and sixty acres worth. The trailer was adequate.

I took out a membership at the YMCA in Lincoln and there, besides swimming and other exercise, I showered on the way to work. A few attempts at bathing in the lake were made but I would come out smelling like a fish, defeating the purpose.

That spring was an especially rainy one, even for Nebraska. Access to our new home was difficult. Rather than deeply rutting the road with the Jeep, I obtained permission to park it on a farm a quarter mile walk away. The short journey was a pleasant one through woods, tall grass and a small plowed field.

For those times that I'd be away at work and not assigned to field duty, I had sunk a steel rod deep into the ground to which the end of Blu's chain was fastened. Otherwise we were always together. Painter was free to roam.

Those first few months that we were down from Alaska had been filled with parties to which Blu was also invited, and visits from long-missed friends. Blu hated to be alone.

One day while away at the office Blu, confined by chain to his circle the radius of which well included the trailer, ripped off the door of our house to gain access to what he considered his.

Upon returning from work through the muddy field, wet grass and thorn-ridden honey locust woods, I found Blu sitting outside on top of a kitchen bench cushion. Littered around him were all of my personal belongings. Pot and pan, guns, cameras, tape recorder and clothes. What really set me off was that my last roll of precious toilet paper was strung out all over our yard. I needed some right then too!

Happy to see me he jumped up and down wagging his tail wildly. He noticed quickly that I was not as pleased to see him. He sulked off to a corner of the trailer, his head and tail nearly dragging the ground.

Memories of Cousin Bill's back door raced through my mind and we were soon involved in another melee similar to the one we had had in Bill's back yard. We wrestled, bit and kicked in the mud and wet grass until I was certain that Blu knew that doors were not dog biscuits.

When I arose and started returning my belongings to the trailer's interior, Blu lunged at my back and, grasping the tail of my brand new shirt in his teeth, nearly ripped it entirely from my torso.

Turning in a rage I saw Blu sitting there with a two foot long piece of shirt in his mouth. I stood a muddy slob with my right shoulder bared, a picture of slapstick foolishness. I surrendered to the best friend I had ever had.

Releasing Blu from his chain I left everything lie while we went for a walk to the lake. Blu swam and I reflected on a friendship that had survived for many years. Old Blu could have done a lot better by having had a different companion. I, on the other hand, knew that the $50.00 investment I'd made had compounded to $50,000,000.00.

After a half hour of romping and meditation we returned to the trailer to restow stuff and repair the aluminum door. Knowing that a dog could break into my home had me concerned as to the security of my possessions.

That spring, summer and fall were happy, carefree times. Trailer living agreed with us. No neighbors to contend with. No yard to groom. No walk to shovel. Time off the job was spent walking, paddling, fishing or reading.

January was another story. On New Year's Eve not only had Painter not returned home for the second night but our heater went on the fritz. For three nights I tried to get it going again but to no avail. It wasn't worth getting it replaced. Our long campout had come to an end. Painter never returned.

Steve Dunmeyer, the last of the frat brothers to remain in residence in a house in town that I used occasionally as a weekend shower, was in need of a roommate. Blu and I moved in. It was a sad day when we towed the trailer to sit, unused, beside the house.

The luxuries of a civilized life once again became addictive. Except for the continual renditions of "Sink the Bismark", sung off key, Steve wound up being an all right guy to live with. When Steve and I would put our heads together we'd even come up with some pretty fine budget style eating. We tried to save our serious money for playing. Once, however, when we tried a frugal breakfast recipe of beef brains and scrambled eggs the result was less than gourmetish.

The smell permeating the house as the concoction sizzled could have gagged a maggot. I think the brains were a tad ripe. Both of us had known meals that didn't smell as good as they tasted, however. We weren't discouraged. We should have been.

Blu had moved from the kitchen at the back of the house to a spot near the front door. That alone should have told us something.

As the meal grew closer to being done, the horrendous odor grew no more delicate. Neither of us was going to be the first to admit that we would rather not give that one a try. We took pride in being able to consume just about anything.

Finally the time came to partake of the abundant and nutritious meal. Filling our plates to beyond there capacity, to give each other the impression that we intended to devour all that had been prepared, we retired to the front room as most unwed and uncouth bachelors do. Blu moved back into the kitchen.

Steve sat with his plate in his lap. I turned on the TV, then did the same. Since leaving the kitchen we had been breathing only through our mouths. We looked at each other, then back at our plates. Sure that we were about to ingest poison, but too proud to cry uncle, we took deep breaths and shoveled in the first unsightly globs.

Beginning to chew at a proper speed, we quickly slowed to a laborious one. We flared our nostrils and puffed our cheeks so that none of the ghastly morsels could accidentally venture down our throats. Any bits reaching our stomachs would have surely caused a slow death or, at the very least, irreversible defilement of our digestive systems—maybe even brain damage, which we must have already had.

We looked at each other with pleading eyes. Discovering mutual concurrence we spit the garbage back into our plates and returned to the kitchen. Blu went back to the front room. Dumping all into a garbage bag we sealed it tight and carried it to the alley. Returning to the kitchen we opened two cans of old faithful chili which we heated on the stove right in the cans. A proper breakfast.

Our relationship was regrettably short-lived. Steve got a job in another town and moved away. Blu and I were alone again.

Our adventures were cut back to a minimum. But then everyone needs easy living once in a while. Besides, Blu had turned eight. He was still pretty tough and performed well, but it was probably time he slowed down a bit. He had always preferred lazing around, visiting friends, playing with children and going to parties over hair-raising ordeals. He had faithfully stayed with me all those years. He'd earned and deserved retirement.

We were fortunate to meet someone who kept a little excitement in our lives. His name was Anthony "Diamond Jim" Hebert. I'd known of him since I had been a student but

I'd never made his acquaintance. He had been rumored as being a reclusive old man who would just as soon put a bullet in your butt as look at you.

Having lived a semi-reclusive existence myself I had learned how a relatively small segment of people, having nothing better to do than mind other people's business, can fantasize some of the most outrageous lies imaginable. Then they transmit them as gossip until even respectable folks begin to believe them as being true. This was the case with Diamond Jim.

Diamond lived on the outskirts of town across the river. His dwelling was an old trailer having no utilities nor any of the other luxuries to which modern man has become accustomed.

As it turned out, he possessed higher standards and cherished greater values than most I've known. To many, his downfall, but to me, his great success, was that he wouldn't sacrifice those values for anything.

Admittedly he was no master of tact. He had obviously alienated some of the most influential people in town. He looked upon wealth and material possessions as meaningless idols. What he held as supreme was virtue and goodness in a man's heart.

A man with only that could have been naked, penniless and diseased and Diamond would have revered him over all other men. But someone without virtue and goodness, but having instead untold wealth, could have driven to Diamond's trailer in a Rolls Royce with thousand dollar bills as handkerchiefs and solid gold, disposable toothpicks and Jim would have spit snuff juice in his eye.

To those few who had been allowed the privilege of knowing and understanding Diamond, the foul language that poured profusely from the lips of that short, slight-built, stooped man was never taken in offense. Even the frequent pieces of Skol that would find there way past his few remaining teeth and into the eyes of a friend were accepted without undue revulsion.

I met Diamond one night at the El Toro Bar and Grill. I immediately felt a liking for the man. I guess it was the introduction that did it. Judy, the waitress, introduced us. The intro. went something like this.

Judy: "Diamond, this is Tedd."

Tedd: "Hi, Diamond. Nice to meet you."

Diamond: "Who the ____ are you?"

A fine example of the tact that I grew to love and respect. You never had to wonder what Diamond Jim was thinking. He would tell you with fine tuned, perfectly developed eloquence that was unabashedly complete. There'd be no room for question.

After I told him who the ____ I was, we sat and chatted over cold beer, hard boiled eggs, Polish sausage and pickles the rest of the evening. He was covered with a layer of soot. I would learn that that was a permanent condition from his cooking and heating fires.

"Well, I gotta get the ____ outa here. Time for bed," he said ending our visit.

"Be happy to give you a ride," I responded. "I need to be goin' too."

"Don't want to cause ya no ____ trouble."

"Won't be any trouble at all. Like I said, I've got to get goin'."

We paid our bills, he'd have no part of me buying any more than the intro beer, and we left the bar for Jeep.

Blu was asleep on the passenger seat. When Diamond opened the door and saw him I was afraid that Jim would be shocked but no such occurrence. There wasn't even a "Who the ____ is this dog?"

"Yah, ha!" Diamond yelled as he grabbed a stunned Blu by

the neck. "Gotcha, dog!" he said just before he grabbed Blu's ear gently with his nearly toothless gums.

Blu regrouped quickly, spinning out of Diamond's grasp and playfully latched hold of Diamond's shoulder.

"Ohhhhh!" Diamond flopped his head down on the seat in mock defeat and Blu let go his hold and licked the back of Diamond's neck vigorously.

From that moment on I was only the chauffeur. Diamond stepped in and Blu crawled onto his lap. "Diamond, meet Blu."

It was love at first sight. All those years I had never known that Blu was partial to diamonds.

That first night at Jim's trailer there was no invitation in. Not even what could be called an authentic good-night. After he gave Blu a hug he stepped out and, with just an overhead wave of his soot-blackened cane, he shuffled away with a hint of a dance in his step.

The next time I saw Diamond he was coming out of the auction house on Main Street. He carried a broken-down suitcase in his cane hand and a wooden box under his other arm. Turning slightly he directed a profane holler back into the building. I pulled into an open parking slot and called to him.

As he turned I said, "Hi, Diamond."

He responded with, "What the ____ do you want?"

"Just thought I'd buy you a beer if you've got a minute."

"After the ____ ____ I've been taking in there I could use one of those," he said making a gesture with his head toward the auction house. "But I'll just buy my own."

"Suit yourself. Hop in. We can drive over."

"You still got that big black dog in there?" he asked as though if my answer was no, his would be too.

"You bet. Rarely go anywhere without him."

"OK. I'll go. But I gotta get my ____ chair out of that ____

_____ place first."

"Take me in and point it out. I'll haul it."

We walked into the auction house. The auction was just about over. Diamond showed me a La-Z-Boy he had bought and I latched hold. After a few vulgar exchanges between Diamond and a woman of his vintage and, I might add, his vocabulary, I carried the chair to the Jeep dumping it in the back with Jim's suitcase and box.

Blu's tail began wagging the moment the door opened. Jim's mock threat with his cane only got it going faster. The two boys started wrestling the moment I closed the door behind Diamond. Blu took great care not to harm his newfound friend but still gave Jim a robust time.

When we pulled in front of Toro's I thought that maybe I would have to have that beer alone. Diamond only grudgingly left his pal behind.

"I don't know why he can't come in. He's a ____ site better for business than most of the ____ ____ in there!" he mumbled, showing his irritation.

Opening the door we were greeted by the usual incoherent chatter and occasional outburst, the sounds that are as much a part of a bar and grill as beer and burgers. We found an empty booth and for the next two hours I heard how the "crazy old ____" at the auction had tried to finagle him out of his La-Z-Boy.

By the time I got Jim home it had grown dark. He wanted his chair by his cooking fire. Carrying that chair in the dark over old bed frames and springs, car parts, farm, garden and shop implements of all descriptions, wooden pallets, piles of used bricks, buckets, dozens of gallon milk jugs filled with water and other items, some of which I didn't recognize as being from this century, was no easy matter even though the distance traveled was no more than forty feet.

By late summer Diamond Jim had become a good friend.

Then came autumn and time to hit the fields and woods once again. That wasn't Jim's cup of tea so it was just Blu and me again.

Blu had slowed down some. He could no longer keep up the hunt all day. But we still enjoyed those weekend mornings when we would rise before sun-up and ritually get our gear together for a hunt. The instant I dragged out of the sack he knew we were going afield. For an old puppy his enthusiasm was overwhelming.

While bathing, dressing, cooking and eating breakfast and loading the car he would follow me as nervously as a puppy-dog. I suppose my teasing didn't help matters any but I so loved seeing him bubbling with energy and excitement, ecstatic every moment. He was gray around the muzzle and his endurance wasn't what it used to be but he still loved life.

With age he had acquired a peculiar trait that set him apart from all other dogs. Toward the end of a day's hunt he would be well done in from having run all over tarnation. At those times, when he needed to relieve himself, instead of customarily lifting a leg and watering a tree, he would lean against the tree and lift the outside leg. If we were hunting with friends, that trick would be the topic of conversation for the rest of the day.

Other than hunting our yen for adventure was filled with more canoe trips down the many waterways throughout the state. And of course every trip to Diamond's was a harrowing experience, what with the unintended booby traps of heaped junk, the worst infestation of mosquitoes I had experienced since the Brooks Range, and patches and patches of river nettles. Don't ask how a visit to Diamond's always turned out to be a pleasure. Blu turned nine that winter.

At work one day, I was assigned the Niobrara River basin. I had hoped for that assignment since returning from Alaska. The Niobrara flowed through beautiful country, as wild as

Nebraska gets, and great water. I was pleased. I couldn't wait to get home and tell Blu about it. Maybe we'd even celebrate with a short, gentler game of puppy-dog football.

As I pulled into the driveway, instead of Blu being there to greet me, a neighbor came walking from around the corner of the house. Oh brother, I thought, Bluper's loose. I'll have to go reel him in down at Jimmy and Helen's.

But then looking closer I didn't like the expression on my neighbor's face.

"Hi, Frank. What's up?" I said as I stepped from the Jeep.

Frank didn't say anything. Seemed he had trouble with words. He continued to look at me in a peculiar way.

Suddenly I began to feel light headed and fear stepped into my soul. "Frank, what's up?!"

He lowered his head. Softly, almost inaudibly, he said, "Blu's gone."

"Gone?" I questioned, demanding further explanation.

"Dead," he clarified looking up into my eyes.

Numb with disbelief, I turned and stared blankly at Blu's collar lying on the ground at the end of his chain.

"How?"

"He jumped the fence." he said pointing at the five footer alongside the dog house that separated our two properties. "His chain hung up on the corner of the dog house roof. It was over quick, Tedd."

Our times together were over. How could he up and leave without me? After all that we'd been through together. Whatever we did we were supposed to do it together. We were always supposed to be together. But then again I guess we still are. There's a place in me reserved for him alone. Nothing or no one else can ever fill it no matter how dear.

I buried Blu in the wide open Nebraska fields that he loved so much.

A few weeks later I left Nebraska to start over, a difficult task because a big piece of me was left behind under Nebraska grass.

Saying good-by to the places where Blu and I had spent time together wasn't easy. We'd done more than existed. We had lived.

"Hell!" Diamond said as I said good-by to him. "I'm gonna miss that big black dog a hell of a lot more than I'm gonna miss you!"

"Can't argue that, you crotchety geezer." We hugged tight for a moment. Just before he turned toward his trailer, I thought I saw a clean spot running down through the soot under his left eye.

Diamond was found dead from a heart attack soon after. Now he and Blu are together in that very special place that God has made for those with hearts the size of Diamond's La-Z-Boy.

When I travel back to the places where Blu and I grew together they still ring with laughter and shouts of joy. I see him running after bunny rabbits with a vision as clear as ever.

My memories of him can never fade. Someday we'll be together again where there will be no more sorrow, only happiness. In that place just now out of reach. Up where eagles cry.

You're missed, Blu.